FROM *Paradise* TO *Hell*—AND BACK

FROM *Paradise* TO *Hell*—AND BACK

Lou Lee James

Copyright © 2012 by Lou Lee James.

Library of Congress Control Number: 2012903773
ISBN: Hardcover   978-1-4691-7602-4
                Softcover   978-1-4691-7601-7
                Ebook   978-1-4691-7603-1

This book was printed in the United States of America.

To order additional copies of this book, contact:
Xlibris Corporation
0-800-644-6988
www.xlibrispublishing.co.uk
Orders@xlibrispublishing.co.uk
303716

to Alice

In his fifty-fourth year, plus three months, ten hours, three minutes, and five seconds, Simon was a normal human being who talked, walked, worked, and laughed.

In his fifty-fourth year, plus three months, ten hours, three minutes, and six seconds, Simon was not a normal human being. He could not talk, could not walk, could not work, and could not laugh.

One second lay between being very happy and very unhappy; being very busy and not very busy; and not committing suicide or committing suicide.

Chapter 1

The plane trees ran endlessly along the tarmac road, which bore the heavy traffic coming up from the mighty river. The autumn afternoon was fine, with a few white and pink clouds scattered in the blue sky above. There were many Indian, Chinese, French, Italian, German, and Japanese people and millions of Britons that were crowding the streets, lanes, and squares.

The city was London, with the West End shops, fish and chips shops, Wimpy's restaurants, cinemas and theatres, pubs and coffee bars, where people were enjoying themselves, away from the worries of life.

Hundreds of pigeons and doves picked up the corn grains scattered by old people, young people, and kids, in great profusion. Trafalgar Square was beautiful with the lions, the fountains, the water, Nelson's Column, the Tate Gallery, and several wide streets.

London is nice when one is healthy and has money. Simon was among these people, but he could not enjoy himself.

He had enjoyed working in London and other places many times, but this time luck was against him.

The previous evening he and his wife were returning back from a machine exhibition in the Midlands, which was successful, with thousands of customers and ordinary people crowding hundreds of aisles, filled with multicoloured lights, machine adverts, machine and human noises, machine agents, directors, and . . . the heat! It was the suffocating heat, the sweat of people, the reel of dirty oil and poisonous fumes.

Simon had gone to the exhibition five days beforehand, without his wife. He had to work at the stands with multicoloured paints, nails and screws by the ton, posters, high stools and low stools, chairs, desks, overhead phone lines, international fitters, workmen and bosses. The halls were very cold and draughty, so everybody felt a chill while they worked. A few stalls served hot tea, coffee, and English sandwiches, which stuck to their palate when they tried to chew the bread. It was the fault of the flour. England yields poor corn because the weather is wet all the time. Good corn needs the sun, as is found in southern countries. The coffee was like hot sugary black ink, and the tea was like hot sugary creamy wall paint. The milk was not fresh. It was a tragedy at the exhibition.

However, when the machines arrived, along came some Italian wine together with Italian cheeses, salami, sausages, and rolls for the workers, fitters, agents, and customers who liked the machines from Italy. They savoured Italian food with satisfaction, because it was very good. Simon was an agent for Italian pharmaceutical machines. He was covering England, Wales, Scotland, and Ireland. His work—with help from Alice, his Irish wife, and their sons—was very rewarding, with hundreds of customers and many orders.

At the end of the exhibition, the customers were happy, the agents were happy, and the fitters were happy to go home, but Simon did not feel happy, because he had a nasty bout of flu with a headache, sore bones, frozen feet and he felt cold or hot at times, a sure sign that he had a high temperature.

They drove to North London that evening, which was fine and mild. Before going home, they decided to eat in an Italian restaurant near their house. The owner was Spanish, the cook was Chinese, and the waiter was an Indian. The meal and the Chianti wine were gorgeous, and they laughed and told each other jokes.

Later, they went home, and they greeted their boys and their cats, which were roaming in their house. Alice and Simon went straight to bed because they were very tired after the ten days' exhibition.

At ten next morning, Alice got up and washed. Their boys got up and washed, and then Simon got up and washed. Later, Simon opened his case, but he felt sick and uneasy. He was very hot at times, he was cold at other times, and he complained of a bad headache. His wife brought a chair up close to him and offered him a cup of tea. Alice and their two sons were very worried and she called the local doctor. The doctor came within five minutes. After he had examined Simon, he said, 'This man must go to a hospital, urgently.'

However, it was Saturday; the local hospital did not have the right equipment, and the ambulance crew rushed Simon to another hospital on the other side of London, near Hampstead Heath.

Did the second hospital find the disease that troubled Simon and did they cure him?

Chapter 2

Simon's story started when his grandparents lived in the country near Padua. They had two sons and their families. The farm had some fields producing corn, fruit, vegetables, and wine. The village bordered a wide river full of fish, many multicoloured wild ducks, and a few white and black swans. Tall trees and low bushes grew close to the river's green waters. There were a few red and yellow boats and several men constantly fishing; however, they caught nothing. The scene was beautiful and peaceful.

His grandparents would work their land with their cows and sowed corn and hayseeds. The hay grew in two months, which was then cut and dried and became food for the cows. Hay is digested and, within a few hours, it is ejected from another side of their bodies and used like manure to grow the new hay. Very clever!

However, one part of the human race, which is supposed to be well off, does not eat good food, because they are rich. There is too much sugar, salt, and too much meat. They drink too much wine, beer, and whisky. They smoke cigarettes and herbs and then are sick from the most fatal diseases, such as cancers, AIDS, diabetes, and heart disease.

Another part of humankind is poor, but they eat wholesome food. Simon thought that it was far better to be a poor man than a rich man, because one's life would be longer and healthier.

Simon's mother and father lived in the Padua village near Venice. He lived in a village too. He was born in his mother's room in his grandparents' house, above the stable, with two cows and one donkey—a bit like Baby Jesus, who performed many miracles. But Simon was not able to perform any miracles at all!

When he was six months old, his parents decided to move to another part of Italy and he decided to follow them, because he did not have anything else to do.

His mother worked as a waitress at the home of an army general, where his father was employed as a driver The general's family was rich and his parents were poor. That is life; however, a waitress, who worked for the general's family, fancied his father. His father was a real man with a moustache, handsome, nice and tall, and she was a dark Slav, full of fire and beautiful; however, she was very bad. But his father was not interested in her fireworks display, because he already had a wife plus a baby. The dark woman caused a lot of trouble for his parents and other people.

While he was out in the garden in his pram, she tried to pour vitriol in his face to destroy him. His mother was aware of the witch. She ran shouting to his pram and the witch ran off. When his parents talked to the general's family about the Slav girl and her wrongdoing, she was sent off from the family.

About the same time, his father got fed up with the general and decided to get a shop for repairing bikes, which he learned from his uncle when he was a boy. Simon's mother had been a dressmaker since she was a teenager and she used her craft, then, to help her family, because they were very poor.

When he was one year-old, Simon's parents moved to a rented flat, close to the avenues of the city and near those narrow streets with the archways. The houses all had internal passages, vaults, walls, gardens, and apartments over one floor, two floors, three, four, and five floors. Their flat was set on top of an existing four-storey house and he loved to look at the red roof tiles, dark chimneys, the orange balconies, and white sheets caught by the wind.

One day his mother introduced him to a nice fat blond baby wrapped in her arms. He did not recall that 'thing', and she told him that a stork had arrived at their flat, by night, with the pram, ten blankets, three pillows, panties, and frocks. 'He' was his brother, who was quiet, and Simon's parents called him John Charles.

It was the season of the whys and whats. Simon was then two years old and he constantly put difficult questions to his mother.
'Why do birds fly?'
'Because they have wings, Simon.'
'Why don't I have any wings?'
'Because God wants the birds to have wings, Simon.'
'Who is God, Mammy?'
'God is the Father who commands all things from the skies . . . .'
'I already have one father, Mammy!'
'Yes, but your father stays under on the earth. Do you understand, Simon?'
'I don't understand! Does God come down from the skies by train, Mammy?'
'God uses the angels.'
'Why does the train have wheels and I have legs, Mammy?'
'Because the train must run . . . . .'
'I too must run when you get cross with me, Mammy!'
'Because you are a terror, Simon!'
Eventually, all those questions from Simon would end, and she would prepare a ham or salami sandwich for him, to eat out on the steps of their flat in the afternoons, during the summer season.
One summer day, when he was eating a sandwich he heard a voice coming from a window on another flat below.
'Simon . . . Simon . . . Come here. Simon . . . here!'

He turned around, and he could tell that the voice was coming from a window fitted with iron bars. Behind the iron bars, there was an old witch without any teeth called Olga. She was fat and small and had been eating smelly garlic. Simon went close to the smelly old bag without chewing his sandwich, but his sandwich flew into the hands of the witch. Then she closed her window laughing her head off.
He had just learned about the wickedness that some people have!

One day his uncle came by train from a village just outside Padua. He was tired and he slept on Simon's bed soundly, while he was looking at him, but before sleeping, his uncle told his mother to remember to wake him up in two hours, because he had to catch the train back to his town. His mother did indeed wake him up, but his Uncle Ernest went off to sleep again!

'Ernest . . . Ernest! You must catch the train, Ernest!' cried Simon. But Ernest did not wake up. Then Simon ran to his mother's room, grabbed a heavy hammer, returned to the lounge where his uncle was asleep on the bed and *bam* he hit him on his head! His uncle jumped up from the bed, with pain, and his mother, who came from the kitchen, was shouting with fright.

'Did you hit your uncle with a hammer? We must call a doctor quickly! The bruise is getting bigger! Virgin Madonna and all the saints! Why did you hurt your uncle?'

'Mammy, my uncle was not getting up for the train to his village and . . . don't hit me, Mammy!'

'Will you leave him alone?' shouted his uncle. 'Simon is only small. The pain is already gone. Yes!' While his uncle massaged the bruise on his head, his mother had already gone to get a piece of brown paper to reduce the swelling. Simon hid behind the kitchen and a large table, and found that his uncle had postponed his return to the countryside because of the pain.

Simon had a friend at the time that lived in the flat below, named Cici. They played together up and down along the hallways or the pavements down on the street. Once Simon saw Cici eating a sandwich filled with dark meat. He was curious and asked him what sort of meat it was.

'It is rat's meat.'

'What? You are pulling my leg, Cici!'

'It is true, Simon. My mother said, 'No juicy cow steaks from now on, because we are at war. Rat steaks will do.'

Was Cici joking or not? Simon would never know.

And Simon would never know why his parents moved just next door. Before the change, they lived fairly well with the dark red rooftops, the sheets picking up the sky, the winds, the cream and yellow balconies, the sandwiches and, of course, the old bag with no teeth—the Lady Ogre—namely Olga. After the change, he found that the landlady was a witch. She was ugly, a miser, bitter and a widow. Her husband was dead and had passed on to a better life without her, he was sure. And he was sure that Simon hated her.

The flat was one half hers and one half theirs. They paid rent to her for it, plus a loft where his family kept some coal, some chickens and one cock, but the 'witch' complained to them about the cock, the chickens, and the coal every day and every night. She was saying that the chicks were dirty, the hens were dirty, and the rooster was dirty. The coal was dirty and she could not keep her bedclothes clean or her floors or the lounge. She was a terror.

However, some friends of his mother—Silvia and Julius—were very nice and very good, because they understood her needs. His mother had two kids, her husband was at war, and food was scarce.

If Simon's mother needed some shopping, Silvia would get the shopping for her. If his mother had a sick son, Silvia would be there nursing him. If his mother had her husband away at war, Silvia would be there talking to her for hours. Their friendship lasted for a lifetime.

There was also a girl called Mafalda who lived next door to them. She was beautiful, dark, and a Spanish type—even though she was an Italian—with her hair blowing in the wind. And yes, she was warm and nice, but she had a . . . moustache? Yes, Mafalda was growing a moustache! She and Simon met in the yard nearly every day. His eyes met her eyes, which were gorgeous and they stood without talking, without breathing, holding hard on to the wire fence, until she or he went home dreaming of those eyes . . .

Christmas came round and Uncle Ernest—his mother's brother—gave Simon a red toy car as a Christmas present, but his mother gave him a black sock full of black coal, because she thought that he was naughty. He was not an angel, but he was not a devil either!

One day he was walking with his mother along the arcade in the street, keeping to the left side of the street. All of a sudden he decided to cross the street and move to the other side, without looking. But a black car came by travelling fast. The driver braked, hitting the corner of the right column. He jumped on to the pavement.

Simon's mother shouted at the driver saying, 'You were driving too fast. My child had an awful fright. And me! Are you all right, Simon?'

'Your child should look carefully before crossing over.'
'And you should calm yourself down—OK?'
The driver said, 'These women!' Then he reversed back on to the road from the arcade, without ever checking the bump on his car. He changed from first gear to second gear and then to third gear and fourth gear, and his ears and his nose were fuming.

While all this was happening—Olga, Simon's brother, Uncle Ernest, the rat meat, Cici, the broken-down car, and Mafalda with the gorgeous eyes—something else happened too, *the Second World War!*

Simon's mother told him about the war. She said it was terrible and horrible, with soldiers and civilians wounded and dead. Houses, schools, places, gardens, and churches were in ruins. 'Why can't the people of this world live peacefully?' Simon asked himself.

Germany started the war by attacking Poland on 3 September 1939 and on 17 June 1940, and Italy declared war on France and England. Then the Germany-Italy-Japan deal was signed. The USA-China deal was signed. Then America, Russia, and Germany were at war. France . . . Greece . . . Italy and Germany . . . Poland . . . The whole world was at war because of the kings and queens who moved the pawns without the least interest for them. It was a huge game of chess with a terrific computer that asked, 'Who wins the war? Who pays for this war? How many lives are being lost?'

Simon's father was called up for service in the war, because he was a pawn, but Simon's father hated this war and all wars. He was in the Italian Army, driving an army lorry up to the northern Greek border, full of lively Italian soldiers. Then he returned with dead soldiers every day.

The same applied to civilians—babies died, kids died, young men died, girls died, men and women died, old men died, and grannies died by the millions.

Men and women make babies; then war destroys men and women. 'The effort to live is not justifiable,' Simon thought. Who invented war? Maybe it was a sick devil, an idiot or a stupid man, certainly not an intelligent and good person.

When his father arrived in Greece, he wrote to his mother that she must go to the countryside, with her two children, to stay with their grandparents and other relatives in the village, away from danger.

Their relatives had plenty to eat. After that letter, his mother had no news from his father. Maybe he was caught by the Greek troops, the English troops, or the German troops. Her husband might be wounded, lying in a hospital bed sick or . . . dead. His mother was very worried and at times she would cry. However, his mother was very brave. Simon saw her at work in their house, cooking meals, making beds, shopping or walking with him and his brother in the parks. They would enjoy the lake, the boats, and the ice creams in the sun, without thinking about the war. After the evening meals and doing the washing-up, she would be busy again making military hats until midnight, one o'clock, two o'clock, three o'clock . . .

Simon attended a nursery school and he remembered a nun who was good, beautiful, and sweet. His brother was little. Simon also saw German, American, and Italian military planes passing over and hitting the city. People went underground to hide at the cellars at three or four o'clock in the morning, with sleeping children and adults. When the bombings were finished, folks exited from the cellars when the all-clear was signalled by the sirens.

It was an awful experience and frightening to be woken up in the middle of the night, and then the darkness, sirens, bombings, broken buildings, people shouting everywhere, and dreams and nightmares about the war. There was a feeling of lack of hope each and every night. Simon could still remember the hospital when his adenoids and his tonsils were being operated on without anaesthetics, by a 'butcher' doctor, while German or Allied planes were bombing the station, which was near the city hospital, and there was great confusion, running and panicking people, soldiers and blood, blood, blood . . .

After the operation, Simon and his mother left the hospital and walked down the avenue, where his mother bought him an ice cream to help soothe the soreness and the pain.

The war continued and it got worse. His mother listened to the words of her husband. She picked up her poor possessions plus her old cupboard, and left with Simon and his brother for Padua village, hoping that the war would be less severe in the country. The village was sited near a big quarry. The stones and slabs from the quarry were used to make tombs for the dead or conduits and pavements for the living people. The people went shopping at the local Co-op. The Co-op was the only shop in the village, apart from a chemist, a cinema, a church, a parish priest, several nuns, and a cemetery, which was used for the dead—for good and bad people! At their grandparents' farm, their relatives and friends wanted to know everything about the war, the German troops, and the Italian troops. They kissed and greeted them with strong handshakes. His grandfather would cut a few slices of home-made salami and some pieces of toasted bread. They drank home-made red wine, which was delicious. The farm was also the home of Uncle Richard and his wife—Aunt Victoria—who had two children, Bruno and Therese.

Bruno and Simon were the same age, but Bruno grew up to be a rough boy and a bully. Nevertheless, he was nice towards Simon's mother, his brother and Simon himself.

Therese was always nice and beautiful. Uncle Richard was Simon's father's brother. Mary was his grandmother and she was very good. She liked black and grey dresses. Joseph, Simon's grandfather, was very good. He was calm and tall. He did not talk very much and worked in the fields.

The farm had seven fields of grass for the animals, and there were fields of corn, cauliflowers, cabbage, lettuce, and potatoes for their own use, separated by rows of vineyards and fruit trees and other trees. The fields were bounded by four narrow ditches and a gate, which opened on to a country road. The house was brick-built on three floors. The kitchen, the cellar, and the stable were big. There were staircases to the rooms. The house was narrow and long. At the front, there was a vineyard of sweet white Muscatel grapes, which would send anybody to the loo fast, because anybody would get diarrhoea. In between the cement manure tank and the loo, there was a nut tree. The nuts were delicious!

During the war, it would appear that the staple foods were plentiful at the start of hostilities. However, as the war continued, it would appear that there was less food. There was less oil, fruit, grain, and coal. The people were left without salt, sugar, coffee, and candles. The terror of the war remained the same or was actually worse, and not for just the children. The grown-ups were frightened too.

There were air fights between German, Allied, and the Italian planes, every day, in the blue or grey or black sky above them. The bombers were dispersing spent bullet casings into the fields, among the living cattle, rabbits, hens, cocks, and ducks, which panicked. Nevertheless, the kids would use brass tubes as whistles, which they played. They could not understand war because kids are good. Adults are supposed to teach young children to live properly without fights, lies, and thefts, but somewhere along the line adults became wicked. 'Why?' Simon thought.

Every night, without fail, a twin-engine plane flew low at midnight, making frightening noises. That noise was the noise of death. The farmers used to call that plane 'Jack'. Because of the plane, they went to bed amongst the animals in the stable. The stable felt a little more secure with the straw, corn, grass, and the warmth given by the cattle. His grandfather would light or turn the oil light down low at nights in the stable, especially when 'Jack' was heard, while the women made up straw beds amongst the animals on the cement floor. The farmers would be afraid of the German soldiers, who would kill without mercy the poor peasants, nuns, priests, and Italian soldiers. They showed no pity and were without any respect for human rights.

During the day, his grandfather would get up at about five o'clock to cut the grass for his animals. At times Simon would get up to watch his grandfather cutting the grass in the wet fields, to watch the red and yellow sun rise, or to watch the crickets come out of the earth. He loved watching his grandfather cutting the grass with his scythe. His grandfather was an expert. With each movement from right to left, his scythe would sweep low and he would be cutting the grass. With each return movement from left to right, his scythe would be high and he would not be cutting the grass. However, the scythe would be cutting, without fail, the fresh grass at the next sweep.

Every day and twice per day, his grandfather would take the dirty straw out of the stable and bring the clean straw in. The dirty straw was placed on the manure heap at the back of the house. Then he would take the eggs from the loft above, where the hens laid their eggs every day. Simon enjoyed the clean yellow straw, the green hay, the brown wooden boards, and the rough grey aluminium sheeting.

At nine o'clock, his grandfather would send the animals to drink water from the wooden barrel, near the cement cistern. Simon was surprised to see how the cows drank enormous quantities of water at each mouthful. After the watering sessions, his grandfather would pull up a wooden stool from a corner to milk his two cows, while the cattle were finishing their fodder. He and the animals were annoyed by flies in the stable. They were a menace. Flies went everywhere. They were messing up the milk in the bucket, the manger, the fodder, the doors, grandfather's nose, mouth, shirt, and his straw hat. Flies could spread awful diseases—diseases in the cows, the donkeys, and people. 'Flies do not serve any purpose in life and God must have made a mistake,' Simon thought.

With the milking finished, his grandfather would get up from the wooden stool, walk on the outside of the farm, and put the bucket containing the frothing milk on the cement sill. The women would take the bucket inside the kitchen. He and Simon would enter the house and sit at the large table to eat breakfast, with boiled milk and toasted maize meal.

After their breakfast they would go outside. His grandfather, uncle, aunt, grandmother, and his mother went to the fields to rake the dry hay and place it on the wooden cart, pulled by their oxen. The cousins would be playing with the crickets coming out of the earth, eating ripe apples, grapes, and nuts or fishing out the frogs from the ditches. It took a big effort to erase from their minds that there was a war raging which could kill every soul in the world.

On Sundays, everybody would walk three kilometres to the village church. They wore their 'Sunday best' clothes and their shoes would be polished as they walked out of the gate, going down the middle of the dusty road. Then it was the parish priest, the candles, the incense odour, and the Mass. They would arrive at the church at eight for the nine o'clock Mass. If anyone got to Mass late, the parish priest would embarrass him or her in front of the people, with a tremendous voice. At the end of the service, everybody would go to the cemetery saying a few Hail Marys, and would light a few candles and bring flowers. Then, it would be a trip to the coffee bar to drink a few grappa (similar to aquavit) for the men. There were drinks for the ladies and a few sweets or chocolates for the younger generation. At eleven, it was time to walk back to the farm, tired and exhausted, to eat the Sunday meal, based on home-made dried spaghetti, dressed with home-made tomato sauce or chicken soup, followed by roast poultry with fried cabbage, mash potatoes, and garden peas dressed in olive oil, home-made wine and cooked apples to finish the meal, and . . . Amen.

Every afternoon his grandfather would retire to his bedroom for his two-hour 'siesta', especially in the hot summer days. Simon's grandmother, aunt, mother, brother, and Simon and his friends, would seat themselves in the shade of a tree or trees. They would be telling stories about the village, the city, the partisans who were fighting the Germans, or the village lovers. The pigs would be eating the rotten apples or leftovers or running after the hens in front of the pigsty.

Simon's granny was very good to them because she realised that her son was away in Greece for the war and they were without a father, for the time being. She tried to help with the food and the money and accepted them within their house. Uncle Richard seemed a bit awkward towards them. He was at home and was very lucky indeed not to get mixed up with the war because he was very astute.

At other times, the cousins would take grandmother to the fields, where there were apple trees, vines, and peach trees. They would sit down on the grass, near the corn or maize plantations. After the midday meal, they would tell each other funny stories, while they were eating peaches from the trees. Grandmother would laugh, and she would fart! But the more she laughed, the more she farted, because peaches had that effect on her.

From the start, Simon attended a nursery school about three kilometres away from the farm. His mother used to cycle to school using a lady's cycle, which he rode on a wooden rest, facing her, with the handlebar supporting him.

One day, his cousin Bruno was playing at school with a raw bean up his nose. Up and down . . . up and down . . . up and down . . . up! The water and mucus stopped the bean from coming down, and Bruno cried and cried. The nuns, the priests, and the gardener tried to help the situation, until a doctor arrived to clear his cousin's nose. The means of transport for ordinary people was the bicycle, in those times. His grandfather, uncle, aunt, and mother all used the bike for shopping, going to the doctors, to the chemist, to Mass, and to the village or to any of the other villages nearby. His granny walked everywhere. The cousins walked along the road or sat on the handlebar of the bike, pedalled by mother or aunt, while their backside and backs took the pain and got sore. Men used bikes which had a tube from the handlebar to the saddle, within the frame. Women used bikes without a middle tube. Families who had money used horses or a cart pulled by horses or a car.

The nursery school had finished and the elementary school had started. During the schooldays, Simon used to wait for the other schoolboys in front of his grandparents' farm. One morning a schoolboy was late. A farmer and a donkey, pulling a wooden cart with a load of sticks and covered by a canvas, were approaching on the dusty road. Eventually, the schoolboy came running, and started to walk on the dusty road, talking and shouting. Suddenly, a big noise came from around the bend, partly hidden by the trees. The farmer, the donkey, and the cart seemed to have vanished. Everybody ran and ran along the dusty road shouting, until they got to the scene. The scene was, indeed, a battle scene. The donkey was dead, lying on his side with his mouth open. The mud—yellow, green, and black—of the road seeped thorough his nose. What a mess! It was caused by a plane—a bomber, either German or Allied or Italian. The farmers were sure that the plane was a German bomber. Maybe it was 'Jack', leaving a great big hole on the road and black smoke over the horizon. People would often talk about the scene. Some of the women and the kids cried, but they tried to live normally in spite of the bomber and the war.

His grandfather liked to follow the phases of the war, which were broadcast on the Italian radio, every day. It happened that Mussolini was arrested on 25 July 1945 . . . Badoglio seized power . . . then Badoglio declared war on Germany . . . At first, the Italian troops were fighting with Germany, and later Italy was against Germany. The Allied forces were in Sicily, Calabria, and Naples, pushing the

German forces to the northern part of Italy and—at last—outside Italian soil. This meant freedom for Italy.

One time Simon was terribly sick with earache and his mother wanted to insert hot olive oil in his right ear, to soothe it a bit. Simon was in his mother's bedroom and on her bed, but he was afraid of the hot oil. His aunt and his grandmother arrived, and with their help his mother nailed him on the cushion. He was screaming, 'Don't use the hot oil, please!' However, his mother managed to empty the hot olive oil into his ear. Was it hot oil? Cool oil, because the hot olive oil—with all the fighting with mother and the two women—had cooled down. And Simon was very lucky!

During the time that they were living at the village, Simon's mother paid a one-month visit to some other relatives on this side of the city, near a river, where another grandmother had lived. She had four girls and two boys, but she had to visit St Peter above, urgently!

Simon played, every day, with two other cousins, who were daughters of his mother's sister, Esther, plus Uncle Ernest and Uncle Renate, who were single. Apart from playing with the cousins, aunts, uncles, and their friends, he went to the riverside shores every day, in the shade of some tall trees. The river was beautiful, but dangerous, for the water swirled near the shore. People said that several swimmers were drowned there.

After the holiday, they returned to the home village and to his grandparent's farm. Since these relatives were farmers, they would do many things every day, from watering to feeding the animals, from feeding to milking, from cutting the grass to harvesting, from breaking the soil to feeding the hens, and from cleaning to drying the fruits. The work made them fit and hard.

When the season was right in September, his grandparents, his uncle, aunt, mother and kids would harvest the grapes using many wicker baskets in the fields. Then the baskets—full of sweet grapes—would go to the farm, with the cart pulled by their two oxen to the porch beside their house. Under the outside porch, the grapes would be pressed, using a large screw and a wooden tub, to produce white or red wine. After the pressing, the wine would be set inside in the cellar to rest. In the following two weeks, one could try the sweet wine. It would be better to drink it the following March, when the wine was mature.

Another system for pressing the grapes in a wooden tub was for one or two persons to climb the side of the tub, get inside with bare feet and legs, and trample the grapes. Simon tried to trample the Clinton grapes in the tub when he was six years old. Clinton is originally an American rustic red grape, almost black, and strongly flavoured. The grapes were OK. He was not OK, because five minutes after Simon got the squashing operation underway, he was itching all over! His legs, his feet, and his arms were itching and he went almost crazy with the pain and the itching, while his rustic relatives were almost crazy laughing! He had learned that town people must not squash any grapes, especially Clinton grapes.

It was Christmastime, and Simon's relatives had to kill the pig to produce chops, sausages, black pudding, salami, and ham for next year.

The first year that he saw a pig being killed, he was seven years old. He hid behind a window in the kitchen. He saw the pig's table. He saw his grandfather and his son preparing a few thick wooden boards and two short steps. He saw the deathbed on which the poor pig had to die. He saw them bringing the pig outside from the pigsty to the deathbed, screaming and shouting like a baby, because he knew that he had to die to make sausages and pork chops for the wicked man. He felt an awful sadness and pity for the poor pig, but he did not run away from the window, because he was curious about what happened next.

The two executioners tied the pig up. The victim screamed, trembling. One executioner, Uncle Richard, tied the feet more securely, and Simon felt those screams and shouts were in his head, his body, in the kitchen, in the cellar, and in the rooms. The hens and the cocks were afraid to go inside to hen house. The hens stopped laying more eggs. The other executioner, who happened to be his grandfather and the father of his father, raised his right arm with a butcher's knife while his left arm stopped the pig from running away. He could see that the weapon fell towards the victim, and the man nailed the poor pig with the butcher's knife on to the boards. The pig's red and black blood poured on to the green grass, turning red. The last cry came from the pig. The last cry was full of pain and death, and Simon felt a big lump his throat and he swore that he would not eat pork for the rest of his life, having seen that scene. (That was a lie, because Simon likes pork meat immensely.)

After the pig was killed, the two men washed their hands inside the house, and then they had a *salami* sandwich and a glass of red wine as a snack. Later, the men went out to prepare three wooden poles to hang the dead pig in front of the pigsty and drain off the blood. The men returned to the kitchen for two hours to have lunch, prepared by his grandmother, aunt, and mother.

The men went out again to fetch the pig.

The pig was inside on the large table and his grandfather cut chops, ham, fillets, heart, and tripe. With the pork fillets, pork fat, and tripe he made *salami* and sausages, adding salt, pepper, and spices, based on his own recipe. His grandfather became famous with his own recipe, because other farmers wanted his help in making good *salami* and sausages, from the village to all other villages and cities.

However, it was the spring of 1944 and Simon was famous. He was famous for his boil on his nose. It was a hell of a boil, red, inflamed, and big, which made him cry by day and by night.

One morning his mother cycled to a doctor in the city with him, on the long road past the big bend and a big farm, before the village.

The people of this farm had been unlucky a few years before. It was a tragedy. The unbelievable story went as follows.

Five men—the father, his sons, and a few uncles—were working in the fields. They went home at midday with their dogs, washed their hands and dried them. They sat at the big table and the wife served their food with *pasta, salami,* and wine. Later, the wife prepared some salad dressing with olive oil, salt, and vinegar. The five men ate the lettuce, but they did not feel well. They were sick and, before the arrival of the doctor, they died an awful death.

Disaster—the dressing was not olive oil, but poison! It was rat poison, and the woman kept it in a wine flask!

A few days later, the wife committed suicide by throwing herself into the well by the light of the moon. This was the story that upset all the people of the village for many years.

After the well-known bend, the road goes straight on until the house of 'the crazy woman' near the local village. This woman had a lonely life since her husband died. They were in love and she wanted to be near her dead husband and the coffin had to be buried in her garden between her roses and tulips. From then on, the people of the village called her 'the crazy woman'.

They were at the village church and the only Co-op shop, where they turned to the right, leaving the village. The road here passes a quarry on the left side and a country inn on the right side. Customers can eat wonderful *pasta*, followed by cooked maize with roasted small birds or fresh fish and drink wonderful local white or red wine. The road went on to the mountainous area of *Colli Euganei* (a local mountainous range). Here, they turned left and joined the main road to Padua. She and Simon met cars, vans, lorries, and many bikes. Suddenly, they heard the sirens from the city announcing an air raid. His mother got off her bike and dived into a ditch with Simon and her bike. They listened for the bombers' engines and watched out for the black smoke, which the planes were making on the horizon. Then the noise grew louder. The fog was thicker. The smoke was harsh. His mother understood that she and her son were in the middle of a serious air raid. She understood, also, that the ditch was safer than standing on the main road from *Tencarola* to Padua and so they did just that!

The ditch was full of the things that one can find at the bottom of the ditches like tall grass, weeds and nettles, river fish, millions of mosquitoes, mud, bushes, small trees and dirty water, while the bombers were above and approaching Padua Airport, dropping their bombs. Allied machine guns were hitting German soldiers. People were running about shouting, with children and babies crying. All of a sudden—silence! The Allied bombers departed, leaving black smoke, a faint fog, and faint noise. The *Tencarola* to Padua road was clear again. However, the German troops stayed in the city, but his grandfather told them, before leaving for Padua, that the Allied forces had gained ground fast in Sicily, Naples, and Rome, while Hitler's troops had occupied Hungary. Many Jews were in prisons in Poland, and English troops had made an attack on Greece. Simon's father was there fighting, wounded, or taken prisoner. Previously, Simon did not realize the pain, the sorrow, and the fear of being at war. Now he did.

He noticed the pain too, which he got by sitting on the handlebars for four hours and the pain in his back. In addition, it was all for nothing, because his boil exploded on his face; they did not visit the doctor in Padua but returned to the farm.

On 28 April 1945, Mussolini was sentenced to die by Italian partisans. On 30 April, Hitler committed suicide. The Nazi Party, the SS, and the Gestapo were finished, according to Italian radio reports. German troops were retreating from Bologna, Milan, and Padua, converging on the mountain passes, which would take them back to their own land, instead of Italy's, at last. Their soldiers and their officers were dirty. Their uniforms were in rags; they had no guns, no machine guns, no tanks, and no motorcycles. They begged from the farmers, because they did not even have any food and water. The soldiers and the officers were afraid of the Italian partisans, who were looking for them by day and by night. Nevertheless, the Germans were wicked, at that time, and they killed partisans, ordinary people, Italian soldiers, nuns, priests, and children, for instance, at Simon's nursery school . . .

It happened that a few German soldiers were attacking the priests, nuns, and peasants, while Simon was playing hide-and-seek in the woods with his friends. The German soldiers ordered the people to stand against a wall in single file, while he and his friends cried silently in the woods. Then the soldiers opened fire on the people against the wall. Some people were dying.

Suddenly, a group of Allied soldiers entered the nursery school and opened fire on the German soldiers. There was a battle. The Germans and Allied soldiers were dying. Shouts . . . crying . . . noise . . . machine gunfire . . . fighting . . . pistol shots and terrible smoke reached in the wood.

For half an hour, the battles went on and the Allied soldiers won the final battle in the nursery school. The Germans were all dead. The priests, the nuns, the peasants, and Allied soldiers who left were counting the dead and the wounded, but Simon and his friends ran away across the fields to their homes.

When he got home, he told his mother crying what had just happened at his school about the battle between the Germans and the

Allied troops, but he did not want to be at that nursery school any more, because he felt all shaken up inside by the fighting and the war.

There have been many wars since our earth came about, but any war marks a defeat for an intelligent human race that is stupid enough to allow this to carry on.

One day, Simon's grandfather's family saw about fifteen soldiers and two officers wearing khaki uniforms in rags. The men were dirty, tired and had long beards. The men were German soldiers.

After a while, the soldiers marched to a big farm, near his grandparents' farm. Two officers walked to his grandfather's door, while the soldiers camped on the bigger farm. The two commanding officers demanded to stay in his grandparents' house, ordered food and wine, and insisted on sleeping in grandparents' beds . . . without the grandparents!

The two officers talked to Simon's grandfather.

'Wez want zhome. You zslep zstable. Underztand? Ja?

Wez want zeat. You little zeat, ja?

Wez want zbedz. You little zbedz, ia?

Wez all zwoman zeat. Underztand?

Wez no hurt you. Underztand? Ja! Jaa! Jaaaa!'

In short, the German officers got control of the house. The women cooked, washed, dried, and cleaned for the Germans. They were eating bread, home-made cheeses, cooked chickens, home-made cakes and drinking beautiful wine, until they got drunk, and began shouting and joking in German. They were hateful.

Simon's grandparents' family was sleeping in the stable among the cows and the donkey. However, the Germans did not know that they slept in the stable every night, because for many months 'Jack', the bomber, would frighten them every night. Luckily, the fifthly Germans stayed only fifteen days in the farm, because it happened that the Allied forces were storming the village only three kilometres away and all the German troops were forced to move out of the Padua area and up into the mountainous area towards German territory. The Italian people hated the German soldiers, officers, and their 'chiefs'; moreover, the German soldiers were frightened themselves of the Italian partisans who were an irregular army.

Hate? Interest can create hate. Money can create hate. Fright can create hate. Love can create hate. What is hate? People do not know. Maybe wicked people hate. However, good people do not hate. Animals do not hate. Animals attack in search of food only.

There is a tendency to love that which creates love, as Simon's mother did, but she had no news from her husband for five years, so she was very worried.

One day, Uncle Ernest arrived from Padua at the grandparents' farm on his bike and was overexcited. He was saying that 'Nini', her husband, was not wounded or killed. Nini, or Giovanni, was in town, but his mother did not believe Ernest, because it would be too good to be true.

'Did you talk to him or did you see him? Are you sure?' she asked.

'Yes, yes. I talked over the phone to him, but I did not see him. I am sure. Your husband will be here on Saturday afternoon, walking from Cervarese village, in two days' time!'

Simon's mother did not believe Ernest. It would be too incredible, her husband and father of her sons! It was after five long years . . .

Uncle Ernest stopped for half an hour. He took a glass of water.

He got on his bike, said ciao, and set off turning to the left on the way to the village and Padua.

It was three o'clock on Saturday afternoon on the dusty road from Cervarese, and Simon's mother, his grandmother, his brother, and Simon were all walking outside his grandparents' farm gate. The dusty road was a desert, apart from a peasant with a donkey pulling a cart. The sky was blue above, but green and yellow at the bottom with corn and plants. His grandmother was sitting on a marble seat in front of a statue of the Madonna, her child, and some flowers. She was praying quietly, 'Oh Jesus, I beg you . . . Oh Mary, Virgin Mother . . . . .'

Simon's mother was standing and looking at the road, where her husband, maybe, would appear. It was 3.30 and the sun was tremendously hot. However, his father was not coming yet. At 4 p.m., you could see the dust being swept by the wind on the road, but nobody appeared. At 4.30 p.m., they saw one yellow-brown figure coming from the Cervarese road. It seemed to be a man with a long black beard, black hair, wearing a khaki uniform with shorts, no hat, shoes white from the dust on the dry road, with his head low probably due to fatigue.

It was their father and their mother's husband, at last.

The women cried by the lawn, while he tried to remember the farm, the grass, the apple trees, the prune trees, the cherry trees, the hens, the cocks, the cows, the donkey, the pig, and the two dogs barking as if to say, 'Hello Nini, you are at home now.' The women cried too inside the house. They cried while pouring a glass of red wine for him, while slicing the bread for him, and while toasting the bread for him, while their father sat down on a chair, made himself comfortable and told them his story.

He said that he was on a ship from Brindisi to Tirana in Albania, and then to Greece with the Italian forces: Salonico, Giannina, Larissa, Patrasso, Athens and the Greek mountains, where he was taken prisoner by Greek troops during a battle.

During the battle, there were rifle shots by the Italian troops and by the Greek troops. One shot caught his father in his right foot, deep inside the flesh. The Greek doctor performed an operation to remove the bullet, and their father kept the shining brass bullet as a souvenir. During his imprisonment, he machined his bullet into a cigarette lighter, because he was a good mechanic.

Later, he got malaria and had a high temperature and nightmares. He lost his hair and became tremendously thin. He was in danger of losing his life.

The English troops then arrived. The Greeks ran away from their hideout, and their father recovered thanks to the care of an English woman doctor. At the end of the war, he walked and walked across Greek soil, until he got to Athens. Then he caught a ship to Taranto. A thief robbed him of English gold sterling on the ship, while he slept, but his father saved five of them inside his trouser pocket. He concluded, 'My eyes saw many wounded and dead people during this war—Italians, Greeks, and German soldiers and civilians. I would like to rest while I am here. In three days' time, I want to go to Bologna to find work and accommodation for my family. In a month, you can join me,' he said to his wife.

Apart from the Second World War and his father returning home, there was a girl who stayed with her aunt during her school holidays. Marie, the girl, had long black plaits. She was tall, robust, and nice and played with them on the farmyard or in the fields every day. His cousin, Therese, used to say that Marie liked Simon.

One day she called him to play in the fields—without Therese. The day was sunny, hot, with no wind and with no clouds. The sky was clear and pale blue. She and Simon were walking down a green path—she in front and he at the back. A field of maize was beside them, and the yellow reeds with their green leaves were five or six feet tall. Suddenly, Marie stopped and said, 'Simon, follow me into the field of corn, please!'

'Why, Marie?'

'Follow me, please. I want to show you some, er . . . thing.'

She led him to the middle of the cornfield, where the crickets were singing like in a chorus. She crouched down and he crouched until they sat on the ground, face to face, but he felt his face go red and she was red in her face too, and she showed him the . . . 'thing.'

'What is that?' He could feel a warm swelling in his groin.

'This 'thing' is a thing that women need to have a baby, Simon.'

'But I always thought that the stork brought babies.'

'You are silly, Simon!'

Therefore, he had learned another 'thing' that the 'thing' could do, not just urinate. Anyway, they heard someone or something walking near them on the path. It was a dog—Uncle Richard's hunting dog—but he wasn't barking. If the dog had barked, his uncle would have discovered them in the field of corn making porridge, and his uncle would have made porridge out of them!

He didn't discover them. They could see his uncle and his hunting dog making their way to grandfather's farm, his gun carried over his shoulder, while Marie and he were wetting their pants in fright!

However, soon his mother received a letter from her husband in Bologna. The letter said that he was ready with the work and the accommodation. She said goodbye to their relatives with thanks for the food and company. His mother gathered a few things and her ancient cupboard, waiting for Uncle Bert to drive them to the city of the twin towers. In fact, the war was over for Italy.

Chapter 3

It was June.

The Second World War was not yet over in Japan, because on 6 August 1945, the Americans bombed Hiroshima with an atomic bomb. On 9 August, another atomic bomb hit Nagasaki. This led to the fall of Japan. The Second World War cost the human race millions and millions of lives, which was terrible.

Even Bologna was not the city it once was before 1945 due to the action by the German troops. There were broken and wrecked flats, broken railways, and the remains of buildings everywhere. The eastern university was a wreck, filled with millions of mosquitoes, millions of bats, and millions of flies, which were eating the filth of the people. The university—and many other buildings—had no toilets, no heating, no windows, no doors, and no ceilings. The people were compelled to throw out the dirt and urine in the open air, between the thorn bushes, long grass, and the low trees or against the walls.

The people who were made homeless by the war included some good people such as the carpenters, painters, fitters, taxi drivers, teachers, and doctors; and some bad people, like robbers, murderers, and whores, who were living at the university. Simon's father went to the university for free accommodation. Their flat was a very large classroom. It was huge and dark, cold in winter, hot in summer, and full of crawling black beetles.

His father and Julius, who was a bricklayer and Silvia's husband, converted a classroom into a flat. Their toilet was in another huge classroom next door to their kitchen. There was no heating, no sink, no bath, and no lavatory, but it had two or three ceramic pots, which they had emptied on the fields, together with other waste and human manure. Logs and coal were stored underneath the massive stairs and along a corridor, outside their flat. Simon recalls still the immense fear he felt to fetch coal or logs for the range in the dark. When he was little, he was afraid of the dark. When he was alone and at night, he would have dreams or terrible nightmares about huge boulders following him down the stairs, standing in his pants talking to his teacher in the school, or those massive logs running after him into the woods every night.

During his stay in the countryside he did, partly, his first elementary schooling. When they moved to Bologna, he was compelled to start his first elementary schooling again!

One day his mother took him to school at the beginning of the school year. They arrived at 7 a.m. and she was talking to some other mothers. Simon was looking at the scene. He saw girls and boys, and other mothers at the school, teachers, the yard, the sun, and a blue cloudless sky. Suddenly, he saw a boy running towards him with his fists clenched, shouting like a lunatic. Before he was ready for this attack, the boy's fists landed on his face and he flew away fast, shouting all the time, while mothers were shouting and Simon was shouting and massaging his nose. Why did the boy beat him? He didn't know him and he didn't understand ever. Maybe that boy was growing up to be a Nazi . . .

The school started very well and he started too, but Simon did not do very well!

One day the sun was brilliant outside and the lesson was not easy inside. The teacher found out that he hadn't studied his lesson properly and asked him, 'Simon, did you study the lesson?'

'Yes . . . no . . . yes!'

'What comes after the letter "F"?'

'Er . . . "M" . . .'

'Nooo! "G" . . . "G" . . . You are an ass! Come here! Put your hands here, on my desk with your palms turned up and here . . . here . . . here and here! You must learn your lesson instead of looking at the birds outside!' The teacher delivered four huge strokes with the cane on his fingers as if he were a criminal.

At the end of the lessons, Simon got home and he decided to tell his parents that he had been beaten by the teacher. His parents were not annoyed with him. They were annoyed with the teacher and in the morning, his father went to the school to talk to him.

'Mr Teacher, you must not beat my son with the cane or anything else, do you understand me?'

'I am sorry, but if a student hasn't studied his lesson, I will beat him with the cane!'

'You won't! You must teach the lesson without using the cane!'

What a father!

Outside school hours, Simon and his brother would be playing or reading at the Church Hall near to the 'smelly university'.

One day he picked out a book from the library. The title was *After Death*. It was supposed to be a true story in which a man died. His relatives were mourning over his coffin. Nevertheless, he—the dead man—climbed out and went to a dark corner of the room. The people couldn't see him. He could see, but he couldn't talk to the people. Eventually, he got down from the corner, lifted the coffin cover, and spoke to all the people, and they almost had a heart attack! The man was dead initially, but he lived later. The story is true as told in the book, but Simon could not check it out.

However, there was a second story that he could check for sure, because it happened to Simon.

His First Communion and his Confirmation were held in the Church, and afterwards, the boys and girls were playing in the hall, while the relatives, priests, and friends were having some biscuits and tea.

Two boys and Simon decided to play ship a rope. Suddenly, the two boys pulled the rope tight causing Simon to fall on the marble, hitting his head and face. He screamed in pain. His mother screamed with worry. Other mothers screamed. The priests shouted. The boys shouted and the two boys who caused the commotion ran away screaming with fright. The fall was severe, because the left frontal bone over his left eye was raised by two to three millimetres and remains like this to this day. His mother took him home because she was very worried.

When they got home, they found his uncle Ernest and his aunt Lena (his mother's youngest sister) had arrived from Padua in a beige Lancia car, with a new square watch as a present for Simon. His uncle did not always have any money. Usually, he only had debts, but he had a new car and a new watch. Uncle Ernest was very good and very astute!

His square watch, with the golden hands, helped Simon to forget his pain and bruise when he fell on the marble. He was sure of that.

The years were passing continuously. Simon passed through his school years'—first elementary, second elementary, third, fourth, and fifth. Anyway, progress was not regular for him. His marks were below zero! However, he used to go—for his summer holiday—to the Falzarego Pass at 1,250 metres in the Dolomites. Here, there was a hotel which belonged to the nuns and priests.

The holidaymakers were allowed to take one rucksack each, with trousers, heavy wool socks, and so forth, on the coach. They would sing, fight, or cry until they went to sleep. Then they would wake up to eat sandwiches or drink water, and they would look at the mountains covered by snow, the animals, the lakes, the trees, and the deer and the goats. It was fantastic!

It was the first time that Simon saw the Dolomite Mountains with their blue, white, brown, and green magnificence and without clouds. The yellow sun was very hot. The mountain air was fresh and clear. The peasants were working their fields with cows and bullocks, dancing to the music of 'dan-din-don-den' coming from the bells hung around their necks. There was a strong smell of roasted maize with ham, salami, or barbecued duck emerging from houses, wooden huts, or open-air fires. It was terrific!

They would arrive at the Falzarego Pass at five o'clock in the evening. Then right away, the priests would say a Mass to praise God His Son, Virgin Mary, the Holy Mother of God, and all the saints.

After the Mass, all the boys would shout, fight, and cry while they retrieved from their rucksacks trousers, woollen vests, gloves, and water. The priests calmed the commotion made by the boys.

Every day the nuns served breakfast with hot coffee, warm milk, ham, cheese, and bread to them. Later, there was lunch with bread, water, hot soup, meat, fruit, cake, and tea or coffee; and evening meals with bread, hot pasta soup, cooked apple, and camomile tea.

They would get up at seven o'clock in the freezing morning, and they would go downstairs and outside—half-dressed and shouting—to get their hands and faces washed with freezing water out of a freezing wooden barrel, while they were looking up those freezing mountains covered with snow at the top.

Later, they would go upstairs to their rooms—half-dressed and shouting again—and then to the restaurant to get their breakfast.

With breakfast over, the nuns and priests would march them to the church to attend Mass—every day! From ten in the morning to midday, the day was theirs: they would play football or ping-pong, darts or cards, fight, cry, or sleep.

In the afternoons, they would go out in their heavy shoes, with wooden sticks, rucksacks filled with a few sandwiches and an orange drink, a few bars of chocolates, and a torch. They would climb mountains to 2000-2200 metres, walk in the woods to see a waterfall, the ibex, the roe deer, the edelweiss, the lakes, or the glaciers. At five o'clock, they would return to the hotel feeling very tired, and at seven, they would eat their meal. At nine, they would retire, with more fights, crying, and more fights.

A month of that life—without school, without teachers, without books, and without parents—would make the boys very good, strong-willed, and powerful. However, holidays must finish. Their coach was full of moody boys without jokes, without sandwiches, and without songs. The boys were bored and sick. They were not ready to go back to the hot cities and were not ready to study. Simon thought, with alarm, about the teacher at the school and the questions he would ask him, 'What is a planet? Who was Julius Caesar?'

He would not go to a planet ever, and Julius Caesar had died more than 2,000 years ago. Julius Caesar did not interest anybody!

He was more interested in his other brother, Julian. He was born in 1948, but Julian was dead before his mother got home from the hospital. His new brother was the image of his father, black hair, thin, and slim. However, the doctors found Julian with the umbilical cord twisted around his neck, and it strangled him.

Two years after the death of Julian, his mother gave birth to a baby boy, whom his parents wanted to call Conrad; but Conrad flew in not through the window, riding a stork. Now Simon knew the truth! So there were three brothers living: John-Charles, Conrad, and Simon, and Julian was an angel.

Before Conrad's birth, the weather was very hot in August and his mother felt very tired, so she moved with Simon up to the hills, which were cool, especially at night. They stayed at an inn and there was a feeling of utter happiness for them, apart from her pregnancy.

After their breakfast, they often went out to the village to go for shopping. Later, they had lunch with pasta, roast chicken, steak, cheeses, lettuce, bread, water, wine, cakes, and coffee or tea, in preparation of the afternoon 'siesta' (a word which Italians use even though it is Spanish). At five, he and his mother took a walk in the cooling forest, near the inn. After a light evening meal, all the grown-up people sat out on the deckchairs, talking, playing cards, looking at the sunset, or playing records, while the children played hide-and-seek, talking, shouting, or fighting. The evenings continued until midnight, because the night was warm to cool. Those evenings were 'electrical' to the people up on the hillside, with their music, talk, playing, and their wonderful wine.

One day, the doctor advised his mother that she ought to travel to the city because her baby wanted to come out, and Conrad was born. His brother had black hair. He was thin, cried, ate, laughed, and slept, had many pees, had many farts, and made many smells, in line with millions of babies all over the world.

After the vacations, Simon went to first year of high school, but one year later, he was back again to 'first year'. He did not pass in workshop mechanics and mathematical study. The professor of mechanics gave him a rusty iron cube to file, and Simon did not understand when the cube with six sides was straight, or crooked! He tried, but the professor shouted at him, because he thought the sides were crooked, and he had to file his cube until the cube was cubical.

The story went on and on, and the professor summoned his mother to the school to talk. 'Your son worked badly, he does not listen to what I am saying, *and* he left the school to play football. I am sorry, but 'signora', he must return to me this September.' And his mother went out crying in front of the pupils.

When his father heard the story, he aimed a strong kick at Simon's backside, a kick so powerful that it gave him a terrible pain on his bottom, which remained with him all his life without doing things wrong.

In mathematical studies, he did not understand the numbers.

There were divisions, sums, multiplication, and fractions, but he tried again that September, and he passed mathematics and workshop mechanics.

In mathematics, the professor was also the professor of art and drawing. Simon liked drawing and painting then and he does even now.

In the second year, he did better in the workshop. Mr Hammer, the professor, gave him a swallowtail to file and to finish. He liked the swallowtail and he liked the files, the squares, and the chalk. He worked hard during the normal school year and Mr Hammer passed him. However, he did not pass in maths and geography that year. He disliked these subjects, apart from the places across the earth, volcanoes, tides, seas, and mountains. Numbers were lifeless figures, so he did not memorise them, and he was 'an ass', according to his teacher.

The professor, who was teaching him Italian studies, was not intelligent. Simon used to wear glasses for his eyesight, and this professor used to call him a shortsighted beast in front of all his mates. Simon would feel embarrassed, blushing like a ripe tomato, and stammering like a faulty engine. However, one day, he decided that enough was enough, and he removed his glasses for good. A forty-five-year-old professor should make it easy for his students, instead of making it easier for a professor.

When Simon went to school in the centre of Bologna, just under the Two Towers, he would sit on the entrance steps of a house, near the school, reading Mickey Mouse magazines during the breaks. One day, a man wanted to gain access through the main door where Simon sat reading. This man asked Simon politely to take a heavy book from the corridor to a small room, because he had back pain. Simon knew this man, because he rented a flat with his wife and had two young kids about his age.

'Please, 'he was saying, 'can I use this chair, while I hold you by your legs, OK? I will close the door because I feel a draught.'

Simon reached up to the place. He noticed that the man below was breathing heavily, clutching his legs and thighs, while he panicked. The man was looking up under his shorts, and . . .

Simon jumped down from the chair and got to the door. He opened the door and ran down the corridor until he got to the entrance, breathing the pure air outside.

He did not understand it then, and he could never understand it. In addition, the Two Towers of Bologna did not understand why dirty men touch boys. Those men are not true men. 'These men have an incurable disease,' Simon thought. They should be quartered and burnt until the dead cinders are blown away by the hurricane winds.

However, the 'shitty university' was there, with the food remains, with the urine, whores, robbers, and the murderers, as always.

His father owned a shop for repairing bikes. He was a mechanic.

Later, he had some vans and motorcycles for hire. He was very busy with his work. His brother and Simon helped their father. They liked to work with the bikes and the customers. The shop was sited in a small square leading up to the avenues, inside the walled city. To the left, there was a carpenter's shop, where his father bought a second-hand, twelve-string Spanish guitar for him and a mandolin for his brother. They did not play a note ever. Next door, there was a shop selling fruit, vegetables, cheese, pasta, salami, and sausages. The aroma filled the whole area and finished at the police station, which made sandwiches with the strong perfume of salami or sausages.

There was also a wine cellar, and the people would buy gorgeous wine by the flask or by the bottle for their homes. There was a crowd here that did not want to go home, drinking all the time and smoking. They were drunken old men and drunken old women.

Next door to the wine cellar, there was a tobacconist, and next door again there was a baker, who baked bread, grissini, biscuits, and cakes so good that they would wake up a body buried in the cemetery for 1,000 years or more with their wonderful aroma!

Near the square, there lived an old man or a saint who helped poor children without parents and relatives, and Simon remembered him riding his old bicycle cart through local streets, carrying his children and begging bread, pasta, and flour from the people. He was Padre Marella, a priest with a long white or grey beard. He was very courageous.

There was also a supposed young Mafia man, who would steal from the rich people and give money to the poor people, and he was called 'Giuliano', but he was killed by Italian police who fired many shots at his home early one morning, near Simon's father's cycle shop.

Simon and his brother learned, in those years, to drive their father's scooters—a Lambretta and a Vespa—and later, they learned to drive their father's Fiat 600. When they got home from their father's shop every day, they went to the shop for fresh bread for the family, but the fresh bread would be finished almost by the time they returned to their home because it was so delicious.

In addition, his father always sent him to the wine shop to get his white wine up to the square near to their 'shitty university'. As they all ate, their mother would rest the wine flask against the right leg of the table. Whenever the father felt thirsty, he would put the flask on the table without looking, unscrew the cork, pour the wine, and drink. It was the same action every day. Nevertheless, once the action was different . . .

Their father got up and followed the same procedure. Then he spat out the wine, which was not wine, went all red, trembling, and got hold of his chair. The chair fell to the ground and he shouted, 'What is this? This is . . . this is . . . petrol! Are you crazy?' Then their mother shouted, 'Sorry, Nini, sorry! I must have poured petrol into the wine flask. Sorry, Nini . . .'

Their mother began to laugh, because she saw the funny side of the story. His brother and Simon both started to laugh, and Nini, after a while, started to laugh too.

However, the war was not a story to laugh about, because the Martyrs' Square and the nearby streets had suffered heavy bombing during the war, and 800 Bolognese people died, in a single day's bombing by Allied planes, striking against German forces, who were fleeing from the station to Germany. However, the Allied bombers missed the station, and instead the bombs fell all over the city. Therefore, the Germans went home to Germany, and many Italians died while they went shopping in Bologna! It was a tragedy. It is a diabolical tragedy to be at war. Soldiers kill soldiers, who were friends before. There are dead and wounded civilians, because a general, a king, or a president gives the order to kill. However, they do not die from wars themselves. Simon was sent to many schools for learning, but he could not understand war. As Simon could not understand anything, like Pinocchio, the wooden puppet made by Geppetto, his father sent him to work in a printing shop, near his bicycle repair shop. He liked the printing shop and he worked with many lead types, but the lead types were not good for his liver. Then the boss gave him milk to drink every morning. Unfortunately, he got attacks of colic when he drank milk. So he lost the job and he was compelled to work at his father's mechanical shop for a month, and then Simon worked at another factory, which everybody hoped would be better than cleaning bikes.

The factory made boilers for home baths and showers. The owner was small with grey hair. He was old, and to Simon he resembled Donald Duck's uncle with his glasses. He was a wretched soul and a miser. He had a son who worked with him. Luckily, his son was different. He was nice and kind to Simon, to the workers, and to the secretaries.

The first job that Simon did was a series of brass washers from their furnace. The heat was terrible all the time, like hell. Later, the boss employed him to wash the finished boilers, using coloured water to see that there were no leaks in the boilers. With the tests over, they packed in straw and cardboard, for shipping on a Saturday and Sunday mornings by him and a young girl, who liked to flirt with the workers, non-stop. He too liked the girl, but she was eighteen, at the time, and he was thirteen.

It was the wrong time!

When the packing was over, they wanted to try him on a lathe, which was like an enormous beast. He had not seen a lathe before. The son told him, 'This is the lathe chuck that holds the bit. The chuck rotates very fast. You must be careful. Those are the cooling water jets to cool down the bits. Those are the wheels that lengthen or shorten the stroke of the chuck. Are you ready, Simon?'

He tried to turn the first brass washer on the lathe, but it was a disaster, because the washer wasn't set at the right measurement.

He sweated and tried the second washer on the machine, but after a check he realized that the second washer was too thin. Simon felt waves of heat and cold terror when he realized that the third washer was too thin.

He turned off the diabolical lathe when he went down to the toilet.

When he returned to the diabolical machine and the diabolical washers, he turned out fifteen washers. One brass washer was all right. Fourteen washers were too thin and the big boss had arrived to check the operation.

The big boss realized that the work was all wrong. He went red, yellow, and blue and he put the blame on Simon. Simon tried to defend himself but the old miser got worse. As Simon was very upset about the lathe and the washers, he vented his wrath on his boss. He saw a heavy hammer on his bench, and he saw that the hammer would hit the boss's head, because the man was a lunatic! If Jim, the son, could not stop the blow to his father's head, Simon would seriously wound the man. Instead, he lost his job.

One week later, a man arrived at the 'shitty university' on his Lambretta scooter. The man wished to talk with Simon regarding the job, which he had lost. Jim said that his father was very angry still. Nevertheless, he wanted him back. The story ended with Simon working at the factory again, but not on the lathe. Jim gave him another job, all right, but he gave him a donkey's job!

The boilers made in the factory were very heavy. Simon had to carry the cast iron boilers on a bike cart to the sanding company and back, pushing, sweating and swearing in the sun or in the rain, every morning. Those were very hard times, and Simon soon got tired of the work and the working conditions. He thought of changing employment.

His mother and a priest found him a place in a company, which manufactured hospital beds, called HosMedBed Ltd or HMB. Here, there were two directors called Mr Pip and Mr Pop who were brothers.

Mr Pip was small and fat with grey hair. He was a miser, and he wandered continually around the factory. Mr Pop was a copy of Mr Pip, but he was the finance director and paymaster. The company was very big and built on three floors plus the factory.

On the first day, Mr Pip showed Simon his workplace and said, 'File those aluminium pieces, please. There are millions of fastenings, couplings, washers, and brackets every day. Do you understand, Simon?' Simon felt sick!

Benches occupied half the factory for filing and the other half was dedicated to many machines: drills, lathes, cutters, and presses. There was a factory store too, a packing department, and a shipping department. The company and the factory were almost new, but Simon disliked them, because they were weird and gloomy. His fellow workers were young, just like him, and they were filing on their vices from 8 a.m. to 5.30 p.m. for six days, with a half hour rest for food and drink. They talked about sport, books, art painting, sculpture, music, home, and girls . . .

There were millions of pieces to be filed. Besides this, Simon used an automatic drill to drill various pieces and an electrical grindstone to grind many big and heavy cast iron pieces. However, grinding one day and grinding the next, he 'ground' his thumb down to the bone. He felt a terrible pain with dark red blood mixed with the cast iron particles. His boss took him to the hospital emergency unit. The doctor said, 'The wound is very deep and is very dirty, due to the cast iron particles. It must be cleaned up and you must attend the hospital for ten days in the mornings.' This almost gave Simon a heart attack.

The doctor started the cleaning operation on his thumb. Simon could move his thumb and his arm on the surgical table. Then the doctor called in two heavy nurses to sit on his hand and arm, and the physician worked on his thumb. It was ten days of pain, and such terrible agony! 'Oh mother, Madonna, and all saints, please help me!' murmured Simon, praying. Therefore, the saints, together with his mother, helped him at home, and in two months he had no pain and, within one year, he had completely recovered.

One day, actually one winter evening, Simon and a friend were talking about the company. The friend worked on a lathe and Simon worked on the vice filing millions of aluminium pieces. They were tired of the work in the company and were looking for a change.

'I would like to be an arctic explorer?' Simon said.

'You must be joking! I don't like polar bears and I hate Siberia,' his friend replied.

'Then an African explorer?'

'I don't like lions, only being in cages.'

'Then a missionary?'

'Yes! I would like to be a missionary.'

'Then you and I will go to the Silesian church tomorrow evening to ask about being missionaries, OK?'

At 9.30 the following evening, they got to the Silesian church.

There was a lot of snow on the road, very few people, few bicycles, few cars, and two trams on the tramway. It was freezing, and two frozen young men knocked on the great wooden door of the massive dark church. The young men had no gloves, no coats, no hats, but had chilblains all over their hands. Those persons had to be . . . them! No answer came from the great, dark, and wooden door.

They knocked again but got no answer, and they were freezing. They waited another two minutes, and still no answer. They returned to the main road, intending to go home. All at once, they heard a cracking noise and saw a small door at the side of the massive church. The door opened and a monk walked towards them.

The monk was wearing a long brown robe, a thick white and yellow rope around his stomach and a pair of brown leather sandals without socks. He had a nice grey beard, but he was not old. He said to them, 'What wind brings you to my monastery at 9.33 on this awful night?'

'Wind? But there is no wind,' Simon argued with him.

'It's a saying. What do you want, please?'

'We wish to become missionaries . . .'

'Missionaries? OK, OK . . . let's go to my office . . . follow me.'

The monk entered the church with them, but the church was freezing cold and was frightening with its marble statues, chilly paintings, and marble stairs. Many wax candles were lit, but the air was freezing. The steps and stairs cast many shadows, reminiscent of tombs. A quarter of an hour passed, and they walked the stone slabs without any sound. There was only the flickering of the candle, which the monk held by one hand.

The office was very cold, with a dim light on the desk plus three dark wooden chairs, a dark wooden crucifix, and a dark wooden wardrobe. The monk sat down in his chair and said, 'Please do sit down . . . Missionaries? I heard that you that you want to became missionaries in Africa, among the pygmies that cut the heads of visitors and missionaries, Later, they place the heads on poles to be eaten by the lions, the hyenas or the vultures, or . . . . . '

'The pygmies? The headhunters?' they repeated.

'Yes! The tsetse flies as big as cows, the malaria, the lions that eat you while you sleep, or . . . . . '

'We are sorry, Mr Monk, but we wish to go home now, please! Sorry.'

'OK, OK. The door here will let you out on to the main road. Goodnight and bye.'

Before, the monk had walked miles with them to his office. Then the office door opened on to the main street: a ten-second job. These monks!

When Simon went to work and returned home, he used his bicycle in springtime, in summer, in autumn, or in winter. It was pale blue with a sports handlebar, a ten-speed 'Campagnolo' gear system, a thin saddle, an aluminium water bottle, and two very thin tires and wheels. He loved that bicycle. He felt like a racer doing the Tour of Italy. In those days, there wasn't much traffic on the roads, just a few bicycles, motor bicycles, cars, vans, and lorries. Simon used his bicycle in the city, in other cities, and out in the country to breathe the pure air which came in from the hills. His brother would cycle with him, at times, and one summer morning, they decided to cycle to visit some relatives who lived in the countryside 120 km away.

They passed some farmers, tall trees, and villages and later, a wide river, the Po. The scenery was beautiful. However, it was very hot, even at eleven in the morning. Suddenly, Simon's right knee became very swollen, sore, and painful from pedalling. He could not make the bridge across the river, even though he'd taken that road many times with his racer bike. So they returned, very slowly, to the city.

While all this was happening, the family moved from the university to a proper flat, and his father moved from the walled city to an area outside of Bologna with his shop.

Simon's work and the trips helped him to make new friends. He had friends at work and friends at home, such as Rolf, Sergio, and Frank, were workers at the company where he worked, and Claude, Raymond, and William were workers at other companies. Rolf used the file every day in the company. He was a painter at home, and he was Simon's best friend.

Sergio used the drill and he smoked cigarettes like a trooper. Frank used the file—the same as Rolf. However, he had epilepsy attacks and went sleepwalking at times. William was Rolf's younger brother and they had a sister as well. Claude was Rolf and William's friend.

Raymond was 1.92 metress tall, very thin, and a violin player.

The Magnificent Seven? Maybe.

Rolf and Simon were going out painting the scenery: ancient houses, gardens, old bridges, views outside the city. Rolf was very intelligent, very good, and liked the arts and classical music—the same as Simon.

If they were doing nothing—apart from working, walking through the city, on trips, listening to music, going to the theatre, eating with their parents, cycling and sleeping in their beds—then it was a good excuse to visit 'the 'Spipola', which was a cave. There were seven kilometres of holes, passages, crevices, small cracks, and big cracks, rocks, lakes, rivers, alabaster rocks, and giant caves, all buried underneath the hillside.

The first time they visited the cave was in August. From home, they took a small tent, drinks, some sandwiches, a torch, and a short rope.

There were four of them: Rolf, Sergio, Raymond, and Simon. Rolf was the 'head' of the expedition and Simon was the 'tail'.

The entrance to the cave was almost obscured by big stones, small bushes, many birds, small black snakes, green vipers, many bird detritus, and the remains of human food.

It was dark in the cave. They saw three branches inside—one level, one going up and one going down. They took the one going down, but in a while the expedition halted. The 'head' was not sure, because it would be dangerous to go ahead into the guts of the earth with only a torch and one small rope.

'I think,' Rolf was saying, 'that we'd do better to visit the cave another time, with more torches, a fifty metre long rope, a few pullovers, more sandwiches, drinks, and one hundred metre long string to guide us out, just in case.'

In September, they decided to inspect the cave again. Unlike the first time, they took one hundred metres of rope and of string, three big torches, food, drinks, and a few pullovers. It was the same boys and the same branch of the cave, plus a stray dog, which wanted to enter the cave. They did not want the stray dog in the cave, and consequently, the stray dog stayed out.

They walked upright for fifty metres without problems, and then they were compelled to crawl on the floor in single file, getting all dirty with the mud and water. The three torches lit the narrow passage. Suddenly, it was raining large, cold drops from the ceiling, and they felt cold. After another fifty metres, Rolf secured one loop of the string around a rock, just in case they could not find the way out and got lost. Another five more metres and Rolf stopped everybody, shouting, 'Stop! Stop! There's a big hole in the ground to the left and a narrow muddy path going ahead. I can feel a draught and hear running water.'

Rolf and Raymond crawled to the large hole lit by the torches and they shouted, 'It is not a hole. It is an abyss and it is frightful!'

Sergio, the small guy, said, 'Let me look at this hole or abyss, and the river. Give me the rope, please.'

Sergio tied the rope around his body. He tied the other end of the rope around Rolf and Raymond. Carefully, the friend lowered himself in the dark abyss, while Rolf passed the torch to him.

The abyss was full of mud and dirty water and Sergio shouted up,

'It is empty here now. The abyss enlarges to a few metres below. It is raining. It is cold. It is very dark. Give me a few centimetres of rope, please . . . ahhhh!'

'Sergio! Sergio!' they called, but Sergio did not answer. There was just dark emptiness and the noise of water.

'I am here! I've dropped my torch in the water. There is a dark river here and I am coming up. Rolf . . . Rolf?'

'We will lift you up slowly. Don't panic!'

Sergio came up from the abyss, with mud all over his face.

'So, Sergio?'

'There were millions of small beasts and there is terrible mud. There is a dark river. Can you hear? I want to go home, now!'

'Why?'

'Because I do not like "the Spipola" cave!'

'And you? 'Rolf asked them 'Do you want to explore the cave or go home? I am prepared to stay.'

'I am prepared to stay,' Raymond said.

'Then I am prepared to stay,' Simon said.

'Then lets go ahead!' said the chief.

To pass the dark abyss, they crawled along a muddy path only a foot wide. Simon was the last one and he panicked, really, when he saw the dark abyss. Slowly, he went past the nightmare and they entered another narrow passage, which contained stones, mud, and water. At a certain point, Rolf shouted, 'Damn! The string is finished.'

Everybody was frightened. Was it better to turn back or to go ahead? However, they noticed that the passage was less dark while they were crawling ahead. Maybe it was a light or the sun.

After another thirty metres, the narrow passage led to a big stone platform. They saw a terrific, immense, and beautiful cave, lit up by the pale of the sun. The cave was full of grey stones, brown boulders, and yellow lumps of alabasters. At the bottom, there was a green, yellow, and blue river, which was beautiful.

Sergio wanted to see the beauty offered by nature. He jumped from stone to boulder and vice versa. They followed him going down. All of a sudden, Sergio fell between two boulders and shouted loudly.

The shouts bounced back between the boulders and the cave. The atmosphere was frightful. Their friend was hurt and he moaned. His forehead, face, arms, and legs were bloodstained, but the grazes were not severe. His torch was broken.

They wanted to turn back in the direction where the original passage was and to go home, because they were tired of the cave.

However, the 'Spipola' was preparing another surprise for them!

When they arrived at the massive cave, there was just one passage, but on going back, there were ten—all the same—all dark, muddy, and black. And they didn't know which one to use!

'I think that the correct passage is on the right,' Rolf said.

'Not at all. I would say that the correct passage is on the left,' Sergio said, massaging the painful parts of his body.

'Then let's climb those rocks beyond, because I can see sunlight. Maybe there's an opening,' Simon suggested.

'What? Are you telling me that we are supposed to lift a wounded man across stones, rocks, and boulders? You must be joking! 'Rolf said, 'we have a poor torch, no pullovers for the cold, no food, and no water. That is a terrible situation for us. I say let's try to use one of those passages, and let us pray to God, OK?'

'But you are a communist and you should not pray to God!' Raymond said.

'Yes, I am a communist, but I want to save my skin!'

They continued climbing with the wounded man. His red blood stained the grey stones. The torch was almost finished. The immense cave was almost black due to the darkness. They thought of reading in the morning papers: 'Four young men lost in the "Spipola" cave'. However, the stray dog then arrived, wagging his tail and barking as if he was calling to them, 'Are you coming out or staying?'

'I will give you one good kiss or, better, 1,000 kisses.' Sergio exclaimed laughing. They thought that the stray dog knew a safer route from the cave. Therefore, they followed the dog, which chose a passage that was dry without mud and without an abyss and they walked straight through. They took ten minutes from the dark cave to the entrance and the tent, thanks to the stray dog, which saved them almost from death.

Simon's friends went to the cave once more without him, and they told him that the 7 km of the 'Spipola' cave, from start to finish, were covered by them without any problems.

At the hospital bed company, Simon worked for three years in the factory's file department. Then he was moved to the electrical department, where he worked on the main electrical switches and wiring to be used on the beds. He liked the job, and he remained with the electrical department for two years.

Simon's boss, named Rusty, was good, but as well as the electrical beds, he worked at making copper umbrella stands for himself using the copper from the factory and the machines.

He was very cunning!

One day, Rusty asked Simon if he would be interested in painting scenery on his copper umbrella stands at Simon's home. Simon liked the idea and he said yes. He would pay him for his work and he would sell the umbrella stands in Bologna's shops. Great!

But one day Mr Pip of HMB found out that Rusty was cheating and he was sacked. And Simon lost his job painting copper umbrella stands. That is life.

In the meantime, Simon attended a technical drawing school for four years and he passed with very good marks, but these very good marks only served him as a hobby.

His friends were the same.

They cycled to the factory and back from Monday to Friday. After the evening meal, they went out walking or cycling to the operas and the concerts or the cinema and the pizzerias, especially in the summers.

In those times, the streets and the squares were safe, even at night, from the thieves, murderers, rapists, and queers. Everybody seemed to be happy.

Simon was eighteen years old when he took his driving test and he toured Italy during his holidays with his friends. His father lent him his Fiat 600. The tour included Pisa, Florence, Lake Trasimeno, Lake Bolsena, Rome, Naples, Sorrento, Paestum, almost to Sicily, and up the eastern half of Italy: l'Aquila, the Great Stone of Italy, Ancona, Rimini, and Bologna, with him at the wheel, always. Pisa's cathedral and the Leaning Tower were terrific in the sun. Florence and Rome were fantastic. The sceneries, the arts, the Roman temples, the beautiful fountains, Arno River and the Tiber, the Fori Romani, Ancient Rome, the Roman roads, Roman and Florence inns, Brunelleschi's Duomo, Giotto's Belfry . . . and the gorgeous girls they saw.

Naples is famous for the pizzas, the sea, and the Bay of Naples looking up to the 1,281 metres of Mount Vesuvius, whose volcano is never quiet; and Naples is famous for thieves! The friends parked their car full of things to see a museum, and they paid 100 lire to the attendant. They went back to their car, but their car had been broken into through a window. The robbers stole Simon's mother's ancient camera, their flippers, and other things.

'I watch over hundreds and hundreds of cars here,' said the attendant, 'and I could not inspect all the cars here, do you agree?'

He was Neapolitan, very fly. Maybe the attendant was the robber!

The camera was a present from Simon's father to his mother on their marriage, so Simon was very sorry.

They left the car park, but they lost their way in Naples. They asked several boys which road to take to get out of the city, but the boys jumped on their car and demanded cigarettes before they showed them the way. They seemed to be gypsies. They had torn breeches and shirts, dirty faces and arms, legs, smelly feet, and no shoes.

'Give me a cigarette! Give me a cigarette!' shouted the boys to them, hanging from the car. They handed over one packet of cigarettes to them and the boys showed them the correct streets.

'To the left and then to the right! 'shouted the boys. But the narrow street finished in a cul-de-sac.

The situation was terrible and dangerous for them. Eventually, they got rid of the Neapolitan gypsies. Maybe Naples is beautiful, but Naples would not catch them again—no way!

They found the road out of the city, running along the Bay of Naples, which was very beautiful. They saw the Vesuvius volcano with the black ash and rocks. The volcano was hellish, all right! The road which they took from Naples to Amalfi is beautiful and fantastic, overlooking the Gulf of Salerno.

Simon drove through 143 bends and he beeped his horn 142 times. At the last bend, he did not beep, and a mounted motorbike policeman, making himself visible with a round red paddle in the middle of the road, whistled them down.

'You did not beep coming round the bend, therefore you will be fined 1,000 lire,' said the policeman and took out his fine book.

'I always beeped!' Simon said.

'Not always. You did not beep on the last bend, and you must pay 1,000 lire, please!'

'So you do fine everybody who fails to beep on the last bend?'

'Of course.'

'Almost all drivers fail to beep on the last bend,' Simon said, showing the policeman the passing cars.

'I know. I cannot stop and fine all the cars that did not beep on the last bend. Do you agree? You must pay 1,000 lire, please.'

'You must be joking!'

'Then you will force me to take you to the police station and the 1,000 lire will be 5,000 lire. OK?'

Simon's friends, who had kept quiet during the conversation between him and the policeman, now spoke.

'Simon, let's pay 1,000 lire.'

'I would not pay in a 1,000 years.'

'Why?'

'Because the policeman should fine all the other drivers, not just me!'

The conversation between Simon and his friends about the fine was never ending. However, his friends won the contest. They paid the fine of 1,000 lire and proceeded on their way.

Sorrento was beautiful in the southern sun, with the luxury yachts traversing the white waves of the Gulf of Naples to the Isle of Capri and, in the distance, the Isle of Ischia. They followed the coast to Salerno and Paestum, visiting the Greek temples of Poseidon and Ceres. They continued their trip inland due north-east to Benevento, Campobasso, Aquila, and then the Great Stone of Italy. Waterfalls, rocks, huts, a great number of animals, great pines and oaks . . . it was terrific where they camped and they thought that Italy was very beautiful.

They bought some new flippers. They would catch fish, which they cooked themselves. It was great.

By the time they got to Imola, near Bologna, they had clocked up 4,000 km approximately without one scratch. A heavy lorry, going fast, scratched his father's car. The impact was harsh and they were wide awake soon, thinking how Simon's father would take the damage to his Fiat 600. Luckily, his father did not turn the accident into a tragedy, because his father was very good.

Their trip to Elba was beautiful too, with their tent. They would wake up in the mornings and go down to the village for shopping, and later to swim, sunbathe, and fish. At night, they walked up to the village again, meeting boys and girls, laughing and joking. Those were the days! Not the days at the factory to drill and to sweat, but, alas, one needs to work in this life to eat, to drink, to dress properly, to go on holiday, and to have kids.

After eating at work, he used to read travel magazines about London, Berlin, Paris, and Barcelona, and noted their languages. If he travelled to England, France, Germany, and Spain, he could learn their languages in the space of two years. Those languages would open up many jobs in Italy, instead of working on the wires and switches for Pop and Pip's miserly company. The more he thought about travelling, the more he thought about the languages, because the languages might improve his working position in Italy, for sure. But one day the electrical department was shaken by death.

The workers were having a meal break. The testers would stop at 2,000-volts, as always. One tester touched two panels with his hands. Everybody heard a terrible bang and the tester fell down with an electric shock. All the people shouted. The man died with his hands and feet black and smoking. Someone had failed to turn off the 2,000-volt current for the meal break, and one of Simon's friends was dead. That tester was very unlucky.

Therefore, Simon left Pop and Pip's company, not wanting to end his life from an electrical fault! He started to think about travel for real.

Chapter 4

Simon could not rest in his bed. He couldn't sleep, and it was as if he had drunk twenty cups of coffee. The old clock on the wall of his bedroom struck 3.30 a.m. He was thinking about his luggage, his passport, his money, the boat, and his father and his little brother, who were accompanying him to the station. His mother wept silently the previous night. He slept on and off. He turned to the right, but he could not sleep. He turned to the left, but he could not sleep. Then he would take a glass of water from his bedside locker every couple of minutes. Every couple of minutes he would pass water in the toilet. He would feel cold and he would feel hot, while he thought about a thousand things.

His father was saying to his mother, 'Our son is leaving us for his travels. However, he will return soon, in two or three months or a year. Our son wishes to improve his working position. Be sensible.'

He was very good to Simon's mother and to his sons. He was a serious person and dedicated to his bicycle work. He was handsome with his black moustache and his black hair, even though he had almost lost his hair in Greece during the Second World War.

At the end of the war, his father was cured by Italian nuns, who had a miraculous oil for lost hair. But Simon's mother wept continually and silently. He could see her cutting, with the big scissors, the blue, grey, or khaki cloth for the military hats. She would use the white chalk to mark the shape and then she would cut again to produce the hat, which she sewed using her sewing machine. Then the hat would be ready.

He thought of her, his father and his brothers. He thought of Bologna too. The Two Towers, San Petronio Church, the Madonna of San Luca, the Margherita Gardens, Saint Peter Church, and the Servants of God Church. His oil paintings. His drawings. His books by the hundreds. Then . . .

Then he did not feel like leaving Italy for England. He had heard that England was cold, always cold, and it rained every day. By contrast, Italy was gorgeous.

Simon could not speak English, at the time, apart from three words: 'apple', 'cow', and 'big'. He was a disaster with English!

However, a young man of 19¼ years, who has been working as a printer, on a lathe, as a fitter, and as an electrician, reaches a stage when he must try to find work overseas.

The time was 6.30 a.m. on the clock fixed to the wall of his room and he jumped out of his bed. He couldn't sleep now, because 'the dice had been thrown', as a Roman said 2,000 years ago, in front of the Rubicone River, near Bologna, and Simon wanted to cross the English Channel and see the Thames River in the morning.

It was 8 a.m. The time had arrived to leave for the station. His father carried an old cardboard suitcase tied with a string. His little brother followed. His mother was crying and kissing him, and saying, 'It is better that you wear a woollen pullover and a coat, because England is very cold and . . . remember your prayers!'

When they arrived at the station, the train was waiting at platform one. Simon said goodbye to his father and his brother while he sat in the compartment. The stationmaster whistled to start the train. It went slowly and then proceeded faster. Simon leaned out of the train window and his hair was in a mess. However, his father and his little brother were not visible.

The train went even faster. He turned around in the compartment and he saw five seated passengers. There were two fat serious men of about fifty to sixty years old sitting on the left. On the right was one man about forty to forty-two years old and two women in their thirties.

None of the passengers in his compartment were talking at all. They were looking at him. It was very embarrassing! He tried to light a cigarette. Unfortunately, he hadn't smoked a cigarette ever since his mother was pregnant with him. After the ninth match went out, the tenth lit the cigarette, and Simon's hands were shaking, He felt his face blush, his legs would not support his weight, and he felt almost faint after making such a bad impression in front of the passengers. He opened the compartment door, opened the window and felt like jumping off the damn train! Instead, he put out his cigarette in the ashtray. His hands were shaking still and he swore that he would not smoke ever again during his life (which was a damn lie!). Slowly, he calmed his nerves and opened the window to look out at the scenery.

'Modena . . . Modena . . . sandwiches, beer . . . sandweeches!' shouted a wandering vendor, when the train had stopped.

'Ice creams . . . ices . . . ice creammmms!' shouted another wandering vendor.

Some passengers got out of the train and other passengers got on to the train. The stationmaster closed the train doors, blew on his whistle, and the train left Modena station.

The train reached Milan station and remained there for two hours to transfer some carriages to the French and German lines. He stayed in his carriage because he was afraid that he would miss the train if he got out of the carriage to get some papers or fresh air.

Such pain! Eventually, the train found its way north to the freezing cold.

Simon dozed on and off and he heard voices. He thought that the train was still in Bologna, or in Milan, maybe. However, his mother was not in Milan, never!

'Customs! Customs! Why are the Customs men here on my train?' Simon wondered, and woke up.

'Customs . . . papers, please.'

He opened one eye. He opened the other eye and he felt cold.

Custom officers on the train kept saying, 'Custom documents, please. Lire, francs, please. Vite, vite! Passport, please. Vite, Vite!' There was great confusion on the train, and Simon felt confused in his head, because he'd gone without food and drink on the train for hours and hours. He was sleepy.

He was feeling cold, and then the customs officers demanded papers or money at 3 a.m. It was too much!

The train stopped for ten minutes. The customs officers got down from the train, and eventually left the station at Chiasso, not Milan.

After two hours, Simon woke up again because he was feeling cold. His teeth were clattering with the frost. Someone had put out the normal compartment light, and he or she had switched the dim blue light on. He could not see a thing, but he could smell the odour of feet. One of the passengers had removed his or her shoes. Help!

The compartment was dark, and Simon saw the window had misted over, because of the cold. With his hand, he wiped his window clear.

The night was freezing. Snow and ice lay on the tracks, farmhouses, people, trees, animals, cars, lorries, buses, and on the mountains very far away. Where was the train heading? It could be Switzerland, or France, or the North Pole, he did not know, and he slept again. The fellow or the woman still smelled of rotten fish manure, rotten Cheddar, and rotten Gorgonzola cheese.

A cold sun rose on the train, which entered a station as Simon woke up. The station was in Paris, and there was no snow or ice, but it was grey and foggy, and the train spent hours at the Paris station. Two hours doing nothing. Eventually, the convoy departed from Paris going to Calais.

After the city of Paris, Simon changed seats and sat next to the compartment window. The scenery was of flat misty fields, lakes, and villages. There were many cows and bulls, out in the open, because he did not see stables. In northern Italy, cows live in stables because in winter it is very cold. The atmosphere was heavy and dark, even when the sun shone. Dark farms. Dark trees. Dark houses with pointed roofs and square dark outside walls. In Italy the atmosphere was light and bright.

While he was looking at the scenery, he sensed that someone was looking at him. Was it the man who smelled of garlic, or the woman of about thirty-five years of age, or the man or woman who smelled of rotten gorgonzola cheese?

He turned suddenly in his seat to face the passenger. It was a young girl of about eighteen years of age, and she was smiling. She had pale blond hair with a ponytail. Her eyes were greenish-blue. She seemed very nice. Simon left the compartment to breathe some cool air, concluding that the girl had got on the train in Paris. Then the girl came out into the corridor as well! Maybe this girl was spying on him, like a secret agent.

Suddenly, she said to him, 'Ver gu ja?' with that smile.

He said, 'Cosa?' (What?) because he did not understand a word she was saying.

She said, 'Italian ja?'

He said, 'Si'.

She said, 'Ver gu ja', and she started to laugh.

He said, 'Tu London?'

She said, 'Jaa! Tu von a London? Wonderful, ja!'

She spoke in a language that he did not know. Maybe it was German, Russian, or Dutch; it was not French or English, but Simon spoke the Italian language only, so it was a mystery how they understood each other so well.

He got her name: Gredel. She was travelling to London to learn English as an au pair with an English family for a year. The English family would send their daughter to Germany to learn German for a year. Great! He could exchange as an au pair in the same way!

However, he did not do that. He wanted to travel to England, to find adventure or adventures, get a few pounds in his pocket; he would look for a job and learn English for three months. Then he would live in Germany for three months and for the same period in France and then return home. On the other hand, he realised later that he was wrong, because it was not easy to live abroad without money and without work.

Gredel gave him her phone number and an address in London, in case they could meet later to see the sights or go to the cinema, and two hours passed like two minutes talking and laughing and they did not realise that the train had stopped at Calais station—the end of the run. Gredel was spending the night with some friends at Calais, and Simon was getting on the Dover boat. The German people couldn't be his friends. They were hard and harsh. Maybe Gredel seemed a bit more Christian, but he would never know.

He got off the train; he walked to the exit with his cardboard suitcase tied across the middle with a string and went to a bar,

because he was cold and hungry.

It was September. In Bologna, the temperature was 22-25 degrees Celsius and sunny, but here in Calais, there was a cold stormy wind, no sun, and it was freezing; and Simon was wearing grey woollen trousers, a blue woollen jumper, and a short coat with a fur collar that his mother had made for him. Therefore, his face, hands, and feet were feeling the cold.

The bar was not one which you'd see in Italy. It was different, with four wooden walls, a wooden counter, many brown wooden chairs, wooden black tables, and a wooden proprietor! It was a beer place with beer, wine, coffee, sandwiches, and various people, who were standing up or sitting down for eating, drinking, or playing cards, talking and laughing with a terrible noise.

When he went in, the place went quiet for five seconds, and a black fly was buzzing around. The men and the women holding their beers and sandwiches in their hands, or in their mouths, looked at him, taking in his eyes, his mouth, his hair, his ears, his clothes, and his shoes in their minds, like inspectors.

After these five seconds, the bar was normal again, with the laughing, the noise, and the smoke, as if he was no longer interesting to them, but he plucked up some courage and asked the woman behind the counter if she would serve him a coffee and a sandwich, please. Five minutes went by, talking in French and in Italian. The other customers went silent with their mouths open, and the coffee and the sandwich arrived on his table, but the coffee was terrible. The ham sandwich was good.

He left the bar and walked to the boat.

Is it a boat? The boat seemed to be a transatlantic liner and he had never seen a boat that size, only in a photo!

All the passengers were walking in single file on to the transatlantic liner.

'Vite, vite! . . . Presto! One line, please!' shouted the officers in French, in Italian, and in English.

He found the first deck, second deck, and third deck. There was an immense space with offices, shops, rooms, lights, sailors, officers, many people, and toilets that smelled of rotten fish.

The boat was nice, but the top deck was dirty. The funnels were dirty and smoking. The green lifeboat canopies were dirty. The talking, laughing of the passengers, and crying of their children were terrible.

On the top deck, he leaned on to a rail to look at the sea and the birds, possibly seagulls. His body was trembling. The deck was wet and slippery. The boat was shaking. The funnels were smoking and he ventured to look down the side of the ship, and he just saved himself in time from falling overboard, but a strong hand pulled him off the railings, while an officer shouted at him, 'Not there, but sit here, please!' and other words that he did not know. The officer wanted him to sit on a bench, away from the dangerous areas. He sat on a bench, following the flights of the seagulls, the terrible noise of chains at the ship's departure, the passengers talking, and eventually he became calm.

The ship left the harbour, and the English passport officers organised the passengers—like cattle—into two columns. On the right went all those passengers who had 'good' passports and an address in England, money, relatives, and friends. On the left went all those passengers who had 'bad' passports with no address, no money, no relatives, or friends. The officers sent him to the left line. But why? He would look for a job right away, and then, Gretel? She was luckier than him. Tomorrow she would visit London by herself and he would visit Bologna! However, the passengers were then directed to a tall hangar. It was 10 p.m., or 22.00, in Italy, but English people, including the Queen, God bless her, can count up to twelve hours, and no more. Therefore, they begin counting from one to twelve again, because the higher numbers are too complicated for them!

Inside there were other passengers from other ships and English policemen, who were all tall and slim, wearing dark blue uniforms and shiny black shoes. Within two hours, all the passengers went out into Dover. Nevertheless, one young Spaniard, two Frenchmen, and Simon did not get out. A few freezing policemen stood on guard. Eventually, one immense policeman, with square shoulders like a wardrobe, was pacing from the hangar door to a wooden counter, continually polishing his boots with a clean rag. He was in love with the boots!

Italian or Spanish or French people would not dream of shining a pair of boots religiously in that way.

Two English inspectors called for the young Spaniard, but within five minutes he was free, because he had contacted some friends who had money.

The inspectors turned to Simon, but they spoke in pidgin Italian, which was desperate!

'Friends you in England, please?'

'No.'

'Money?'

'30,000 lire.'

'England stay you long?'

'Three mesi . . . months.'

Damn! He should not have said, 'three months', but he should have said, 'one week', because to live in the UK with his 30,000 lire, at that time, meant he would starve or become a thief.

The two inspectors continued, '30,000 lire no money. You sleep night station of police. Morning, you Calais.'

Then a policeman escorted Simon to the police station down at the harbour, which did not look like a police station, but the blue sign on the lamp post did say 'Police Station', so he believed it.

At the police station, the police officer handed him over to three other police officers inside the building and the customs police officer returned to his boat.

A police officer offered Simon a chair, and Simon was given scrambled eggs and tea with milk! Italian people drink tea with lemon, like the Russians, not milk. How disgusting! Anyway, he retired to his 'room', fitted with large and robust bars. He tried to force open the bars, but he was very tired. He slept until seven the following morning, dreaming of thousands of cows spoiling his tea with milk.

At 7.30 a.m., a police officer escorted him down Dover Harbour to get to the boat, which went to Calais.

Once at Calais, he walked the streets looking for a place, which could offer him a job and a place to sleep. He did not like to sleep in September in northern France near the northern sea. He tried inns. He tried pubs, but the answer was the same, non, rien, and non, rien.

A Frenchman, who spoke a little Italian, said to him, 'Try the Italian Consulate here in Calais.'

The consul was sitting at a desk full of pens, rubbers, pencils, his pipe (or his secretary's pipe!), and many blank sheets of paper. Behind the consul's desk, there was a large map of Italy and a small map of Europe. His secretary was sitting at her desk with a typewriter, but she did not use the typewriter. She was filling up spaces in a French puzzle magazine.

The consul invited him to a chair and said in Italian, 'Er, what do you want?' Simon thought that he had a face like the London strangler!

'I am looking for a job, and I thought that the Italian Consulate would help me.'

'Calais has no work. One piece of advice; you should return home to Italy, because you have no money, food, or hotel room. Am I right? You must return home while you still have time,' the consul said.

'You do not want to help me, am I right? However, I will try again for a job, and at 6 p.m. I will tell you that I found a job by myself., Ciao,' Simon replied.

He left the consul office, but he knew that a job on Saturday afternoon was very difficult to find. The church clock struck 1.30 p.m. Slowly, Simon walked—his suitcase with him—down to the harbour, while his mind thought about 1,000 possibilities. So Simon said, 'Will I drown in the Northern Sea?'

His mind said, *'I should not, because I am very cold!'*

He said, 'Should I steal because I am very hungry?'

His mind said, *'My father taught me not to steal, never!'*

Simon said, 'Should I return to Italy?'

But his mind said, *'You must be joking!'*

While he was thinking on the sand by the seashore, he saw a few anglers working with two or three fishing boats and nets, and one idea came to his mind.

If he paid the men, they would take him across the Channel and after two or three hours on the water, he would make it to Dover, which is England, but that was not right, because he had no money.

He walked back to Calais, where he saw a four-storey grand hotel.

Outside the hotel, there was a man cleaning the windows and a short-skirted French woman aged thirty years. She was blonde-haired, very nice, smoking a Lucky Strike cigarette, and telling the man what to do. The hotel was called Hotel de la Ville.

He asked the boss woman if the hotel had any work for him.

'Work for you?' answered the woman in French.

'Sure. You can wash the plates, forks, spoons, and knives for 30,000 francs per month. In the nights, you can sleep in the toilet up on the fourth floor. The rooms are not vacant, *hai capito?*

He understood, *capito*, for sure. He would sleep in the toilet equipped with the water closet, bidet, and bathtub. At nights, he could use a mattress, pillows, blankets, and sheets in the bath without water. He had succeeded in obtaining work and accommodation in France, thanks to Madame, who was very nice, and he felt like kissing her. First, he would deposit his suitcase with the hotel for an hour. Next, he went to the Italian consul to tell him that he'd found one very good job and would start at 5 p.m. The first thought that crossed his mind was this man wants to strangle me, but the man shook his hand and said *bravo!* Then they showed him the office door.

After he went to the shops to buy some items such as bread, ham, milk, drinking water, fruit, a toothbrush, and a toothpaste tube. He had got through his money, but Madame would pay him later, he hoped.

Madame, with the help of a waiter, had brought up two wooden boards, a mattress, pillows, sheets, and two blankets, which Simon used when he went to bed. Then, when he took a bath, he would remove the blankets, the sheets, the pillow and the boards from the bathtub. This woman was very intelligent! His mother, if she were present in Calais, would have said, in her dialect, 'Santa Madonna e Cristo, a bath to sleep!' However, her son would reply to the same mother, 'Dear Mother, it is much better to sleep in a bathtub than to sleep on a street!'

At 5 p.m., he went to the kitchen to see his duties for Madame, who told him that the first job was, 'Lavez des assiettes . . . vite, vite! quite seriously. He washed 300 plates, forks, spoons, and knives, which took him three hours, without removing the new blue pullover, knitted by his mother. He thought that the washing-up was finished! Another load of washing-up was waiting in the line for him, from 9 p.m. to 2 a.m. However, the hotel chef, once the customers had gone to bed or gone home, would take from the fridge sandwiches, brioches, coffee, and more coffee to eat and drink before they went to bed. Simon thought it was all nice and tasty.

On weekdays, the restaurant was not so busy, and he wouldn't have to wash continuously, the chef told him. From 6.30 a.m. to midday, he helped the cooks by sweeping, floor washing, and cleaning the ovens. Later, 'laver et laver' breakfast plates, small plates, saucers, saucepans, small coffee cups, large cups, glasses, and cutlery.

At midday, the cooks and the waiters had a meal in a hurry, because the customers had lunch from 12.30 to 2.30 p.m., and Simon washed up. There was a mountain of dirty plates, cutlery, glasses, saucepans, empty wine bottles, full water bottles, pieces of bread and crumbs, pieces of meat and fat and grease—and always the same cold water.

'The washing-up water must be used until exhaustion at night—hai capito?' Madame shouted at him. The hotel was the most expensive in Calais. The food was sublime. The wines were heavenly. However, the plates, cutlery, glasses, and so on were sublimely dirty.

Then the chef shouted at him, right, left, and centre, 'Dustpans out! The cats out! Plates and cutlery in. Uniforms clean. Butter out from the fridge. Meats out. Fish in . . .' The chef was like Napoleon with his sword (in truth, a wooden ladle to stir the soup) and his white horse (a white stool) charging 101 Dalmatians.

About 4 p.m., the atmosphere was quiet. The chef, the waiters, and the cooks went off for their *siesta*, and Simon stayed in the kitchen wandering into the cold room for a piece of chocolate, cakes, or a roast chicken leg. The cuisine did not offer anything to calm his hunger. At times, he read French books. He did not know French. Nevertheless, his brain became used to French words and sentences.

Christmas 1957 drew near, and one day in November he wrote to his parents to tell them about the train journey and his work in a hotel in Calais. In reality, he wanted to go to London as soon as possible and he asked for their help. His father had many customers with his garage, car hire, and workshop. One woman customer had relatives in England, and, maybe, she would be willing to help him, through his father.

While he waited for an answer from his father, his life in Calais was normal. At times, he walked to a bar at night, which he found was filled with cigarette smoke, French wine, old men, old women, and drunken people. It was very cold in Calais, every day and every night, and the Channel was intense with cold and damp wind, which would compel people to shut the doors and windows of their houses.

There were lots of people in the bars but very few people about on the streets.

The letter from his parents arrived at the end of November. His father had contacted Mrs Rossi. Mrs Rossi had telephoned her aunt in Northampton. The aunt had telephoned an English friend, who was interested in employing a young Italian man to help their cook and work in the fields. He would look after the hens, ducks, horses, and donkeys. Her aunt said, 'Yes, I have the sort of person you are looking for'. Consequently, the English friend had arranged for a work permit for Simon from London. In fact, a letter from Dover did arrive with his work permit in just three days, which was good, and Simon was ready to travel to England after his many adventures. First, he wanted to cook a meal of Italian spaghetti for French cooks in the hotel. The cooks and the chef had never eaten Italian spaghetti with Italian tomato sauce. You could call it, 'Forget me not spaghetti!'

A cook made ready the Italian spaghetti bought at a Calais shop, adding a few grains of salt to the boiling water. Another cook prepared the sauce with tomatoes, good oil, salt, pepper, and spices, following Simon's instructions, then adding the pasta. To eat Italian spaghetti properly would be an adventure for the French cooks or for anybody else. The cooks watched him when he rolled up the spaghetti on his fork and ate. They tried but they failed. Then a cook got up and reached for a pair of long scissors. He sat down at the table. He picked up some spaghetti, and cut it off using the scissors near his mouth as he ate it. They all laughed!

France has an excellent cuisine: *coq-au-vin* or *escargots* or *fromage frais* and wines, etc. The people of France love *le beurre*. Butter is excellent, but it is fattening. It is fat and it is not terribly good for you.

The last morning in France—the last morning in Calais—arrived.

Simon wanted to go to England, immediately. However, the hotel, the French cooks, waiters, the chef, his toilet-cum-bedroom, his bath, his bed, and Madame wearing the short skirts meant someone liked him and, sooner or later, would be impressed for good.

Nevertheless, he did not know England. He did not know the language and he could not understand those English police officers.

Here in France the people were nice and friendly. They laughed from the heart and were similar to the Bolognese people with their language and culture.

So should he stay or should he go?

To be or not to be? To die or not to die? To stay or not to stay? . . . He felt like Hamlet.

Simon saw it as a dilemma.

On the other hand, he wanted to see England, the Queen, the tremendous fog, the smog of London, and he wanted to learn the English language.

When he arrived at Dover, the queue was never ending. He was sweating because he was afraid that one of the custom officers would not like his face, or that his documents were wrong, like the first time. However, thanks to the work permit, the door was opened for him, and he passed through at Dover Customs Checkpoint like an express train.

He was in England.

It was 10.45 a.m. on a Saturday. The white cliffs of Dover were beautiful. The sea was choppy and the air was windy. The first job for Simon was changing francs into English pounds at the bank in the station. The second job was to get a map of England. The next train to London was departing at 11.10 and it was about to leave the station when he reached the platform. It was old, green and black outside and brown inside. The compartments were very hot. The seats were three on either side with the corridor in the middle, like a Wild West train of the 1860s with the Red Indians galloping on their horses without saddles to reach the train . . .

He opened the glass top window to let a bit of air in. The stationmaster whistled and the train departed slowly. The train gained speed sweetly, as if it ran on rubber wheels. The first stop was Canterbury East, then Sittingbourne, said his map.

At Sittingbourne, two passengers entered his carriage. One was a young man, tall with blond hair. The other man was about forty-five years old with grey/black hair of medium height, not fat, but not slim. He smoked a bent pipe, and Simon guessed that the stranger was an Italian.

At Chatham, he dozed off with the movement of the train. It was very hot and he was tired. However, the young man offered him a piece of chocolate. The man was either English or Scottish, and he could talk some Italian, so the Scot told his story to Simon, and Simon told his story to the Scot.

Then they reached the outskirts of London, and the train pulled into the station. Then his train companion told Simon, 'I have a flat near the station. You could rest after the journey, the ship, and Calais, if you stopped the night. In the morning, you could travel to Northampton, OK?'

'Thank you, but the signora will be expecting me tonight, sorry!' Simon answered.

'Well! Do call me, please.' The Scot wrote a note on a piece of paper. 'I had better give you my telephone number—ciao, and the best of luck, Simon.'

'Thanks, ciao.' replied Simon, thinking that Sam, the Scot on the train, was nice, kind, and pleasant.

The station was ten times larger than the one in Bologna. It was London's Victoria Station. There were hundreds of passengers: working men, women, girls, students, children, and babies. There were English, Italians, French, Germans, Chinese, Japanese, Tibetans, and Africans; black, brown, white, yellow, and red people. Some were dressed in the European style. However, many were dressed in the clothes of their original countries and spoke many different languages, as the people got on or off the Undergrounds and the trains; some walked out of the station, to the left or to the right, in total silence.

In Italy, train passengers would eat a brioche or a sandwich with an espresso coffee waiting for their train, and they would talk about sport, their wives, and kids. Here, people did not talk. The station seemed a place filled with robots, with their cold eyes, missing noses, thin mouths, screw necks, and metallic legs.

Simon left the station and found himself in the middle of a host of London buses, which were single-decker and double-deckers, and black taxis, which to him seemed like hearses. Taxis were white, red, or yellow in the rest of the world, not black.

Then he thought, 'This is London with its thick fog, black chimneys, and no sun.' The people were grey. They seemed, with the smoke, like chimney sweeps. The houses and flats were built of dark red, grey, and black brickwork, but had no porches. 'No blue sky here, only grey fog,' thought Simon.

These English people! They use cars with a right-hand drive, but everybody drives on the left of the road, unlike the rest of the world. The men dressed in black, always, and the women were dressed in the 'rainbow' style. They use the pound and their basic number is twelve. The ancient Romans invented, over 2,000 years ago, the decimal system. Maybe the mighty Saxons have twelve fingers, but Simon would not know!

He woke up from his fantasies and recalled that he had to get to Euston Station, to get a train to Northampton. He decided to walk to the station, because walking is good for the legs and the system. However, it's not good for the lungs among all those cars, vans, and buses. Simon walked and walked, until he got to Whitehall, and saw a church to the right. It was Westminster Abbey, where queens, kings and earls are married, and later they are buried. Then he saw Westminster Bridge, and on the right, a big square tower, which supported Big Ben with four clock faces. It was a very good idea, because people could see Big Ben from north, south, west, and east without changing position. Saxons are a clever race!

He continued walking until he saw some French tourists stopping. A tourist commented, 'C'est la maison du Prime Minister! C'est Downing Street. Mon Dieu!' The road went uphill. Simon's sweat was dripping on the pavement. Then he saw two horses beautiful, majestic, huge, and motionless, as if they were made of stone. One horse was black and another brown. On the big horses sat two horse guards, motionless, without eating and drinking, without moving their eyes, for hours and hours. If a guard was itching on his chin, his leg, or he felt a fly on his right or left ear, he must suffer, because he was guarding the life of Queen Elizabeth the Second.

After 300 metres, he saw four gigantic beautiful bronze lions, which supported the statue of Admiral Nelson, the Duke of Bronte, covered by the droppings of thousands of pigeons. Admiral Horatio Nelson fought naval battles against the French ships and won at Adukir of Egypt and at Trafalgar, where he was killed. Poor Nelson! It would have been better for him if he had stayed at home eating pigeons with roast potatoes, instead of fighting the French Navy!

Nevertheless, Trafalgar Square was very beautiful.

Simon left all the above and finally reached Euston, with his tongue between his teeth because he was thirsty. His shirt, his pullover, his trousers, his socks, and his shoes were in a mess. He went into the station and to the ticket office, where he bought a single ticket to Northampton. The train was due to depart at 7.10 p.m., and it would mean that he had time to eat a snack in the station bar.

He sat at the bar counter and ordered a toasted ham sandwich and a beer, thinking about Calais, the ship, the train, and his friend.

A man sat at the bar near him and said in English, 'Are you Italian?'

Si, said Simon. He was thinking, 'This man knows that I am Italian. Maybe I had it written on my forehead'

'Are you traveling to Liverpool?'

'Northampton.'

'Today?'

'Si—ore sette'

'It is cold in the bar and you would be better in my place!'

'No, no. Grazie.'

'Three hours. Three cold hours. My place is warm, and you could get some rest, yes?' said the man, laughing.

Simon did not understand the man, because he was an Englishman and he himself was Italian. He could understand a few words: 'my house', 'three hours', and 'rest'. Nevertheless, Simon accepted the offer.

The man lived near the station in a ground floor flat. The stranger was fat, short, shortsighted, nearly bald, and over fifty years old. He gave the impression to Simon that he lived a lonely life, with no wife and no children. When he opened his flat door, the impression turned real. The man became mad and red, like a hot pepper. His eyes were weird and he was stammering as he said, 'My boy . . . my boy, I . . . !' He was a queer, a coward with no courage in front of women and men. A false man.

Simon opened the door, picked up his suitcase, and ran out of the flat, back to the station to get the Northampton train, but he was worried about some characters who were walking slowly in the station, looking at him and other men. These characters were queers or pederasts, for sure.

At that time, Bologna did not have any queers, because the Bolognese and Italian people hated queers. They believe that God made real men and real women, not weird characters.

The 7.10 p.m. train from Euston arrived at Northampton in a thick cold fog at 9.47 p.m., and at 10 p.m., Simon got a taxi to drive him to Shoremore, a tiny village of Northamptonshire, then to Corn Manor, where he would be working in the farm for a rich woman and her husband.

The taxi driver got in his car, and he had decided that he must drive Simon, at all costs, to Corn Manor, in spite of the thick fog. He drove very slowly, chewing on a cigarette butt, and in silence. At times, he wiped the windscreen with a dirty rag, following the cat's eyes in the road. It seemed to Simon a very good idea, but Italy does not use cat's eyes. Perhaps Italy should urgently use them to reduce accidents on the roads.

There was an Italian story or legend, in which the people of Vicenza,—up in the north—ate cats in winter, because a cat looks like a rabbit and tastes even better, once it is cooked, but cat's eyes are not the same as the cats Italian people cooked, and Simon had never lived in Vicenza . . .

However, the taxi driver kept his car on the carriageway until they reached Shoremore, which was twenty miles away from Northampton.

Chapter 5

'The village was tiny,' he thought, 'with four houses, forty-four cats, four dogs, and four pubs.' The lights of the houses were off, or seemed off due to the fog. Nevertheless, one light was on in the village, coming from a pub. The driver was exhausted from driving in the fog and his eyes were red, not having eaten and by now very thirsty. He knocked several times at the door and silence reigned in the village, but one black rook on a tree answered. The driver, Ben, knocked one more time and the pub's door opened to show a man aged about forty-seven years with a grey beard, dressed in black, with a black and white shirt, shining his torch on the taxi man.

Who's there?' said the pub owner in a deep voice.

'Sorry! Corn Manor, please . . . We are late . . . foggy . . . sorry!'

'Corn Manor? Yes, you turn off to the right at the churchyard. Then it's three miles to Corn Manor. I am sure that the people must be asleep.'

'Maybe. Thanks for your time. Bye and good night.'

Ben drove his car down from Shoremore village, following the bends of the road, which went downhill.

'The churchyard . . . a bend . . . other bends . . . this is it! We have made it, at last!' Ben whispered to himself, as always chewing his dead fag end, and stopped the car in the yard. He got out and said, 'See, we have made it to Corn Manor in spite of the damn fog, and a damn Italian!' Ben teased Simon as he knocked at the door, but there was silence from the mansion. It was 3 a.m. Sunday, and quietness from the hamlet, but all of a sudden, a third-floor window was opened, and the face of a woman appeared.

'Who is there—the devil?'

'It is the Italian for milady!'

'At this hour? It is 3 a.m.? At seven I must cook breakfast for milady and her family and . . . OK, OK! I am coming down to open the door for you.'

While the woman was coming down, Simon asked Ben how much it would be for the taxi fare.

'The signora will pay me tomorrow. It's all right, Simon. The fog has lifted slightly. I will make it to Northampton. Bye, Simon, and goodnight.'

'Bye, Ben.'

Ben drove his automobile up to the exit from the farm, while the woman opened the door.

'Shush! The family are asleep . . . Shush . . . Your room is on the third floor. Tomorrow I will wake you at 6.30 a.m. Now, quiet. I am the cook for the family, and I come from Florence. Now, your room. My room is at the opposite end. Goodnight.'

Simon left his suitcase on the floor and he took a long look at the room. They climbed many stairs in total darkness. They walked up and down many dark corridors and narrow places. To him, the house was an immense weird castle. The room was very big and was actually an attic. There were two windows, a big bed, and a wardrobe with a mirror, a washbasin, a small table, and two broken chairs. There were no heaters; that was why he felt very cold when he entered the room! Simon was so freezing up that he removed his coat and the shoes, but he did not remove his pullover, his trousers and socks, and he got into bed. However, the bed was an iceberg, but he was able to sleep.

Early in the morning, someone knocked at his door.

'Who is it?' Simon said.

'The cook. It is 6.30 a.m. I will go down to the kitchen, while you get dressed and . . . *hurry up!*'

He got out of bed. He did a pee using the pot. He washed his face. He brushed his teeth. He dressed himself. He went out of his room. He locked the door. He hung the key on the nail. He ran down the corridors, stairs, etc. and, *voilà*, Simon was in the kitchen at 6.44 and twenty-six seconds!

The kitchen was nice and spacious. A large window looked at an enclosed garden and the left side of the house. Beyond, there was a hen house and another hen house on the right. Then there were two very old, gigantic oaks on the exit road from the farm. This farm was nice, but dirty, with straw, cow and horse dung, dry leaves, diesel oil, dirty tools, and potato bags.

Simon's grandfather kept his farm clean and tidy, always. On the other hand, this farm's kitchen was very tidy and clean, thanks to the efforts of the cook from Florence. However, it was a pity that the cook was atrociously ugly!

The kitchen walls were painted in dark green and pale green.

There were drawers at the bottom and shelves at the top. One of the shelves was dedicated to the radio, which broadcasted every day. Later, he discovered that English programmers were good for him, for the pronunciation, and for the language.

On the first morning, the cook served him toast, jam, yogurt, and tea, adding milk. Then she said to him, 'You must work right now for me, for milady and her family, and for the gardener, today and every day. Today is Sunday and we must prepare Sunday dinner for milady, the Admiral, and their sons, Colin and Flip.' She paused.

'Hurry up, Simon. You must wash your hands, wash and peel the potatoes, and wash the courgettes and the sprouts. Every morning you will get out of your bed at 6.30 a.m. At seven, you must come to the kitchen and prepare your breakfast. Then you must clean up the kitchen and empty the rubbish bin outside. I haven't stopped a minute this morning! You are young, but I am old, but milady wants turkey in the oven with roast potatoes, sprouts, carrots, and bacon. *Mamma mia!* Then, cakes and coffee. I want tea now and some biscuits, because I am tired—and you? Tea, Simon?' she asked him.

'When the family have had their Sunday dinner,' she continued, 'you wash the plates, cutlery, and glasses. Clean up the kitchen and empty the rubbish. Milady likes the kitchen to be spick and span, with no crumbs on the floor or on the furniture. Afterwards, you and I can eat. OK, Simon?'

While she was talking at one hundred miles a minute, Simon thought that she seemed like a robot, not an Italian woman. She was, without any doubt, very good at her work. On the other hand, she was terribly ugly and certainly not sweet. She was very thin and bent, like the hunchback of Notre Dame in Paris. She had a moustache, a beard, no teeth or boobs, and thin hips. She had drooping shoulders. She invariably talked like a machine gun and without smiling. Simon did not know if she had a husband. If she had a husband, he must surely be dead from fright!

At about 11 a.m., milady came into the kitchen.

'Good morning! A nice day!' she said to the cook. '*Buon giorno*, Simon,' she added, 'you were very late last evening, or last night. Foggy?'

'Si,' Simon answered.

The *signora* had black hair with a touch of grey. She was tall. Her face was beautiful. Her eyes were black. Her mouth was shapely and her teeth were even. She was about fifty years old, and she was very nice. Simon liked her.

'Is the turkey ready, please? We would like to eat at 12.30. Is it OK?'

'Yes, yes. 12.30 will be OK,' answered the cook.

Loud footsteps now approached the kitchen, and a man appeared in the doorway. He was nearly sixty years old, fat and robust. He had a face that resembled a pig, with red cheeks, red nose, red chin, red ears, red neck, red hands, yellow hair, and yellow eyebrows. He wore green trousers, a black waistcoat, a pale green shirt, and brown Wellington boots. Simon thought that he was some clown that the *signora* had invited, because it was Sunday, but the clown was in fact the Admiral!

The Admiral came into the kitchen and said, 'Ah, the Italian boy. Great, great. We need some help over Christmas. Great, great. Is our turkey ready? I'm hungry! The boys and I have been out since seven o'clock. The horses, the cows, the bulls . . . You know, Lucrezia.'

'Sir, the turkey won't be ready for one hour at least.'

'Hummn! OK. Then I will grab one of those juicy apples. I'm going out to the fields. Bye.'

The Admiral went out by the kitchen's side door, while Simon swept up the earth and the mud left by the clown with a broom. Simon would have liked, very much, to hit the Admiral with the broom on his head, if milady hadn't been present. Simon did not like him—no way!

The *signora* then left the kitchen, saying, 'We will be back for our dinner, Lucrezia.'

'Ciao, Simon,' she added.

The cook prepared the table in the dining room, while Simon took out the turkey from the oven to test whether the meat was cooked or not. The meat was not done, and the turkey had to go back into the oven again.

Lucrezia was sixty-five years old, she told Simon, and she was the cook all right. However, as well as being the cook, she had to wash the linen, polish the boots, wash their clothes, do the ironing, feed the cats and dogs, and so on.

If Simon left for good, Lucrezia would be on her own.

By midday, the turkey was done and the peas, carrots, sprouts, roast potatoes, bacon, and gravy were ready in the low oven. They awaited the Admiral's family.

At twelve o'clock, twelve-and-a-half minutes and twelve seconds, the dining room door opened and four persons sat at the table, without any noise.

Milady called from the dining room, 'Lucrezia, pleaseeee. We are ready. Bring in our Sunday lunch—the turkey, please!'

The family started to eat, drinking and talking, making terrible noises, like grinders harvesting the corn.

Simon thought that Lucrezia and he would be free for an hour or so. Instead, the cook began ordering Simon to bring cakes in from the pantry, coffee or tea and milk, gather the rubbish, and boil the water, but then she said, 'I'm tired, Simon. Tea and biscuits would be very nice now.' And they had tea with some biscuits in the quietness of her personal lounge.

After the rest, they cleaned the pots, pans, and the oven and swept the floors. Lucrezia was so exhausted with her work in the kitchen, non-stop, that she took a little nap in her own room, and Simon went outside to the garden, but she wanted to be awakened at 6 p.m. without fail.

The farm was big. The house was three storeys high with a slate roof, which was black. The walls were dark brown. The windows and the frames were black. The front yard was dark grey. The house was not painted. In Italy, houses were yellow, red, ochre, blue, beige, and green, which are the colours of life. To Simon, the mansion was weird and ugly. Anyway, his place of observation was near the gigantic oaks, which dominated the farm, the gardens, and the fields.

He walked the short distance to the first hen house. As he drew nearer, a man began talking to him.

'Hi, you! Maybe you are the Italian. Are you well?'

'Si . . . your name?'

'My name is Dick. I am the gardener's help. You know, I cut the grass, cut the flowers, harvest, slaughter the hens, pick up the eggs. There are hundreds here every day, the damn things and . . . your name?'

'Simon,' he said.

Dick was 1.80 metres tall and about thirty-five years old, slim, with yellow and red hair, red cheeks, red nose, and red ears. He had on a pair of dirty brown trousers and a dirty yellow shirt, a dirty coat and a pair of dirty boots. The dirt was tremendous and the germs would dance with Dick forever!

'Great. I have to pick up these eggs for Mrs Morgan, who then goes to Northampton to sell them. Do you want to help me, please?'

Dick went in to the hen house bent in two, because the hen house was very low. Simon tried to enter the hen house, but in vain.

'You must bend your head, put your arms forward, bend your legs, and your knees must be up. Now push and you've made it!'

Dick talked in English and Simon talked in Italian, so they did not understand each other properly. With some signs and a few words here and there, they communicated.

The hen house walls were 1.10 metres high and thirty metres long. The hens, cocks, brooding hens, and the chicks were very happy, but Simon did not feel happy. The hen house had windows, but they were closed.

'Is something wrong, Simon?'

'I am all right!' However, he tried to swallow a big wave of vomit rising in his throat, until he could not resist any more. He ran the length of the barrack and was sick outside the hen house.

'Are you OK? Is it the smell? Every morning you'll have to pick up those eggs by yourself. I am sorry, but I have many things to do in the fields. The corn, potatoes, cows, bulls . . . OK, Simon?'

If Dick said that Simon must collect those eggs by himself every day—with or without the smell—he was ready to commit suicide!

Dick told him that his day would involve certain things, such as collecting the eggs, helping Lucrezia, lunch, helping Lucrezia again, helping the ducks at the lake, painting the ducks' houses, and so on. There are some special days when we all help, said Dick. Mrs Morgan, Lucrezia, you, and I will help to slaughter, pluck, and wax the hens, to be ready for Mrs Morgan to take to Northampton or London to sell.'

After this important speech, Dick was away and Simon walked to the service door. Soon Lucrezia appeared.

'I told you to wake up me in one hour and now it's 6.30 p.m. Why?'

'I do not know. I felt sick. I am sorry, Lucrezia.'

'Sorry, sorry! We need a cup of tea and some biscuits in my room. OK, Simon?'

Her room was between the kitchen and the hall. It was a small lounge with a deckchair, two ordinary chairs, a wardrobe, a radio, and a table. The walls were covered in wallpaper. A Persian carpet covered the floor.

After her tea and biscuits, the cook talked to him like an Indian chief.

'Milady goes to Northampton every Monday to sell eggs. Furthermore, every Christmas she goes to Northampton and London to sell hens, cocks, and chicks. We all help to slaughter, wax, and . . .'

'I know, Lucrezia. Dick told me the hen story. My uncle used to kill his hens by pulling the head and . . . . .'

'Agh! It makes me sick, Simon! I must drink hot tea, right away. That is disgusting.'

Someone knocked at the door and Lucrezia went to open it.
'Molly! Do come in, Molly!'
'I walked from my home. I can stay one minute. Who is this nice young man? Who is it, Simon? The Bolognese guy? Do you like Bologna, or here at Corn Manor? Do you like Lucrezia? Lucrezia is a very good cook. My husband, Pia, our daughter, and I have been waiting for you at Shoremore and . . . . .'
'Molly, here's a nice cup of tea and Italian *biscotti*.
'Thank you, Lucrezia. I had my tea before I left home.'
'But it's cold outside. Tea is good for you, Molly!'
The visitor remained for fifty minutes over tea, the biscuits, the weather, and the small talk amongst women. She got up from the chair and, still talking, she opened the door.
'Remember, Simon. We've been waiting for you at Shoremore.'
Molly was very nice. However, she was fat, tubby, and round, like a football. Walking to Corn Manor, the road was easy. Nevertheless, returning to Shoremore, the same road was very difficult. Poor Molly.

After the visit, milady wanted to rest at 9 p.m., because she was off to Northampton early in the morning and Lucrezia gave Simon permission to retire early. So, wishing a very goodnight to them, he walked the dark cold corridors and stairs to his room, which frightened him, as always. He tried to open the door, but he was sweating as he went inside. He thought about Italy, where he was not frightened to enter any room in Bologna, Rome, Sorrento, or walk on any of Italy's streets, by day or by night. Here, it was a different matter. His room at Corn Manor resembled a room where ghosts were walking about, so he was looking under his bed, in the wardrobe, and out of his window at the dark night, but he saw nothing! The silence was broken only by his harsh breath and the rooks cawing on the tree near his room. The rooks almost gave him a heart attack with the noise they were making.
'Be quiet! I must get up at 6.30 a.m. Do you understand me or not?'

Hundreds of rooks stopped in a second, and they did not bother him for the rest of the night. It was just amazing!

Simon got up at 6.30 a.m. He went to the kitchen to his breakfast, and later he went to collect many dirty eggs from the hen house, without Dick. He was surprised that he didn't vomit. On the other hand, he got back pain from bending down a hundred times. The smell, the heat, the screams of the hens, the fighting of the cocks and the chicks, he could not cope—no way!

Life at Corn Manor was OK. There was Lucrezia, the masters, the gardeners with their horses, hens, cocks, geese, and donkeys. The farm had another hen house. The noise was terrible, with flying hens, fighting cocks, screaming chicks, and a few weak hens, which were tortured by the strong hens biting their backsides, until they were almost dead. Simon was shocked!

At times, he would take twenty-four geese to the pond. There they swam or played out of the water or in the water. He would look at the oak, pine, and fir forests, the wild free deer, bulls, cows, horses, and the donkeys.

Another time he would draw in his sketchbook the gardens full of flowers, thinking about his mother, father, brothers, and friends;

Bologna and the Two Towers; Rizzoli Street, the train, Calais, 'Madame' and her short skirt; Ben, the cook, and many other things, until his geese came out of the water and he said, 'Ua, which in goose language means 'ready'. The geese would answer him, 'Qua!' (yes). Then he would say, 'Qua, qua!' (go!) until the geese went into their houses on the lawn to sleep.

The work with the geese had ended. Nevertheless, he must do another 1001 jobs, seven days a week, every week, almost without food, drink, or adventures, with little sleep, and without money.

One day, while Lucrezia and Simon were having tea and biscuits in her private room, he ventured to ask the 'SS captain', 'Do you mind if I spend one hour visiting Molly at Shoremore, Lucrezia?' She spat out her tea and a piece of biscuit into her teacup. She turned pale and red with blue, green, and white dots, stammering, 'It is cold, Simon. It is 7.45 p.m., almost 8 p.m. I want you to tell me why!'

'Listen to me, Lucrezia, please. We've had our food and tea. We've cleaned up the kitchen and the rubbish bin is put outside. Milady, the Admiral, and the two boys have gone to bed. I wish to go out for one hour. It is all right, Lucrezia?'

The cook thought for two minutes. She took off her glasses to clean them up, and said to Simon, 'One hour!'

'OK, Lucrezia. You are great!'

He ran along three corridors like the wind, and climbed three staircases. He washed his teeth and he washed his face, and pulled on his new shirt and his coat. He left his room, said 'Bye' to Lucrezia in the kitchen, and ran away from the farm—at last!

It was almost 8 p.m., and being winter, it was almost dark. He realised that he had not ever passed the two big oaks by day or by night. The road went uphill, following numerous bends. He saw many trees, bushes, and fields gleaming in the moonlight. The moon was bright. There was no noise, only one or two black crows on the branches, and his slow steps on the road. The scenery was beautiful under the full moon.

He reckoned that he'd walked four kilometres, and a dim light appeared on the left, a second light to the left, a third, and a fourth . . .

However, these were not house lights. It was a graveyard! He was scared, as if he had seen a lady called . . . *death*.

He had reached Shoremore village and the land of the living. He knocked at Molly's cottage and heard, 'Simon! Come in, Simon! The Italian from Bologna is here! Pia, will you please make a cup of tea for Simon and, maybe, two eggs with cheese or ham, or . . . . .'

'Thank you, Molly. I've had my dinner, thanks.'

While Simon and the mother were talking, Pia was preparing two fried eggs with onions. Later, she came from the kitchen with the food and pushed an armchair to sit in front of the TV, without talking. She looked at him, continually, as if she had seen a beautiful ghost. He wondered about her. Was she dumb or could she talk?

Pia, he thought again, was nice with her long blonde hair. Her beautiful oval face and her intelligent expression with an open smile were truly Italian. She was of average height, and slim, and . . . he liked her! He ate the omelette with onions and watched the TV with his right eye, but with his left eye he watched Pia. She was sitting in an armchair near to him still without talking, and she was watching the TV with her left eye, but with her right eye she was watching him. So they became cross-eyed for that night.

On TV, there was a film called *Wagon Train*, starring Ward Bond.

Molly watched the film, sitting in her armchair. Molly's husband slept, embracing an empty Chianti wine bottle. However, Simon was more interested in her. Did Pia talk or didn't she? Was she normal, or was she moody? Was Pia moody about him or someone else? Pia kept quiet in front of the TV, so everybody kept quiet.

It was 11 p.m. almost. His eyes watched and admired a beautiful, sweet, intelligent, smiling Italian girl, who did not talk, but . . .

'Your next visit to Shoremore, I will cook for you a scramble egg with ham, OK, Simon?'

Then Pia was not dumb. She could talk!

'OK, Pia. Thank you for a wonderful evening.'

He left his friends' home and the road passed the graveyard. He was not frightened, because the dead people were sleeping. However, bad people, who would scare good people, frightened Simon.

When Simon got to the farm, the kitchen and the stairs were almost dark. He went up on the third floor. Instead of going straight to his room, he turned left for the toilet, near Lucrezia's room. As he walked in the dark, he almost felt the handle of the toilet door with his right hand. However, his left hand felt another hand, which gave him one hell of a fright.

A shout broke the quiet darkness. Actually, there were two shouts: his shout and another person's shout.

He heard a click and a light went on. A door opened and Lucrezia appeared in a dirty nightgown. Her grey hair was in a mess and she had no teeth, just like a ghost. The cook was addressing a man—maybe her husband or a lover—who appeared in the doorframe. She said to the man, 'You go into your bed now, OK? How many times have I told you that the light must be on when you go to the toilet?'

Then she said to Simon, 'Sorry, Simon . . . sorry!' and she closed her bedroom door.

The shouts in the middle of the night gave him a terrible fright. He went to the toilet and washed his hands. Simon switched off the light, closed the toilet door, and then closed his room door with twenty-two turns of the key. He rammed a chair underneath the handle, checked underneath the bed, in the wardrobe, and then checked outside his window, in case ghosts appeared.

Simon undressed himself before getting under the freezing bedclothes. He was thinking about Lucrezia's man, or husband, who seemed not to be normal. He was sure that no man would sleep with Lucrezia, apart from a blind man or a dead man.

He was thinking about Pia too, and her scrambled eggs, and then Ward Bond, *Wagon Train* . . . and he got the train to go to sleep!

One day, milady brought a waiter's black and white coat for the Christmas season. She and the Admiral would like Simon to wear it, for any special occasions, not every day or every night. 'Wear it every weekend, please, Simon!'

They asked him impossible things: he had to deal with rotten eggs, hens' and goose shit, food for the geese, and tea for Lucrezia. Milady needed her Sunday turkeys and Admiral needed his cognac, etc. However, he refused to wear the black and white coat for them or anybody else—no sir!

But milady had a strong hold over him (because he liked her!) and the next weekend 'he' was acting the waiter for the family, with black trousers, white shirt, black tie, black socks, black shoes, and the damn black and white coat for evenings and nights.

Milady trained him two hours before the event.

'You should put your feet together . . . the left hand carries the clean napkin . . . the right hand carries the plates, the glasses, or cutlery. Do you understand?'

'*Ho capito*, milady!'

'Well!'

The guests arrived, but . . . they were dressed like him! With black trousers, white shirts, black ties, black socks, black shoes, and black coats. There was no difference at all! Therefore, they could serve at the table, like so many waiters. Lucrezia and Simon could retire to their beds!

Instead, the guests sat at the table. The cook and the waiter would serve them loads of carrots and sprouts. It was three tons of boiled and roasted potatoes and thousands of bacon rashers. It was six turkeys, twenty partridges, ten pheasants, twenty quails, and all the sauces. Ten cakes, four barrels of white and red wine, five bottles of cognac and brandy, and five gallons of hot black coffee.

At 2 a.m., nothing of the stuff was left on the table, only tap water and nibbled bones. The English guests were swearing and burping like the devil. The devil turned red with shame. All that noise, all that laughter, and all those cigarettes, cigars or pipe smoke made Simon almost crazy. The women enjoyed themselves for sure, because they were drunk.

The Admiral had said to Simon two or three days beforehand that Italians eat and drink for the joy and English people eat for need. However, Simon thought that the Admiral and his guests were eating, drinking, and shouting for the joy of it, like so many pigs!

At 3.30 a.m., Lucrezia and Simon climbed the stairs without being able to follow the corridors, bends, steps, or the doors properly, because they were so very tired. All they could see was the beds with the blankets, the pillows, and the sheets.

That was the first evening of 'heavy eating' at Corn Manor. There were another two feasts before Christmas and one after Christmas. Three feasts, all the same as the first one. The guests ate turkeys, partridges, pheasants, quails, and two tons of potatoes and drank ten barrels of wines, whisky, rum, and coffee.

No wonder that the Admiral's guests and the Admiral grew like hippopotamuses!

While all this was happening at the farm, Simon managed to find the time to visit Molly, her husband, and her daughter. Molly had a 'golden' Italian family. Pia, who worked in a hospital nearby, wanted to go to the hospital's dance before Christmas. She did not have a boyfriend. Her mother would be keen if Simon would accompany the girl to the hospital, and he said 'Yes' because he liked Pia very much.

As Simon walked in the moonlight down the black tarmac road towards to the farm, he realised that he did not have a decent suit, a white shirt, or a pair of shoes to wear for the party. He could not use his white and black waiter's uniform. He would look ridiculous!

Simon had decided. He would use his worn black shoes, his worn black trousers, and his worn white shirt. For the coat, he would wear his short black coat with the grey beaver fur collar, which his mother had made for him.

It was Friday morning and Simon asked Lucrezia, please, to iron his white shirt for his evening date with Pia. The cook was sewing a pair of lady trousers. She looked at him and said, stammering, 'With Pia? Are you crazy? She has a good and a fine boyfriend. Why don't you go to your bed and sleep? And no, I will not iron your shirt!'

The beast, Simon thought.

'You will not iron my shirt? OK. I will iron my shirt myself, and I will go, with Pia, to the party, do you understand? Her mother asked me to accompany her to the hospital, that is all! She is not engaged to me. Do you understand, Lucrezia?'

That Friday afternoon, Simon ironed his white shirt. It was passable, or bad, or very bad, with atrocious cuffs and an atrocious collar, but Simon left the farm for his appointment with Pia. The cook hated him for this incident, until he left for London in March 1958.

Pia was ready with her white woollen frock, covered by a blue fur jacket, and shiny black shoes, and Simon had to admit that the girl looked a treat, with her blonde curly hair, and always smiling. The night was cold, and calm with a yellow moon. Simon trembled and his teeth were shivering with the cold, but they did not hold hands. The girl, the beautiful moon, the shining light, or the darkness, the black trees, the small houses, the yellow stars on the blue sky . . . the scene was terrific, like a Technicolor film.

Simon thought about her boyfriend. Maybe he was Italian, English, or Chinese; tall, small, handsome, rich, or poor. Simon did not know.

At a certain point, Pia stared talking about him, and Simon stopped his teeth shivering from the cold. Pia seemed to read his mind. She said that he was English, very nice and tall. He worked in the same hospital that she worked at. The two of them went out together to the shops in Northampton, and to the cinema, but you would not call it 'love', she said.

One day, he fell ill with a terrible disease and she found that she loved him. He was still ill. 'Life can create problematic situations,' Simon thought.

At 9.30 p.m., they arrived at the hospital in the confusion made by many shouting people. Nurses, doctors, patients, tea and biscuits, milk, orange juice, whisky, brandy, and stuck in a corner of the large room there was a band and a male singer.

First, Pia wished to go upstairs to visit her sick boyfriend. 'Only one minute, Simon, sorry!' she said.

To him one minute seemed like ten hours, because he did not know anybody, and he only knew forty or fifty English words, at the time.

Simon sat in a chair away from the confusion, like a white rabbit facing a black wolf, until Pia came downstairs again. He was happy, and she was happy, because she invited him to dance. However, she did not know that he could not dance at all!

'Simon, it is easy . . . one, two, and three . . . one, two, and three . . . it is very easy! *Hai capito*, Simon, do you understand?'

He tried to dance with Pia to the music—a waltz. He was sweating, he was cold, he was hot, his tongue was dry, his eyes were watering, and his collar and his cuffs were dirty. Simon's head, neck, and arms were stiff. His backside was like a rocket pointed at the moon. His knees and legs twitched like a monkey doing a dance. His feet were wooden, like Pinocchio, the puppet made by Geppetto. He was feeling terrible, and fell on to the wooden floor. However, one fall, two falls, or ten falls, Simon danced with Pia at the hospital's 1957 Christmas Dance. It was midnight and she went upstairs to see her boyfriend and, later, Pia and Simon left the hospital, at last.

The night was very cold. After a while, she took his left hand, squeezing it and saying nothing, just walking together in the moonlight, which was beautiful. He had lost his power of speech, and with those looks and touches, she thawed him, like an icicle in the sun. He felt like kissing her, and probably she was hoping to be kissed by him, and moreover, she did not know that he had never kissed a girl, ever, apart from his mammy, his aunts, and his grandmothers. He did not kiss her and, he thought, 'How do you kiss a girl? Does your mouth go underneath, on top, or at the side?'

At nineteen years old, Simon did not have any kissing experience!

When they arrived at her door, she said, 'Sorry, Simon, about the noisy people. The hall was very hot, and I'm sorry my . . . boyfriend.' The night was very frosty, and then she kissed him like . . . her mother!

'The night was cold, but you were warm and charming, Pia,' said Simon. 'Your boyfriend will get better, I am sure . . . Ciao, Pia, and goodnight.'

He walked down and passed the gloomy graveyard to Corn Manor, thinking about Pia's sick boyfriend, the party, the people, her and her 'maternal' kisses. Why had she held his hand and squeezed it in the freezing cold from the hospital to her house? Maybe Pia was starting to love Simon, in spite of the English boyfriend, because the English boyfriend was very ill and Simon was very healthy from his head to his feet, *and* Simon was single. Anyway, he did not know. 'The secrets of women,' he thought.

He knew that milady wanted to slaughter one hundred hens and cocks for Christmas and the New Year. Poor hens and cocks! They start as baby hens and baby cocks, so sweet, so nice, and so yellow. Then, suddenly, they're killed by the wicked gardener, put in boiling water, waxed, and ready to sell in the shops for the wicked men to eat.

Christmas in England was different from Christmas in Italy in the year of 1957. Italian families and churches prepared a crib only, not a Christmas tree. Later, people got used to the tree, like England or the USA, with plastic decorations such as multicoloured balls, triangular stars, and wax candles.

Milady gave everybody presents. It was a bottle of rum for her husband, a book each for her sons, and a clean shirt for Dick, the gardener. For Eddy, the other gardener, a new pipe, for Lucrezia, an English book, and for Simon a pair of woollen gloves. This lasted him for thirty years. It was a very good present.

The last party having passed—thanks to Almighty God—Simon was keen to visit London, very soon, to see Gredel, the German girl whom he met on the Paris-Calais train. He telephoned her, and she could not believe that it was he.

'Simon, it is really you? From Corn Manor? When can I see you in London, Simon?'

Gredel had made great progress in English while she was in London talking with people. However, Simon had made great progress in his English too, talking with the cows, horses, bulls, deer, and geese.

'I shall arrive at Euston Station at 9.44 on Wednesday morning. OK, Gredel?'

'That's fine, Simon.'

She and her English girlfriend would meet Simon at Trafalgar Square, near the fountain and the lions, at 10.30 a.m.

When Simon arrived at the Shoremore crossroads on Wednesday, the bus had just arrived at the bus stop. It was pale green in colour, old and had one deck. It was half empty and very cold. The passengers were frozen and some were sleeping. Some were talking amid the noise of the motor, which sent out suffocating black clouds of smoke. The driver was an old man, and Simon was not sure if the bus, the motor, or the driver would give up first.

The bus took one hour to cover eighteen kilometres without fog, without traffic and without rain, but with plenty of cows, sheep, and donkeys, in time to catch the train to Euston, London.

At Euston, he got out from the station and walked to Trafalgar Square. The lions, Nelson's Column and his 10,000 pigeons, two fountains sprinkling the people, the shining rays of the sun, the morning traffic, and the mobility of the people on that winter's day were all there. Unfortunately, Gredel and her girlfriend were *not* there!

Trafalgar Square was wonderful. He looked, and he looked again, but Gredel was not there. He looked at the sky, the fog, and London's black smoke. He looked at the houses, shops, pubs, and the yellow trees. He looked at the cars, black taxis, red buses, blue coaches, lorries, and motorcycles . . . white, black, yellow, and red people; however, Gredel was not there.

Simon made up his mind: the two girls had not come for their appointment! They had made him travel from Corn Manor to London on the lousy green, frozen bus and on the hot express train. If that was the case, those girls were terrible.

Maybe they had been to Trafalgar Square and they'd missed him, because of the crowds of people walking on the pavements in the square. Perhaps Gredel and her friend were sick or, worse, the girls had been involved in a road accident . . .

In that case, maybe he should ring Gredel at the house where she worked. On the other hand, he did not know how to use a phone in England with shillings and pennies!

On the Paris-Calais train, Gredel had written on a piece of paper the address of the London family where she was supposed to work: 34 Haddington Rd., Camden Town, London. So, maybe Simon should visit her at Camden Town.

OK! He would visit her. Should he travel by bus, or take the Underground, or walk? A bus was dirty. The Underground was scary, so he chose to walk! Nevertheless, his feet were not happy.

After one hour of walking in the traffic and sweating in the sun, he felt very tired, thirsty, and hungry and . . . stupid—stupid for running after a German girl and her English girlfriend in London on that freezing day.

However, he reached the house, and a woman opened the door and said, 'Are you the Italian young man whom Gredel was waiting for?'

'Yes.'

'She went to London to wait for you there . . . and you are here! Moreover, you are on foot. That is amazing!'

Simon went into the house. The woman, Mrs Spencer, offered him a cup of tea and some biscuits, which he politely refused. He could have eaten three roast chickens with roast potatoes, carrots, peas, bread, and a glass of wine, because he was ravenous with the hunger. Anyway, he left Mrs Spencer's house without seeing Gredel, and eventually, he went to a snack bar to have an English ham sandwich and a German beer, instead of the German girl, in the city where Queen Elizabeth II reigns, and was due to travel to a village where Lucrezia reigned . . .

Simon's trip to London had been a waste of time.

The train taking him to Northampton arrived on time. There he boarded the old pale green bus, which seemed like the type used during the wars between the Christians and the Muslims in the Middle Ages. The passengers were, mostly, farmers and farm workers. Some of them were not very clean. Amid these awful smells, he smelled the scent violets and lily of the valley. 'Strange,' Simon thought!

There was a girl sitting on the seat next to Simon, smiling at him.

Now, Gredel was a blonde. Pia was a blonde, and this girl was a brown-haired young woman. He tried to talk to her, partly in English, partly in Italian, and partly in Spanish, even though Simon could not speak Spanish. She was twenty-one years old, and she worked in the same hospital where Pia worked, but in the kitchen. Her name was Sierra. Her family was in Spain and she was single. Sierra loved animals, trees, flowers, and forests and said to Simon, 'Simon, do you like nature, forests, trees, and flowers?'

'Yes, Sierra. I love the forests and animals.'

'Then would you like to spend a few hours with me, in the forest near here, one day, Simon?'

'OK, Sierra.'

Before the pale green bus had stopped at the hospital bus stop, Simon had an appointment with Sierra for 1 p.m., on the following Saturday, to admire the forest, the animals, and flowers.

As he was going down to the farm, he sang happily. Sierra was a beautiful Spanish girl and he liked her.

At 1 p.m. the following Saturday, Simon walked slowly back and forth in front of the hospital, feeling the cold. The forests, flowers, and animals were there all right. The kisses and the hugs were not. She had not turned up for their appointment! Why did Simon date girls who did not turn up for their appointments? Maybe he was ugly, dirty, and smelly, amid all those hens, geese, cocks, and cattle!

Sierra did not appear at the hospital, on the roads, or on the buses. He did not want to tell Pia about the girl because she might have thought that he was dating any girl, which was wrong. He liked Pia very much. However, her boyfriend seemed the problem.

He took the dusty road to Corn Manor, whistling an Italian song that says, 'Women are changeable . . .,' trying to forget his annoyance.

Life at the farm continued in automatic fashion, because the feasts and parties were over. The cook was calmer without the Christmas guests. Milady would entertain friends. Her husband would 'entertain' whisky bottles, and their sons would enjoy their school with paper balls or black ink thrown at other pupils. Dick had his hens, eggs, and ducks, and Eddy, the main gardener, had a wooden hut, his dirty black teapot, his dirty cup, and his black spoon, and he liked tea with milk every day, and a hundred times a day, without changing the water or the tea bags. He sat on his wooden chair smoking his new pipe and looking at the sun, at the rain, at the storm or the cows, horses, and donkeys. He was, indeed, very astute. He was married, but had no family.

Everybody seemed reasonably happy without Simon, and he was reasonably happy to leave the Corn Manor farm with its cattle and forests. In March 1958 he decided to travel to London to see what the world offered him. He would be sorry about Pia and her sick boyfriend. They were living their own life, and Simon was living his own life.

On his last day, Dick used his dirty old Jeep to take Simon to the station. He was a lonely Englishman and had no girlfriend, because he said that women caused many problems. Maybe he was right. Simon thought, at the time, that Dick caused many problems to the people around him with his dirty clothes, and not washing his hands, his face, arms, or smelly feet and pants, from morning to night. Simon witnessed Dick's dirty habits during his four months at Corn Manor.

Chapter 6

When Simon arrived at Euston Station early in the afternoon at the end of March—with his worn suitcase tied with string—he did not know where he could put his head down to sleep at nights. He wrote to St Mary's Hospital in London, but the hospital did not reply. In any case, he had to find lodgings, because he did not fancy sleeping amongst the vagrants down the mighty river. Simon walked along Euston Road, went uphill to Islington, to the northern part of the city, until he came to a large square. It was Claremont Square. Five streets on the left of the square were full of houses, pubs, shops, many people and trees, bushes and seats. Almost every house had two gardens—in the front and rear—and two and three floors.

He saw a girl standing on a chair, with no shoes, on the second floor of a house, apparently cleaning windows. He stopped and he asked the nice blonde girl, 'Do you know if people here rent rooms?'

The girl was sixteen, or seventeen years old, and she had a ponytail. She was smallish and thin. She wore a pink blouse and short black skirt.

'Yes. My mother rents rooms,' she said, and Simon realised that the girl was from Scotland. 'But she's out. Try in an hour, OK?'

To kill time, he walked down to Islington town centre, where there were Indians from India, Chinese, blacks, Irish, Scots, and English people, doing their shopping. One hour later, having killed the time, Simon knocked at 39 Claremont Square, their house, and the girl's mother had arrived back from the shops. She was a forty-five-year-old blonde, rather nice, thin, and of average height.

She was Scottish, too. The mother and the daughter were two drops of the same water; however, the daughter was fresher and younger of course.

'Yes, we let lodgings here, are you interested? It is £1 10s a week and £6 in advance. Do you want to see the room? Yes?'

The room was big with two single beds. Then there was a small table, two armchairs with worn and old cloth covers, a broken mirror and, underneath, a gas fireplace and gas meter. There were windows, and they and the carpet were very dirty. Simon had in mind to refuse the room. On the other hand, his mouth said, 'Yes, the room is nice, very nice' and he paid the rent, because he did not want to sleep where vagrants, thieves, murderers, or drug addicts slept, among rats, mosquitoes, mud, and filth.

Another reason was that Simon liked the girl from Scotland, and Mrs Ballantine, the landlady, used clean teacups and a clean teapot in the room; therefore, he was lucky.

Later, he visited many coffee bars, restaurants, and hotels in the Euston area, looking for work. He was not lucky. He talked to the porters and they would always say, 'No vacancies here at the moment. Sorry.' Porters were very fly.

In the afternoon, Simon was starving. He changed his tactics when he entered an Italian coffee bar at the Strand, very near to Trafalgar Square. The bar was full of people, and there was a man who gave orders to the waiters; maybe he was a head waiter or the boss. The man was short, with a 'pear head', and with an immense stomach, no visible feet, and nearly bald.

'Excuse me. I am a waiter and I am looking for a job,' he said to the man.

'Are you prepared to work for me from today?'

'Sure!'

They shook hands. The man had a problem with waiters and he had a problem with work. The man was a short Sicilian with a big black moustache.

The Italian coffee bar was very busy from morning until very late. They would get passers-by, bricklayers, painters, hotel porters, and clerks. His wage was £2 15 shillings a week during the fortnight that he worked there. On the sixteenth day, he changed his job and he worked at the Falstaff pub, which was English, for £3 15 shillings a week, which was across the road from the Italians.

The Falstaff pub was very nice, and as a plus, he used his white and black waiter's coat which milady had bought for him at Corn Manor. It was a 'VIP' bar and pub. There were three large rooms furnished with three mahogany and oak counters, many multicoloured settees and chairs, Persian carpets, marble statues, big and small lamps, which cast different shades of red, yellow, or green. The food was marvellous. English, Italian, French, Chinese, or Japanese dishes could be washed down with Italian, French, or Spanish wines or beers. The clientele were bank managers, doctors, beautiful airline stewardesses, captains, and tycoons loaded with money and power.

Money and power could resolve all problems. 'Nevertheless,' Simon thought, 'they cannot resolve youth, illness, and death.'

By the end of April, Simon had worked his socks off, after serving a huge amount of people from 8 a.m. to 6 p.m., and he was very tired. He called at the Strand Employment Bureau to see about another job.

The secretary told him that St Mary's Hospital had 'Male nurse helpers' vacancies at £4 per week, food included. St Mary's Hospital was on the other side of the River Thames. Simon didn't mind the distance, because he was young. He gave notice at the Falstaff pub that day because he would be working at St Mary's Hospital in the morning for sure.

But that morning would be a bad morning for him!

In the morning he went to the hospital at 7 a.m. He saw many people: doctors in white coats; nurses in white and pale blue uniforms; staff nurses in dark blue; patients in clothes or otherwise; workers and porters, crying babies, and crying adults. The hospital was massive, with waiting rooms, narrow corridors, vast wards, toilets, and offices upon offices.

An office secretary told him that the wait was about three hours and, later, he had a terrible shock when they told him, 'We have been told that the hospital has not got a place for you here. Sorry!' 'What? The girl at Strand Employment Bureau told me that the hospital had vacancies for sure!'

'We are sorry, but there are no vacancies here.'

Well! Simon had given up his job in the Falstaff pub and he couldn't get work in the hospital. His notice at the bar should have been after, not before changing his job. And now? Without work, without money, and in two or three days from now, he'd be without food and maybe without a room. He decided to call at the Strand Employment Bureau for another job in a hospital, bar, or pub.

The same girl told him that the London Homoeopathic Hospital, near Russell Square and Pentonville Road, would have vacancies in ten or fifteen days' time.

The girl suggested that he could telephone or call to their office every day. Mrs Ballantine, the landlady, was not aware that Simon had lost his job in the bar. Every day he walked from Claremont Square to the Strand. He would say to the same girl in the office, 'Any luck with my job?' and the girl would answer, 'No luck, sorry!'

No luck with bars, pubs, hotels, and restaurants. For ten days he did not eat. He 'ate' a pint of milk every day. It was good, but it was only milk. No bread. No meat. No chickens and no bananas. No nothing. Just walking and walking through the streets of London.

Simon remembered what his mother had told him, often, that milk made him sick, because he had colitis. Then, in London, he drank milk by the gallon! Life is strange.

On the eleventh day, the employment bureau's girl said, 'No luck with your job at LHH—I am so sorry.' The girl was nice and pleasant. She was only an employment girl, not God!

On his first day in London he found work at the Italian coffee bar 'just like that'. A fortnight later he found work at the Falstaff pub 'just like that'. Now, when he really had to find work in order to live, the work was escaping him.

He did not want to call his father to ask for some money. He did not want Mrs Ballantine to lend him some money. He did not want to live amongst the vagrants under the bridges of the Thames River. He did not want to die. Simon had to live in hope.

He had a beautiful new coat, which his mother had bought for him in Bologna for Christmas. However, he was starving and hungry in London. He was so thirsty that his tongue was stuck to his teeth. He had a stomachache. He had a headache and felt suicidal, unless his life improved a lot.

On the twelfth day, he went to a pawnshop near Camden Town with his coat.

'How much for this Italian coat?'

The man was sixty-five years old, short, with an ugly belly, and two piercing eyes, behind two black-rimmed glasses. He said, 'One pound.'

'What? The coat is Italian and it is new,' Simon said.

The miser lifted one hand and said, 'One pound—you take it or leave it.'

That evening he absolutely had to eat. Maybe a Wimpy and chips. *Mamma mia*, his beautiful coat and his big hunger!'

As he walked towards the shop exit, he said again, 'One pound?'

'One pound, right!'

And he said (sighing), 'One pound.'

His coat went to the ogre and one pound went into Simon's pocket. He swore that his coat, one day, would return to him. Instead, his coat did not return to him because the miser kept it!

Anyway, he went out of the pawnshop and into a Wimpy Bar to get two Wimpys and two orange juices, which lasted him the twelfth and the thirteenth days, Thursday and Friday. On Saturday he got one bottle of milk, but on Sunday, he was skinned to the bone. No money, no food, no drink, and he was afraid that Mrs Ballantine would throw him to the rats, because he could not pay the rent.

On that day, at about midday, Simon went out. He didn't have a watch. To tell the time, he looked at the sun. If the sun did not appear, well . . . bad luck! He walked up to Camden Town and he noticed that every place was closed. His steps grew weaker and weaker on the pavement. He thought that he was fainting. Nevertheless, he woke up to a beautiful scent of fresh rosemary, ripe tomatoes, pungent onions and garlic, like in Italy.

In Great Britain there was an awful smell of mutton fat, always, which they used to fry sausages, tomatoes, bacon, and eggs. Houses, gardens, roads, people, companies, cats, dogs, and rubbish bins, all had an awful smell of mutton fat, which made Simon vomit his soul. It was disgusting!

However, following the wonderful scent, he discovered an inn. 'Is it real?' thought Simon. No hallucination? A hallucination brought on by his hunger?

No hallucination, because it was an Italian inn and bar. The door was open and he heard voices. The voices seemed Italian, while the perfume of garlic and rosemary was very strong. The inn was not busy and a woman, presumably Italian, said, 'Hello!' The woman was quick to see the situation. She saw a young man, presumably from her own country, all skin and bone, very hungry and very tired, who was glued to the inn's door by some miracle of Saint Peter or another saint.

'Please . . . a glass of water,' he said to the woman. 'I do not have any money . . . . .'

'First, the water. Second, you must eat quickly and, later, we'll think about the money, young man,' said the woman.

'Thank you. You are a kind lady.'

The woman went to the kitchen to order food for him from her husband, who was the cook. Then she returned to prepare the table for him with cutlery, fresh bread, a glass of red wine and water, like they do in Italy.

The grub was a plate of hot spaghetti with Italian sauce, which the cook served on the table, while the woman said, smiling, 'Eat in peace and drink your wine.' Her husband smiled at him from behind the bar counter. Simon ate the spaghetti and drank the red wine, while he looked at the woman and the man.

The woman was middle-aged, not fat, with black hair. She was small and she looked nice in her Italian dress. The man was about fifty and nearly bald. He had a thick black moustache. He was of average height, and was wearing a clean white apron.

After his meal, he burped with satisfaction. If he had not bumped into the Italian inn, the Italian woman, a plate of Italian spaghetti, the Italian wine, and with everything closed on Sunday in Camden

Town, he was convinced he'd be keeping company with the devil, and without a return ticket. The devil stayed away from him, and early on Monday morning, he went to the Strand Employment Bureau. It was the sixteenth day that Simon had gone without food. However, the London Homoeopathic Hospital had accepted him, at last! For fifteen days, he had suffered with his hunger without talking to anybody, and he had carried his hunger around the streets of London, walking hundreds of miles. It seemed that he had reached the end of the road, but Simon won, because he hated to lose. He tackled the problem completely on his own. No stealing, no drugs, no calling his father.

The LHH cured patients, but not by using ordinary medicines. The hospital used homoeopathic remedies. The first day, Mrs Hartland (the matron), old, dry, and fat, gave him a short list of the jobs he would have to do and a starched coat to wear. He was not quick at the beginning. One week later, he became very quick making the beds, with a nurse, without patients or with patients, young, and old and doing other jobs.

Every day at 10 a.m., a professor, ten doctors, and twenty student doctors, with Mrs Hartland, went around visiting the patients. The professor looked at the clinical card for a patient, while the professor murmured, 'Ah, humm . . . Oh, ah, eh? Aah!' Then he moved to another patient with all the doctors and student doctors. It was like a stampede of cows and bulls let loose with no water.

At midday, the food arrives for the patients, carried on a steel trolley, while Mrs Hartland said, 'Not so much eating. Drink plenty of water. No smoking. No whisky. Plenty of urine—in the toilet and not on your bed! Open your bowels every day and get plenty of sleep. Then you will be happy every day.'

Mrs Hartland resembled a Gestapo captain during the last war.

From 2 p.m. to 4 p.m. every day, the hospital staff had their lunch break on the fourth floor, the top. They climbed or went up and down eight flights of stairs making a terrible noise, similar to monkeys shouting in the jungle!

One day Simon met a nurse at a table, and she seemed very serious while she was eating her food. The girl was very nice, very young with blonde hair, rather small and slim.

'Are you Dutch or German?' Simon asked her. She looked at her plate without talking. Then he said to her, 'I am Italian!' But she looked into her plate, eating her grub. So he thought maybe she is deaf or dumb . . .

Suddenly, she stood up and said nervously, 'I am German! Do not dare to speak to me like that! Do you understand?' And she turned on her heels and went down the stairs, while Simon stood there embarrassed, glowing like a fire in a loft.

Another day the German nurse met him in his ward. She was not serious now, and she was smiling at him. He realised that he did not understand women, like the majority of men.

Apart from normal patients, the hospital had 'special' patients. One had a stroke. One had serious arthritis and another had a serious itch all over his body. Within three months, the men were cured by homoeopathic remedies. This was amazing!

And it was just as amazing how Simon swam for the first time in his life down at the Islington Town Swimming Pool with no staff, attendants, or other people.

He undressed and he remained in his black swimming trunks. The pool was dark. The pool water was scaring, cold, and still. He thought, 'Shall I dive, or shall I not dive?' It was a question at the moment, but Mr Archimedes had taught that, 'a body immersed in a fluid gets a vertical lift from the bottom to the surface equal to the weight of the fluid displaced'. So Simon dived!

He dived into a corner of the swimming pool, supporting himself with his right hand on the concrete, and he floated using his left hand, while he took some sips of the pool water. He was not afraid of swimming or of the pool. 'That was how he learned to swim by himself in the Islington Town Swimming Pool, and Mr Archimedes was right,' Simon thought.

The weeks passed working at the LHH, making 7,000 beds and wheeling 7,000 patients to the toilets.

One spring day an ambulance crew brought in a very tired and very old man, who was dressed in dirty clothes without shoes, but with socks. He had dirty toes, dirty hands, and a long, dirty yellow beard.

The old man was a vagrant, who would sleep among the rats at night. He ate from hotel dustbins and begged from ordinary people walking in Trafalgar Square and the Strand during the day.

The German nurse and Simon undressed and washed him, scraped the black dirt from his feet, knees, and hands using sandpaper. They disinfected him with an atomic bomb, but he could not talk, or maybe he did not want to talk. Eventually, the German nurse went out and Mrs Hartland, the matron, came in shouting at Simon.

'Simon, could you please gather his old clothes for washing! Sweep and wash the floor. Open the window until the stink gets out of here. His documents and any money go in my office, OK?'

Having said all that, the Gestapo chief flew away like an express train without even moving the curtains. Such a woman!

While Simon was folding up the man's dirty shirt and his dirty trousers, he felt two bundles in the vagrant's pocket. He emptied his pockets and found, to his amazement, a lot of money! Maybe £3,000 sterling or more neatly folded in £10 and £20 bundles. He sensed that the vagrant's eyes were pinned on his back, because it would be easy to steal his money. Simon was honest, and later he gave the money to Mrs Hartland.

Every day he went to the LHH to work, apart from his days off—Sunday or Monday. He walked down to Pentonville Road and Euston Road, left at Woburn Place, straight along Southampton Row and into Kingsway. Then he went to the Aldwych and the Strand, looking at the shops, bars, people, pigeons, and the water in the fountains where the water poured endlessly at Trafalgar Square.

At other times, he followed The Mall to Buckingham Palace, where Queen Elizabeth II, Prince Philip, and their attendants lived. He liked the parks and the zoo too because the city was now entering the spring phase. Also, he visited Regent's Park. At times he walked through Hyde Park and Kensington to see people running in the park after breakfast or before breakfast, hoping to slim.

He walked everywhere in London. He looked and looked until his eyes almost popped out of his sockets. He saw monuments, statues, the Thames River, the guards, the Big Ben, and the lion statues. Nevertheless, he was like a lonesome polecat.

At last, he decided that he wanted a feminine polecat to brighten up the days for him.

It happened that LHH gave a party for its working staff: doctors, nurses, cooks, and Simon from 9 p.m. to midnight. The night was organised by the matron. Simon thought that he wanted a female and he found plenty of females.

The party was being held in a big room in a house, near the hospital. The big room was dark, with a few electric bulbs. There was no bar, two toilets, maybe sixty chairs set against the four walls, and a jukebox.

The music started to play, and Cliff Richards sang 'Living Doll' on the juke-box. A few couples started to dance. The girls were laughing and more couples began to dance.

A girl and Simon were not dancing at all.

She was an Indian from India and had olive skin. She was smallish, slim, with dark hair like ebony and a large red caste mark on her forehead. She looked beautiful with her sarong, which is a Malaysian dress. Simon looked into her black eyes, which were beautiful. She looked into his eyes, which were dark brown, and she asked him, 'Do you want to dance with me?' in a sexy voice that would rouse a dead man from his coffin.

Her name was Jasmine or the Fragrant Flower in the Indian language. As they danced, she told him her story. Jasmine was studying to become a staff nurse in London, after which she was going to return to India to tame tigers. While she was talking to him, Simon thought that Jasmine was mysterious and so beautiful. Her exotic perfume pervaded the dance hall, the people, and his head, so he asked her, 'Would you like to meet me next week at Piccadilly Circus at 4.30 p.m.? We could go to the cinema, Jasmine.' She answered, 'Yes, Simon!' and his day was complete.

They watched the film. However, he was not interested in the film. He was interested much more in interesting things she gave him in the dark cinema! He ventured to ask her for another date the following week. Jasmine replied, 'Simon, no more dates. I am very sorry. In a few weeks I shall leave London to go to India then . . . will you be dating me there, Simon?'

Jasmine was very nice, but he thought that she was not telling the truth. Maybe she had another man, a husband, a child or fourteen children! Simon did not know and he would certainly not go to India for Jasmine or the Fragrant Flower's dates. He would be scared of the tigers!

A few weeks passed, and he got the dancing itch. He went to Tottenham Court Road Dance Hall, near Trafalgar Square. After taking three steps, he met a man dressed in black who said to Simon, 'Your tie, please. If you do not have a tie, the shop near here will sell you one, OK?'

He understood! If you didn't have a tie, a big Negro sent you to a shop to buy one at an astronomical price at 10 p.m.!

He returned to the hall, obviously after putting on his tie, because he had the dancing itch.

The hall was dimly lit, with few settees and many chairs. There was a bar with a few mirrors. Young men and girls crowded the large wooden dance floor, stood at the bar or sat on the settees or on chairs, talking or laughing. A few people were sitting in a corner, because they were afraid to dance or some other reason, like Simon! Why? He had danced before with Pia and with Jasmine. He noticed that he was blushing like a red tomato and sweating like a steam train. His hands, arms, backside, legs, and feet shook like a boiling kettle. The thought of dancing with those nice girls made him crazy!

After ten minutes of sitting there, a girl sat on his settee, and she looked into his brown eyes with her black eyes, black hair, and sexy looks. She wore a green coat, a short skirt, and shiny black shoes. The girl was seventeen years old or less. She was beautiful and wore no lipstick. Her name was Nancy.

The check on Simon's entire body was over, and she led him to the dance floor without talking, to dance cheek-to-cheek with him.

He remembers that the disc jockey announced that the next three dances would be ladies' choice, and his girl chose him.

She stroked his neck and his hair, and they danced close together for two hours, because Nancy liked Simon and Simon liked Nancy.

At the end of his last dance session with her, she said, 'I like you, but I should get back to the Nurse's Home. It is late, Simon.'

'I could accompany you to the Nurse's Home, Nancy.'
'I live at the Royal Free Hospital, Hampstead.'
'I know London. Do not worry, Nancy.'

They got an Underground, then a bus, until they reached her destination at 2 a.m. The buses and the Underground trains had gone home for the night, so Simon had to walk for three hours before he got to his bed.

Nancy was beautiful. On the other hand, he was not prepared to travel mile after mile for dates every weekend. Simon was not prepared for an engagement to anybody as yet.

It was May 1958. His lodgings at 39 Claremont Square were nice, because his room overlooked the square, the gardens, the shops, and the houses, with no fog and no sign of London's smog. Simon could see the division between the fog and the sun, which would make a beautiful subject for a painter. If he had brought his oil paints from Italy, he could paint the scene, which presented before his eyes, 'London early morning in the fog'. He did not have his oil paints at the time, so he depicted the scene using his pencil.

It was time to learn English properly, with all the verbs, numbers, and sentences. Therefore, he joined an English course in London, near Piccadilly Circus. The school employed English teachers, English books, and films. He made good progress learning the language, because he hadn't talked in Italian for two years. He only spoke English until he learned the language.

It was time now to get friendlier with Mrs Ballantine's daughter, who was called Lucy. Lucy was sixteen years old at the time and blonde. Her eyes were pale blue and her skin was pink with a few freckles. She was quite small and she was beautiful and sweet, like honey.

One day Simon was shaving down the communal bathroom, overlooking Mrs Ballantine's rear garden, which was full of roses, lilies, and daisies. He was whistling an Italian tune. Suddenly, he heard a sweet voice from the garden below. It was Lucy who said, 'Simon, you can whistle very well! When you've finished your shaving, do you want to come down here in the sun with me, Simon?'

So they began a love story on the Ballantine's rear garden pulling tufts of grass, laughing and joking. He was worried about her mother, but her mother did not worry about them, so they continued their love story.

For a month Lucy and Simon went out together during the day—never by night—to see London, its cinemas, parks, and the zoo watching the giraffes, the lions, the monkeys, and the bisons. Lucy was a young and sweet girl and Simon took her, at times, by the lake among the garden daffodils or the reeds. She was terrific. But one terrible day, Lucy was ill.

On that dreadful day he was in his room, and he heard knocking on his door. 'Cup of tea, Simon?' It was Lucy. Lucy? Lucy never came to his room . . .

He was about to open his door when he heard a funny noise. Quickly he opened his door and he found Lucy had fainted on the wooden floor. The hot cup of tea had spilled. He heard Mrs Ballantine from downstairs calling, 'Lucy . . . Lucy!' Then her mother came running upstairs, panicking. Lucy's face was pale. Her eyes kept rotating. Mrs Ballantine was upset. Simon was upset too and Mrs Ballantine called an ambulance. Lucy had a headache. She felt like vomiting. 'She must have a serious disease,' Simon thought. The ambulance arrived for the girl and her mother.

The following day, her mother returned from the hospital. She said that her daughter was fine, but he could not see her for a month, on the doctor's orders. So Simon was suffering a lot.

During June, her mother agreed to visit Lucy in the hospital with him. Her hair was cropped, and her head had many white bandages. Simon was shocked, and he thought that Lucy must have had a cancer operation or a brain operation. The specialist, who cured her, assured them that the operation was a success, but within ten days Lucy went home to Scotland and their love story was ended forever.

During that month, Simon also got 'sick' because Mrs Ballantine rented the second bed in his room to a man. The man was about fifty-five years old, big, fat, and bald. He was an English waiter, and his garlic breath would kill a robot. For three or four days, he seemed OK. One night, Mr Lovejoy (yes, really!) came into their room very drunk from a pub, while Simon was in his bed reading a book. Mr Lovejoy undressed himself and, wearing just his dirty pants, walked towards Simon's bed. He spoke to him and said, 'You are a man, but I am a queer and I am fond of you, Simon.' His voice was slurred and he was falling all over the place, because Mr Lovejoy was heavy on the beer in the pub.

'Stop, stop it, Mr Lovejoy,' Simon told him, 'and get back to your bed, OK? I am not a queer, and I cannot stand queers!'

Mr Lovejoy returned to his bed and then went to sleep on the floor, until the morning.

On the following morning, Simon went to Mrs Ballantine downstairs and explained to her what happened after his complaint about Mr Lovejoy. Simon said, 'Mrs Ballantine, either he or I will occupy the room.'

'Simon, you stay, but he must leave. I do not like queers,' she said.

After the queer, Mrs Ballantine let the room to a young Scottish man named George. He was good to Simon, and eventually they were good friends. George liked beer in the pubs, where he could stay for hours and hours drinking. He was an amateur boxer and he had a younger brother, who lived in Scotland, named Mickey. Mickey was extremely fond of beer, whisky, or rum, like his elder brother. George had been in love with a Scottish girl in Scotland for three years. Later, the girl fell in love with Mickey. Anyway, the brothers remained friendly or seemed to remain friendly.

One Saturday afternoon, Mickey arrived at Euston Station from Glasgow and they decided to go out to the pub together. At midnight, the brothers returned to the lodging, full of beer, whisky, and rum, quarrelling and fighting. Mrs Ballantine had retired to her room, but she heard all the noise. The two fighters burst into Simon's room. Suddenly, Mickey drew a knife from his trouser pocket and attacked George, who was defenceless. The excuse was the girl and the drink. Quickly, Simon jumped between the two fighters. He pulled away Mickey's knife and put it on his own bed, shouting at him, 'Mickey! Do you want kill George, who is your brother? You are stupid, Mickey, and I want to sleep, now! In a few hours I have got to work.'

While Simon was scolding the two brothers, Mickey had decided to sleep on the floor. George had decided to sleep on Simon's chair, and Simon had decided to sleep on his bed.

The following morning at 6.30 a.m., Simon left the two fighters sleeping and he went to LHH. When he returned to the lodgings, he found the brothers still asleep. Mickey had to catch the train to Scotland, but they did not mention the fights, the drink, the commotions, the knife, or the girl. Then they left the lodgings to go to the station.

When Mickey left London, George and Simon went out often to the pubs and to dance down at Islington Town Centre. One night, a girl made eyes at Simon, smiling. The girl was young, pleasant, and a bit fat with black hair and black eyes. He moved his drink over to her, 'Do you want to dance with me?' Simon said and she replied, 'Yes!' They danced in the middle of the dance floor. Suddenly, she stopped dancing with him and walked out of the hall quite mad. Everything seemed OK while they danced. He had a shower before they left. His teeth were white. His feet and socks were clean, and he had not any bad smells on his body. Simon thought that the girl was very moody, but why?

However, Simon and George went out from the dance hall to a clean pub, which had three rooms. The main room had a bar and five big live green plants in vases. George wanted a drinking session with Simon, so Simon bought a Guinness and a whisky for George and a beer for himself. Later, George bought a beer for Simon and another Guinness and rum for himself, and so on, during the night. The sessions were fine for Simon, because his friend was drunk and he was sober. Simon poured some of his drinks on the plants without George noticing!

At eleven o'clock, they heard a terrible noise. Men and women seemed to be fighting in the middle of the pub. Chairs, tables, lamps, empty bottles, and glasses flew over the wooden counter, among the plants and the people. There were shouts, cries, and laughter, and then someone yelled, 'Police! Police!

At least ten officers fought some pub customers, and twenty people were charged for being drunk, including his friend, George.

Simon went to the police station that night. An officer told him that his friend was in hospital.

In the morning he visited George. He'd been mauled by the police and an English drunkard. The doctors said that his face would be fine, given one week . . . if he would stop drinking. However, the doctors did not know George! Simon did not like drinking, apart from water and a beer or one glass of Italian wine at the pub, that was all. He read a book in his room instead or listened to radio programmes. George did not listen to the radio, but he smoked non-stop, like a steam train. He used loose tobacco and thin rice paper to produce a thin cigarette with one hand. George was an expert at this, and of course they were cheaper! George was twenty-seven years old, and Simon was twenty, at the time.

However, the LHH was fine with Mrs Harland and all the nurses, doctors, surgeons, cooks, porters, and patients. Patients define a hospital—no patients, no hospitals. But there was a hospital and there was a new English staff nurse called Alison, and there was Tony, an Italian male nurse, all working on Simon's ward. Alison was nice, tall, and blonde, but she was very moody all the time towards all the people.

One day Tony was washing his hands in the shared sink in 'B' ward. Alison needed to wash her hands at the same time, and she looked in the mirror, smiling at him. Tony looked at her in the same mirror, smiling at her. Quite suddenly, she said to him, 'You've made me pregnant.'

'What?' Tony said.

'Yes! You got me pregnant!' and the English nurse started to cry. Then she ran into the nurses' pantry. In fact the pantry was empty, and Tony closed the door.

'I do not understand,' he said to her. 'I was in Italy for twenty years until I came to England. I am living here for two weeks. Do not try to put this on me!'

Luckily, two nurses came in and Alison went out of the pantry and out of Tony's life, for ever. Alison had tried a trick, but Tony was not stupid. She got drunk and a man made her pregnant. Tony told Simon this story about Alison, her crying and the pregnancy at the tea break.

Then Alison was moved to another ward and another English staff nurse took her place. Jane was blonde, nice, kind, and witty and he liked her.

One day she was smiling continually at him across the bed, which they were making. Her eyes met his eyes, and he had a date with her, which was very quick.

'I will wait for you at the Woburn Place bus stop, near the LHH, at 2.30 p.m. OK, Jane?'

'That's fine, Simon.'

Sunday afternoon, he got to the bus stop at 2.27 p.m., but Jane had not arrived as yet. He was dressed in a pair of beige trousers, a white pullover, white shirt, and brown shoes, all bought by Simon in shops in Bologna. The street, shops, pubs, and church had a deserted look.

There were no people about.

The air was warm.

At 3 p.m., four young men stopped at the bus stop, dressed in black from their shoes to their coats, apart from their white shirts, which were dirty. They had four black cameras, apparently new. The young men were, apparently, English and smoking Marlboro cigarettes without filters.

Two minutes later, two black police cars braked at the bus stop. Four police officers came out, and the four young men—and Simon—were pushed into the cars and taken away to the police station.

At the police station, things became a bit clearer. The young men were robbers, who had broken a photographic shop window to steal the cameras. One of the robbers swore that Simon had nothing to do with the robbery. The police inspector agreed and Simon was allowed to leave. That robber was a gentleman!

Simon walked back to the bus stop at 3.15, but Jane was not there.

She had arrived at 3.10 while Simon was at the police station, and having stopped a while, she went home.

The timing was all wrong.

On another date, Jane wanted to go to Epping Forest, on the northern edge of London, with old oaks, old pines, old villages, and old pubs. They were travelling on a red double-decker bus, and Jane talked and talked because she wanted Simon to study to become a doctor.

'I will lend my medical books to you. Then you can study, start a course at a university, and you could become a doctor. OK, Simon?'

'I was at the University of Bologna.'

'You! When?'

'I was there from seven to thirteen years old.'

'You must be joking! Here in England you must be eighteen or nineteen years old to start a university course.'

'I am serious, Jane! After the war, the university could not have lessons because the teachers were missing and -'

'You're joking, Simon! Try studying to become a doctor. You could study in my room.'

'Maybe, Jane.'

'We are at Epping Forest now,' she told Simon 'with our picnic basket.'

She walked into the forest in the sun, among the plants, the flowers, and the dry grass, until she found a sheltered place.

'We can sit here, OK?' she said, and she took from the basket a few bananas, ripe apples, bread, and orange drinks. The green pines and the broad oaks were beautiful with their coolness and quietness. Every so often, they could see deer or squirrels in the depth of the forest.

Jane had on a white blouse, a wide blue skirt, and tennis shoes. Simon was wearing a pair of brown trousers, a white shirt, and brown shoes.

Jane blushed and moved closer to him. He moved closer to her, and a ripe red apple fell to the ground.

Jane's hold around his neck became stronger and he protested, 'Jane, you are strangling me!'

'Sorry, Simon, but I am so in love with you!'

Jane laughed with a wicked laugh, and Simon touched the rigid garment that women wore—at that time—underneath their skirts to safeguard their valued goods. A chastity belt? He did not know, but the 'chastity belt' got rid of his urge to make love to Jane in Epping Forest.

Jane and Simon continued going out to the markets, to the cinema, walking, or in the parks, but he could not feel at ease with Jane.

Lucy, Jasmine, and Nancy were much better. Jane was hard and harsh, like being dated by a camel, which lived in the Sahara desert!

On the night shift at the hospital, the night staff nurses would need help from the male nurses, who were young men from Italy, France, and Spain. At the outset, an Indian staff nurse selected Simon. She was small and slim. Her skin was brown, her hair was black, and her eyes were black too. Sadly, she was married. She was thirty-two years old and beautiful, and was called Kamali, which means 'full of desires' in the Indian language. *And* Kamali was full of desires . . .

For one week, Kamali was kind to the patients and to Simon. She and Simon did the rounds among the patients, taking the pots to the toilet or bringing water or Ovaltine drinks to the sick men. Later, they would go into the nurses' pantry to have tea and biscuits. But one night—it was midnight—the street lamps were swinging in the wind, a few boats were floating down the river, trains were moving down the tracks at Euston station, the full moon hid behind the clouds . . . and Kamali closed the pantry door. She turned in Simon's direction and said, with a sexy voice, half in Indian and half in English, 'Simon, I like you! I would like to make love with an Italian man. You are handsome. You are strong and you are tanned.'

Then she pushed him violently against the wall and the table, where there were apples, kiwi fruit, and ripe bananas, so he could not escape her embraces.

'Kamali! . . . Kamali! If your husband came here, and . . .,' Simon said.

'He's working in another hospital on the night shift,' Kamali said.

'Kamali, if the staff nurse comes, and . . . . .'

'The door is closed, and I am the staff nurse for this ward, OK?'

'Kamali, I am already going out with a girl, and . . . . .'

'My kisses are better and sexier, Simon!'

'Kamali . . . Nooo! I am serious.'

'OK! My 'Italiano'. You are handsome. Ciao!'

The little Indian woman was beautiful and sexy, but he could not afford to sacrifice Jane for a night with Kamali. Besides, her husband might be a strong Indian man, who would kill Simon with a knife if he messed with his wife.

For the following nights, Kamali was moved from his ward and another staff nurse arrived. She was young, nice, English, blonde, and unmarried. She had no funny ways and was quite normal, and was called Lily.

One night Simon felt very tired and asked Lily's permission to go to a small room to sleep. While he was sleeping, Simon had a nightmare of a girl in the sea, being terrified by sharks. Then the scene changed. The girl was afraid of Indian tigers. But the girl changed again into a staff nurse. This nurse was Lily, who was afraid of the hospital. He woke up from the nightmare to find Lily frightened, in front of him.

'I had a fright, Simon!' Lily said.

'Shush, Lily! What's happened?'

'Listen! Listen!'

'I am listening, but I do not know, Lily!'

The patients were all sleeping, but their heads, blankets, beds, and pots all seemed bigger with the shadows. Lily was frightened and cupped her two hands ready to shout, while a patient shouted in fear, and Simon laughed at the scene. The patient chewed his denture's rubber shield, non-stop, while he was asleep making the noise that frightened Lily.

After this adventure, they retired into the kitchen to have tea and breathe London's cool night air, while he looked at the street lamps, a few cars, and a girl—young, blonde, and white—being kissed passionately by a tall, thin, and tanned white man, down below in the street. Simon knew the girl. The girl was Jane! So she was a bad girl! Lily pulled Simon's trousers quickly, in case he wanted to jump through the window at seeing Jane being kissed by another man.

'Simon, what happened?'

'Nothing, Lily.'

At 8 a.m. on that unlucky day, Simon waited for Jane at the entrance of the LHH, because she went in as he went out, and she said to him, 'Good morning, Simon!' and tried to kiss him. He pushed her away and she said, 'Why, Simon?'

'Who was the man you were kissing last night, Jane?'

'What? I did not kiss a man last night!'

'You are a liar, Jane! I saw you, and that man, from the hospital kitchen window.'

'Last night? Ah! My cousin.'

'At 3 a.m. being kissed passionately? I am not stupid! You were cheating on me. Bye, Jane, and now I'll have to look for a "nice girl"!' And Jane walked away angrily to her ward.

He started going to the pubs and dancing places, again with George. One cold and foggy night, George and Simon left the Round Tower, which was an Irish dance hall. It was 2 a.m. From the bus stop, they saw two girls running towards a black taxi that was for hire. George and Simon ran towards the same taxi and asked the girls if they would mind sharing the taxi.

'We'll be stopping at Islington. And you?'

'At Euston.'

'OK, Euston and Islington are near.'

The two girls weren't sure. Maybe the young men were drunk. However, they took a chance because the men seemed honest and nice. George was sitting opposite a small girl named Brigid and Simon was sitting opposite a tall girl named Alice. The girls were Irish and they worked in London, near Euston. Before the taxi arrived at Islington, they had made a date to see Alice and Brigid. George's date was a disaster. Simon's date was a success because Alice was genuine, good, sweet, intelligent, witty, and smiling all the time.

Christmas came with perfume, coats, furs, and money, but not for them. They had nothing, at Christmas and any time. They could afford two Wimpy burgers and two orange juices, to go to a cinema or walk in the parks. For Simon, those times were magic, walking on the streets of London without a penny, but with his Alice. Who cared about the money, coats, furs, and posh restaurants? They cared about their love.

The spring of 1959 arrived, and the daffodils and daisies came out again. Simon liked Alice a lot and he thought about getting engaged to her. But a voice deep down in his stomach said, 'Simon, are you sure?'

'Yes! Alice is the girl for me.'

Another voice in his brain tried to warn Simon, 'You must be crazy, Simon. You are only twenty. You're in England, away from your native land, away from Padua. You make me cry! No, Simon!'

Nevertheless, one day they were walking near Euston Station. His hand was in her hand. It was 5 p.m. at the end of April. She was wearing a blue dress and he was wearing black trousers, a white shirt, and a grey coat made by his mother. The sun was pale. The air was breezy. There were bikes, motorbikes, cars, buses, vans, and lorries in the roads. There were babies, young persons, men and women, pigeons, doves, cats, and dogs. There were rats also coming out from the sewers of London, and they all listened to what he said to Alice, 'Alice, will you marry me?'

Alice stopped and looked at him without moving her eyes. She found his heart, which beat on the left-hand side. She returned the look in his eyes and said, 'Yes, Simon, for always.' His hand was in her hand. No shocks, no cries, and their walk continued.

Summer came, and Alice found a hotel in Newquay, Cornwall, to work as a chambermaid for the season. Alice was a staff nurse, but she could earn more money at a hotel. Simon was not ever in Newquay, and so he decided to visit Alice by the seaside.

Simon got a train just before one o'clock on Sunday morning. It ran from London to Truro, calling at Reading and Exeter. Between Truro and Newquay, there was another steam train due to depart at 10.30 a.m. When he arrived at Truro at 6.40 a.m., Simon was very tired. The station was empty, and it was freezing with the wind coming off the Atlantic Ocean. No papers, no bars, dirty toilets smelling of stale human urine. Dogs urinating on a tree would be much cleaner. However, Simon had to wait almost four hours with twenty cows, thirty sheep, two horses, and one donkey . . . SIMON!

Should he wait for the train or should he walk down the road? He did not like waiting, so he decided to walk.

The road went uphill with a series of bends. It was almost dark. The sun tried to break though a bank of purple and red morning clouds.

Later, he saw a road sign which said, 'NEWQUAY, 17 miles' or twenty-eight kilometres. He pulled off his coat, because he was hot, sweating, and tired. The clouds were disappearing and the sky changed from dull grey to brilliant blue. He sat on a rock beside the road for a while. He saw dirty houses in ruins and many dirty rooks, which flew away screeching, but he decided to move to another place with less dirt.

He took the road again and the sun was very hot. His steps were weak. His eyes were not bright and his head was dizzy. No people; no farmers. No cars. No tractors. He was not sure he'd see his Alice, because of his tiredness. He heard a noise and he smelled smoke.

The noise and the smoke drew nearer, like a dream or a mirage.

It was a van which had stopped, leaving a cloud of dust with a stink of dead pigs, apples, pears, milk, bread, newspapers, fresh tomatoes, and old diesel. The driver said to him, 'Do you want a lift on the back? I could leave you at the next village, because I'm going back to Truro. Is that all right for you?'

'You're saving a dying man. Thanks!'

While he sat on the van, Simon thought what a man must do to love a woman. When he left Italy, Silvia, his mother's best friend, had said to him, 'Simon, do not come home with a foreign girl, because *oxen and wives are better in your own country.* You must remember that, Simon.'

Simon thought, OK. But he was sure that Alice's love was genuine. Not Silvia's oxen!

He got off the van and went to the village shop to buy a sandwich and an orange juice to help him on the long road which awaited him. It was 10 a.m. He found that his steps were quicker and brighter and—with the sun, the mild wind, and the thoughts of his girlfriend—he arrived at Newquay on his feet. It was 12.40 p.m.

Alice had told him that the hotel was called Ocean Hotel. He asked a policeman directing the traffic where it was. The hotel was grand and overlooked all the cliffs down to Newquay, the sea, the Atlantic waves, and the black rocks. It was a scene of blue, purple, green, yellow, and white with the wind, grey/black sand and the white water, but Alice was keen to see him, not the Atlantic Ocean. He walked up to the hotel, where a man was washing a big blue car on the street. Simon asked, 'Is this the Ocean Hotel?'

'Yes.'

'I am looking for a Ms Alice, who works here . . . . .'

'Yes. You are Simon from London, am I right? She's waiting for you down the chambermaids' house, just opposite the hotel. I am Mr Horn, the owner of the Ocean Hotel.'

On the way from Truro, Simon thought that if he could be a waiter for the season, at the same hotel, he could see Alice every day and every night, so he said to Mr Horn, 'Could I be a seasonal worker at your hotel, Mr Horn? I am a waiter.'

'A waiter? I should think so. When?'

'I could start in one week.'

'OK.'

'OK, Mr Horn, I will see you on Sunday.'

When he got to the chambermaid's house, he found his girlfriend on the doorstep waiting to greet him. Later, they walked to a large cave with no people to see the Atlantic Ocean, the sands, and the multicoloured waves. Alice was sweet, tender, sincere, and passionate to Simon until the evening. Then they walked to a bar to eat some small cakes with yellow Cornish cream, which was very good, and later, Alice and Simon went to Newquay Station.

The steam train was ready, engulfing them and other people with smoke. The stationmaster closed the train's doors and blew his whistle. Alice blew kisses at him and the train began to gain speed, while smothering itself and all people at the station with dirty black smoke. Alice was there, on the platform, to see him away.

On Monday evening, Simon talked to Mrs Hartland and Mrs Ballantine, who agreed that he could return once he had finished his Newquay job, but George was not happy. Simon talked to his friend and he said, 'George, it is my life, not yours.'

One week later, Simon got the train from London to Newquay without walking on the roads, and he presented himself to Mr Horn at the Ocean Hotel. The owner taught him how to wait at the table and how to wear the black trousers and the white waiter's coat. He was to put his feet together and not to spill red wine on the ladies' dresses, because the ladies would get angry.

The hotel's restaurant was big and grand. Ten large windows and balconies let in light from the sea and the sky. The Indian carpet was in two halves, joining in the middle of the room. The kitchen was big. Three foreign cooks and one French chef prepared the food.

Simon did not like the French chef because he annoyed Alice. On that account, Simon fought the chef on the kitchen table and the floor, until the cooks separated them. The chef was a bad, dirty man.

Apart from the fight, the work seemed OK. However, a week later things began to happen pretty fast!

On his first job as a waiter, he was serving four chicken pieces with a garlic sauce from a silver serving plate to four English guests—two ladies and two gentlemen. The silver serving plate was in his right hand, but the halves of the Indian carpet were not straight under the table, and Simon tripped on the folds. The garlic sauce and the chicken tipped out of the tray, causing a red mess on the table and on the ladies and the gentlemen, who did not complain about the sauces spilt over their evening dresses and dinner suits. Simon's guests were nice about it, because they were aristocratic English people.

Meanwhile, the seagulls flew over the Atlantic Ocean, the weather was fine, the waves ran over the dunes, and the hotel lights twinkled like diamonds. It was a marvellous night and the 'Italian waiter' had ruined it all! And Mr Horn came running to the table. 'What happened? It was like a bomb!'

'It was not a bomb, Mr Horn,' a waiter tried to explain. 'It was Simon, the sauce, the chicken, and your guests.'

'Then my guests were at fault,' said the owner.

'The chicken was at fault,' said the waiter.

'But the chicken is dead! I do not know, Simon, but in the future, it is better that you serve at 'our' table, near the door. OK?' And to the guests he said, 'Sorry for the trouble. The waiter has no experience, sorry.'

The four guests insisted that the havoc was their fault, not Simon's.

If Italian guests had an experience like that, first they shouted at the waiter; second, they fought with the waiter, and third, they shot the waiter with a six-barrelled gun!

After his accident with the chicken, the red sauce, and the silver tray, life at Newquay returned to normal. Alice and Simon had the afternoon of every day free plus one day off per week. They would go on to the beach or to the shops, to see the horses and the river, or sit on the rocks for many kissing sessions, because they were young and in love with each other.

One day they hired a car to go to Land's End, which is the most western point of mainland England, full of cows, sheep, donkeys, crows, and seagulls. There was nothing else, apart from the ocean, which was blue or green or grey or black.

The roads were very narrow by going too near to the verge, so Simon drove very carefully.

At a certain point, a blue coach came fast speeding along in the opposite direction round a bend. Simon saw the milestones on his left-hand side and he tried to avoid the impact, but it was too late. He heard the coach's horn. He braked. He got out of his car and viewed the possible damage.

The possible damage was real. Two wheel rims were damaged.

All the way to Newquay, Simon thought about the cost of the repairs, money which he did not have. However, the garage man did not ask for money. Some people were still very nice.

On another occasion when they were walking about the seaside resort, where they saw a tall, thin man, dressed in black, standing in front of a circus tent, and saying, 'Folks, come in, please . . . come in, folks, please . . .' And they went in.

The tent was small, with about thirty wooden chairs and thirty spectators. The doors were closed and the show presenter called four people to sit down on chairs on the stage and said to them, 'Do not worry, folks! When I say 'Pop' to you, you will fall asleep. When I say 'Pip' to you, you will wake up. Are you ready?'

The people on the stage fell asleep and later were woken up. And the audience was amazed.

'Second test,' said the man.' When I say 'Cro' to you, you will cross your hands behind your backs and you will not be free. When I say 'Cra,' you will be free. Are you ready?' And the audience was not able to free their hands, but the presenter spotted two persons whose hands were free. They were Alice and Simon!

'Do you feel some itching on your hands?' the man asked.

'No,' they said.

'Maybe you are nervous.' Then he said to the audience, 'These two persons do not feel my power. Let us carry on with the show.'

Simon and Alice thought that the show presenter was a cheat and the people in the audience were stupid!

The season was soon over, and Alice and Simon returned to London. She was working with an Irish family, near Euston, and he was working at LHH. However, it was October 1959, two years and one month since he'd left Bologna. Alice wanted to visit her relatives in Ireland for a month and he wanted to visit his relatives in Italy for a month. They left London, travelling by train and by boat—one day and one night—but she went further north, and he went south and east, which seemed strange. In a month's time, Alice and Simon would return to London. Before leaving, Alice gave him a gold signet ring, which was a token of their love.

Chapter 7

From London, Simon went to Dover, then by boat to Calais and, by train again, through Paris, Bern, Turin, and Milan. He arrived after twenty-four hours of travel at 3.37 a.m. in Bologna station, where he took a taxi.

His middle brother opened the door of the flat, and greeted Simon for about two minutes, because it was four o'clock in the morning and they retired to their beds.

During the following days, he told his mother, father, brothers, relatives, and friends some of his adventures about London, Calais, the pubs, the hospital, Pia, the hens, and the geese. But his mother was not interested in how English people or their geese lived. His mother was interested in Alice's life, and she wanted to write a letter to the priest in the Irish village where Alice came from to find out more about her.

The letter was in Italian. Simon's mother wanted to know what religion she followed. Was she good or bad? Did she have parents, sisters, brothers, and friends? Simon's mother was like a female Sherlock Holmes.

'Mother, Alice is good, intelligent, honest, sweet, and beautiful,' he told her. But his mother would have preferred an Italian girl or a girl from Padua or from Bologna, not an Irish girl.

'Where is Ireland? Is it in Africa or in the North Pole? I don't know, Simon!'

'No, Mammy. Ireland is near England, where I was last week. You look at the map. Here is Italy. Here is France, and here is Ireland, which is an island, the same as Sicily. However, Sicily is hot and Ireland is cold. Do you understand, Mother?'

The parish priest from Cracklegs in Ireland answered his mother's Italian letter in English. Simon's mother did not know the language. So together with his brothers, she took the letter to the priest of the local church, who knew English. Simon knew English, but she did not trust him, for obvious reasons.

The Irish priest said in his letter that Alice was very good, honest, intelligent, and sweet and a devout Catholic. She had a mother, sisters, brother, relatives, and many friends, so Simon's mother was very happy. She herself was very pious, honest, and nice and wanted Alice to be the same.

Simon got in touch with his friends too, who asked him questions about France and the Italian consul in Calais, about London, the geese, and Newquay, all the time, because they hadn't had a chance to travel abroad as yet. Anyway they might fall in love with an Irish, English, or German girl—you never knew!

One day, he saw a uniformed man walking down to his father's garage. The man was a *carabiniere*, or an Italian police man. 'Good morning. I am looking for Mr Simon.'

'That's me,' he said to the man.

'Then you must go to the Bologna Military Hospital this Wednesday for military tests. Could I have your Italian passport, please?'

The *carabiniere* flicked the pages of his passport and said to him, 'The police station will keep your passport. Thank you and good day.' The *carabiniere* went away up the garage's slip road and disappeared.

Simon was astounded! Many thoughts flashed though his mind, like lightning, about Alice, London, and how they were happy before the *carabiniere,* the forces, the navy . . .

'Simon, you must do your military service, maybe for twelve months or more,' said his father.

If Simon had stayed abroad and if he hadn't left London, the *carabiniere* could not have held his passport. His father guessed the thoughts that were on his mind and said, 'My son, you believe me. If you do your national service now, you will remove a thorn from your brain.'

He knew about the thorns, but . . . his sweet Alice? He promised to her that they would meet again within a month in London. Now, the military bosses wanted him to embrace a gun or a cannon to shoot the enemy. They must be crazy! He hated weapons for killing people or animals. One day, a long time ago, an uncle had taught him to shoot with a hunting rifle. He was seven years old. He saw a bird on the branch of a tree and his uncle had ordered him to shoot it, but he shot into the air. Why shoot a bird? Birds are unarmed and are not wicked. Humans are very wicked and wicked to compel him to do the military service, but he knew that he must complete his national service. It was compulsory and there was no escaping from the army or the navy or the air force.

He went to the Military Hospital on Wednesday, Thursday, and Friday. He saw many young men—like him—waiting for the hospital tests. The tests were OK and the military chiefs put him down as a sailor for twenty-five months, instead of twenty in the army and air force. Simon thought that was wrong. The military chiefs should call up youths, who wanted fights, battles, and wars, not normal people.

Later, he was sent to the harbour at Ravenna, on Italy's eastern seaboard, full of golden sand. He saw gunboats—for the first time in his life—ready to sink or to destroy the enemy's gunboats. He hated the battleships, because they spelt out the words *War and Death*.

The naval barracks were full of officers, who walked miles and miles inside the corridors or the offices of the port authorities, and they did nothing, apart from drinking espresso coffees, smoking cigarettes, cigars, and pipes. The heating was on in the offices, but the heating was off in the corridors, so the recruits were shivering with the cold in autumn, while they collected naval documents for hours and hours without any coffee.

A week later, the big chiefs moved him—by train—to La Spezia harbour, on Italy's west coast, full of black rocks.

It was Christmas 1959.

At the barrack in La Spezia, all the recruits had to do the 'Recruits Training', which involved undressing naked in front of a navy doctor, who gave a breast injection with his left hand and, at the same time, felt your testicles with his right hand, while he tested your temperature with a thermometer stuck under the armpit.

If someone was missing one testicle, the doctor would send that person home crying. If someone was without testicles, then that person, maybe, would change into a girl.

Simon's mother had made him with two testicles and he passed the tests without crying. Many big and strong recruits fainted on the floor, seeing the big injection needle.

On the same day, Simon posed in the nude in front of a female officer, who asked him many personal questions like, 'Why are your testicles so small and full of wrinkles?'

'Because it is mighty cold,' he said.

The officer looked straight into his eyes and asked him, 'Have you ever had measles? Has any doctor treated you for venereal diseases? Have you ever slept with a bad girl?'

'I would not sleep with a bad girl,' he said, and he went out holding his trousers, while a sergeant ordered him, with a sardonic smile, to put on a blue uniform and a blue round cap with a black ribbon bearing the words *Marina Italiana* or Italian Navy.

Simon hated uniforms. Nevertheless, the sergeants, captains, and the admiral at La Spezia's naval barracks insisted that he must wear the uniform.

'If you do not wear the uniform, we jail you—do you understand?' So he wore the damned mouldy uniform, which smelled of dead rotten sharks.

On the following week, the recruits took the oath in front of the captains, officers, and the admiral, and the families were invited.

'Love your country . . . duty . . . respect . . . solidarity. You must say: *We will take an oath to the Italian Navy!*'

Many would-be sailors took the oath. Other youngsters were joking about the oath and others did not want to take any oath at all, like Simon.

But since he must join the navy and since he must wear the uniform, he decided to be awkward with the naval doctors and he went on a hunger strike. Simon drank coffee and whisky to raise his blood pressure. He urinated in his bed every night on purpose, so that the doctors might think that he had a disease and send him home.

Instead, the doctors were clever and he was stupid! He endured the pain and discomfort for ten days. On the eleventh day, his mates took him out to a pizzeria to eat a Neapolitan pizza, and the Neapolitan pizza cured Simon's uniform disease.

After three months, Simon was moved to Taranto in the south of Italy. He was another 1,500 kilometres away from his Irish girlfriend, almost in Sicily! They wrote letters to each other, but it wasn't the same thing.

The barracks were massive. The admiral was very strict with the recruits, who ran miles and miles with their rifles, wearing a woollen coat, because Taranto was very cold, especially at night. If Simon was on guard at night, he looked at the moon, the same moon that Alice saw in Ireland, 3,500 kilometres away, which was an amazing thought.

Apart from the distance, Simon suffered terrible toothaches every day and every night. If he had toothache during the day, he jumped like an Australian kangaroo. If he had toothache during the night, he was like a woman having birth pains. But he couldn't have birth pains because he was a man! He had a terrible toothache, and Simon decided to use the navy dentist.

'Open your mouth!' the dentist shouted at him, armed with his pincers, his needle, and chair with the brake and clutch. The nurse, who was very ugly, looked like a German SS trooper. The navy dentist hooked Simon's bad tooth with a thin metal hook, and Simon yelled like Tarzan in the middle of the jungle. The SS nurse was laughing, like the German soldiers and officers who laughed in Auschwitz in Poland, when they killed millions of Jews, by poisoning them in the gas chambers and burning their bodies, which was horrible. Those barbarians were devils, burning in hell for ever.

Simon was not a Jew.

Anyway, the navy dentist and the SS nurse wanted to kill him, so he yelled again, 'My tooth is very painful!'

'I know! I will remove your tooth from your mouth with the pincers and you will feel better, OK?' The dentist pulled and pulled his tooth and, eventually, his tooth came out of his mouth. He saw blood and he yelled out, 'Aaargh!'

'I must grind two more teeth with the electric grindstone, OK?' said the dentist.

'Will it be painful?' said Simon.
'Open your mouth wide, please.'

The electric grindstone was on, but Simon's nerves made him go rigid, like a male porcupine that saw a lady porcupine naked for the first time. Simon almost yelled again, but two steely hands (the SS nurse) compelled him to be quiet during the dentist's work. Eventually, the dentist spoke, like a Redskin Sioux chief.

'Are you OK?'

'I am *not* OK!'

'Try some water. Then the paste, all right?'

The dentist used some grey paste on three of his teeth to protect them and said, 'We have finished with you. You were very brave.' Meanwhile, the nurse smiled at him like a hyena and said, 'Do not eat or drink for two hours. Ciao!'

At seven he ate and at ten he was on guard with his woollen coat, his rifle, and a severe toothache! He was very tired in the wooden hut, in front of the Taranto barracks. At midnight, you could find him sleeping! All recruits on guard would be the same.

At seven the next morning, Simon could not sleep because the post arrived in the yard, delivered by a postman who would call for sailor George, Fred, or Jim for their mail from their mothers or their girlfriends. If a sailor did not get any mail, he was desperate.

Simon's mother sent him 1,000 lire every week. The Italian government would pay fifty-five lire plus seven cigarettes and seven matches per week to an unqualified sailor like him, so one would of course become very rich. Nevertheless, the food, water, and a bed were free of charge.

The food was very good: from *spaghetti* or *macaroni* with tomato sauce to beefsteaks, from veal chops with fried chips to boiled potatoes, bread, lettuce, wine, and coffee. It was all good, but the sailors had to wash their plates, cutlery, glasses, and pots with cold water. No soap and no kitchen paper. The sailors would pick up sand from the yard, and use it like sand paper for the cleaning operation.

The day began for the recruits when a sergeant pulled them at 6 a.m. from their beds where they dreamed of their 'mammies' or their girlfriends. If they turned over to go to sleep again, the sergeant would hammer them with a thick stick until they woke up. Then wash, uniform, eat, train, and guard. The life of recruits in the Italian navy was not easy!

One day, a captain was talking to Simon and said, 'Sailor Simon, are you interested in doing a typewriting course?'

He thought for a moment and said, 'Yes, Captain.'

'The course will start this Wednesday, from 2 p.m. to 3 p.m. OK?'

On Wednesday, the classroom was full of unqualified sailors, sergeants, and officers, worse than a bunch of three-year-old babies!

Anyway, in two months he could typewrite, 'Simon Simon, Abc street, Italy,' but very slowly!

The Taranto barrack's admiral was very impressed with his performance, so Simon was moved to Rome to the Italian Naval Headquarters.

The INH was on the right bank of the Tiber River, while the naval barracks were on the left-hand side. Simon had been in Rome previously, when he toured Italy in his father's car with his friends in 1955. He was eighteen at the time. Now he walked every day in spring from the barracks to the Naval Headquarters to work as a naval clerk, and he was twenty-one.

Spring was terrific that year. The swallows were making their nests under the roof tiles and twittered happily. Leaves were starting to appear. Boats sailed up and down the Tiber, and the men whistled happily 'Old Rome'. The sun hid behind the clouds and showed up again with the brilliance of the day.

However, every day, Simon was buried under a heap of mouldy military files about warships and cannons. Life was not fair to him.

He worked in a section of the INH where an office girl and a thirty-five-year-old 'land' captain, without a ship, were working. He was quite tall, his nose was in the air, and so was his head. He had a crooked mouth and a sadistic laugh. Simon did not like the captain at all! Simon did not greet him when he came into the office. He went to the toilet or he pretended to use his typewriter, but the captain wanted him to greet him every morning, and that made him furious.

'Sailor Simon, I expect a "Good morning" from you every day, OK?'

'Captain, I say "Good morning" to everybody, but I talk quietly.'

'Sailor Simon, loudly, OK?'

The captain was not happy and he reported Simon to the admiral, who called him into his office.

'Sailor Simon, I heard a story from your captain that you refuse to greet him every morning. Is that true?'

The navy admiral was a good, honest man of about sixty, and his white hair made him look like Father Christmas in a white uniform. Simon liked the man.

'Sir, I greet everybody, but the tone of my voice seems too low!'

'Sailor Simon, speak *loudly* when you greet your captain, OK? Maybe some captains do not hear so well, or maybe captains hear sirens' music only. I do not know, Sailor Simon.'

'Sir, I will try to talk louder to my captain.'

Nevertheless, the land captain did not feel happy with Simon, though Simon carried out his work every day for the captain.

Why was his captain so unhappy? It was true that when Simon was on night guard at the barracks, plus doing his office work at the Naval Headquarters, he was very tired, so he managed to find a place to rest during the night watch. The place was a cupboard with blankets and pillows, but a sergeant caught him snoring! However, the sergeant was kind, and Simon did not go to the naval jail. He was lucky!

Alice and Simon wrote long letters to each other. They decided that she would travel to Rome. Since Alice was a staff nurse, she could work at the American hospital in Rome, looking after American patients.

The train journey left Alice very tired, after twenty-five hours of travelling from London. Rome was very hot in August and Alice got dysentery.

Before Alice arrived, Simon sold three navy books to a pawnshop, because he had not the money even to buy two pizzas! They ate two beautiful pizzas in an inn beside the Tiber. Later, he took her to a Roman family who had a B&B place to sleep, and he returned to the naval barracks to dream about his fiancée in Rome.

The following day, Alice worked at the American hospital all right, but later, the officer in charge told her that the American patient was leaving for USA suddenly. It was same story as Simon's. He couldn't work in London a few years back. So strange!

Simon looked for another job for her in the city and they were lucky, because a Roman lady was looking for an English girl to teach the language to her little boy. The lady was married to an Italian TV show producer. The family lived next door to the Italian Naval Headquarters. Alice went out with the boy to the Villa Borghese park every day, to play in the fresh air, and Simon walked to the Italian Naval Headquarters office.

At midday, he went to the barracks to eat a plate of *macaroni* or *spaghetti*, and he would keep a beefsteak or a pork chop with a sandwich for her, every day, because although the family was rich, the food was not enough for a young girl.

Some nights, they went out courting. One night, two MPs found him not wearing his navy cap. He argued with the MPs, but the MPs were big and strong, so he was jailed for fifteen days in the navy barracks.

The navy jail was a proper prison with wooden benches 60 cm from the concrete floor and big iron gates. There were no windows and the light was on all the time. Under the benches, there was a population of beetles, large rats, huge spiders, and little beasts, which had soup with breadcrumbs and milk that the recruits ate for their breakfast, lunch, and supper. In the cell, there were wooden beds, one wooden pillow, one woollen blanket, and two occupants, who would fight all night long over the blanket. After fifteen days in jail, some sailors went crazy. However, the jail sergeants gave them another fifteen days in jail, then a court martial.

When Simon got out of the jail, the barracks and the headquarters were all the same in Rome's sun. His girlfriend was better with her Italian, and he found that she was more beautiful than ever. Simon's mother and his brothers got down to Rome by car, because the mother was curious about his Irish girlfriend. Was she thin or fat, tall or short, attractive or ugly?

He showed his relatives Rome first, and then took them to a country inn to eat, drink, and talk. He noticed his mother looking at the food plate with her right eye, but she was eyeing Alice with her left eye during the entire meal. He thought that his mother was impressed by Alice, who had dressed properly. She was tall, attractive, and honest and was not dumb. Later, his brothers and his mother left the capital of Italy and he concluded that his mother was happy with the girl.

However, his captain was far worse towards him. He was furious and quite mad, and he reported Simon to the admiral again!

'Sailor Simon is OK and he says hello to everybody. The sailor's voice is just a bit too low.'

'Sailor Simon does not greet me *ever*, sir.'

'Are you sure?'

'Yes, sir! I would like to move him to the Manfredonia Port Authorities, down near Sicily, as a punishment, until the end of his naval service.'

'Calm down, Captain! Erm, Captain, could you send the sailor to my office *alone, please*!'

The captain's steps sounded like a deranged elephant on the corridor, until they stopped at the office door.

'Our admiral wants you, *quick*!'

Simon walked slowly into the admiral's office and said, 'Good morning, Admiral.'

'Good morning, Simon, or rather a bad morning for you, because your captain does not want you here in Rome, and he would like to move you to the Manfredonia Port Authorities next week, until you are dismissed. I cannot prefer an unqualified sailor to an Italian Navy captain. I am sorry, Simon.'

'I know, Admiral,' said Simon. He stood up and looked through a window overlooking the Tiber, and he would have enjoyed, very much, drowning 'his' captain with his hands using a ten-ton concrete block.

In the evening, Simon told his love about the wicked captain, who wanted to station him in Manfredonia, deep in the south of Italy with giant spiders, cockroaches, and green vipers. She decided to tell the woman and her husband, who knew some very important people at the Naval Headquarters. Also, Simon telephoned his parents in Bologna. He told them his story about the captain. His father told the woman, who had helped him to get the work permit in England in October 1957. Her husband was an admiral, and maybe he could help Simon's situation. But the days passed without news. Two helps never helped. Alice's woman said that the important people were on holiday and his father's friends said that the former admiral was abroad. Simon thought, at the time, that Alice's woman was better off without him, and his father's woman was better off if Alice went back to London without him for ever. Why? It was women mysteries and jealousy.

He left Rome bound for Manfredonia on a slow ten-hour train journey.

'Did you gain anything by being offensive to your captain?' said a deep voice down inside of Simon.

'I didn't!'

'Then?'

'Then I was very stupid.'

Manfredonia's Port Authorities barracks were in fact a two-storey house, located at the docks, which also had three small multicoloured boats and two large naval motorboats. On the first floor of the barracks there was a hall, a telephone room, the toilets, a kitchen, and two sleeping rooms for twenty-four sailors.

The second floor of the house was a flat, which housed the captain of the barracks and his wife. The captain suffered from 'Mad Dog Sciatica'; when he shouted like a mad dog, the people of Manfredonia, within a thirty miles radius, could not sleep. His wife had to call the fire brigade, and the barracks sergeant dressed in his pants, because the havoc happened only at night. The sergeant was small and round like a football. His wife was tall, big, and fat like a hippopotamus. Poor sergeant!

The food was very good, because two or three sailors went to the market every day. They ate fresh tomatoes, fresh beans, fresh bread, fresh chicken, fresh fish, and beautiful southern wine.

Simon's job at the Manfredonia barracks was as a telephone operator, which he liked very much. One day he was having some fresh sardines. Someone telephoned and it was Alice from Rome. Such was Simon's surprise that a sardine went down the wrong way in his mouth.

'How are you, Simon?'

'Sardeee . . . !'

'*Simon!* Are you all right?'

'*Feeesh* . . . !'

A sailor who understood the situation gave Simon a hard blow across his back. His mouth became free from the sardine bones and he could talk to his Alice easily. But he had such a fright!

At times he drew, with his pencil, sea scenes, boats, or the Manfredonia harbour, when he did not have anything else to do.

At times the barracks sergeant watched his drawings, and one day he said, 'You can draw very well, Sailor Simon. Can you paint using oil colours?'

'Yes, Sergeant.'

'Then, could you paint a picture for me?'

'OK, Sergeant. I need brushes, oil paints, canvases, black chalk, turpentine, and a palette.'

'On Monday I shall buy everything for you. The painting is for the fortieth birthday of my wife in November.'

'I will try, Sergeant. What is your wife like? Maybe a river, a house, or some deer?'

'Yes!'

'OK, Sergeant. I will start as soon as possible when you deliver the stuff to me.'

The barracks sergeant had a nickname. It was 'Mr Wee', because he needed to urinate continuously, like a broken water tap. If someone called him by his nickname, the sergeant went all red and blue, spat on the ground, stamping his feet, and shouted at the sailors, '*What?* Who dares offend me?'

'It was the Sicilian sailor who went to the toilet to do a wee, OK, Sergeant?'

The Sicilian was over two metres tall and very big. He had a face like the Abominable Snowman. On the other hand, he was very kind, but the sergeant was not courageous enough to face him, because he was too little.

The sergeant brought the stuff in on Monday. Simon started the picture on a canvas measuring 100×70 cm and he used an empty warm room. The picture showed a river, some green and brown trees, and yellow and orange bushes. Some deer were grazing near the river under a pale blue sky. Everybody agreed that the landscape with the animals were beautiful, but Mr Wee did not pay for the work, because he was a miser.

Christmas 1960 came round, and with it winter. The snow did not fall, but it was freezing cold. Many new navy recruits came to the barracks and Simon gave many injections on their breasts.

Simon learned this from Jane, when he worked in the London hospital, before he knew Alice.

But all the recruits were afraid to see the big syringes and some of them fainted like little boys. Why? They were local farmers or shepherds and living rough with wild wolves, brown bears, and snowstorms. Therefore, they weren't afraid usually, but they were in fact afraid, and Simon thought that it was odd.

After the injection sessions, a doctor asked them if they had a bad tooth, flat feet, venereal diseases, or not. Venereal diseases were common amongst sailors or all soldiers. They wanted nights of love with young whores, who were nice, or their mothers and their grandmothers, who were wrinkled and ugly, like old kangaroos.

There was a 50×70 cm hole in the perimeter wall to allow them through to make love in the moonlight. Simon did not know this, because he did not mess about with the whores. One sailor, who enjoyed nights of love with the young whores, got a terrible disease in his sexual organs. When he was very sick, they carried him to Saint John Rotondo's hospital, founded by Padre Pio and the nuns, to cure him. The doctors gave him many blood transfusions. That huge strong sailor, who had a massive chest like a wardrobe, in two days, was dead. The nuns at the hospital put him in a black coffin, not in a wardrobe! Think of him. Think of his parents, brothers, sisters, and friends. He wanted to love a nice whore. The whores were not bad. They needed money mostly—money for old mothers and old fathers, for sons and daughters, and to cure diseases.

Springtime in 1961 came round, and the barracks captain, who had the 'Mad Dog Sciatica,' wanted to send to the 'Father Christmas' admiral in Rome two large glass containers full of white southern *mozzarella* cheeses. They were friends and the southern *mozzarella* cheeses were very tasty, much more than the Italian northern *mozzarella* cheeses. The shipment went with Simon by train, which ran slowly as always. Simon was starving on the way and he ate a few pieces of *mozzarella* cheese from two containers, thinking that the admiral would not notice. The admiral loved Manfredonia's special black buffalo white *mozzarella* cheese and the captain from the south of Italy went crazy for the cheese.

However, Simon and Alice went up and down across the Roman hills. Many times they stopped at a country inn to eat, under the shade of the trees, to avoid the hot sun. It was beautiful!

In the evening, they went out courting, under the light of the silver moon at the Villa Borghese gardens, until he left her to return to Manfredonia.

Those trips were customary once a month, to take the *mozzarella* cheese to the big navy chief.

Between May and September, many tourists went to the Tremiti Islands, about one hour from Manfredonia, on fast motorboats in the hot sun, twice a day, skimming the water on the salty seawater. They would enjoy the mild breeze blowing and the people grew tanned. The sea bottom at ten metres or more was visible because the water was very clear, with no rotten fish, no green seaweed, or no rubbish. There were a few houses, a few seamen and their families, and a hotel. The islands were a beauty spot . . . in the 1960s!

One sunny day, Mr Wee approached Simon and said, 'I can see that the white writing on the harbour wall is faint. You are a painter. Would you mind giving the letters a fresh coat of paint, please?'

'Yes, Sergeant. However, I'll need some white paint and bricklayers' brushes.'

'By Wednesday I will get the stuff you need, Sailor Simon.'

By Wednesday, Mr Wee got the stuff and Simon started to paint on the harbour wall big white letters, which occupied three weeks of his time. The writing read: *Manfredonia Port Authorities*. He used the small boats to paint on the outside of the harbour, jumping from one to the other, trying to tan himself. If he was too hot, he would swim for a while, then he would paint a while, then swim, and so on.

Life in the Navy, down in southern Italy, was not hard, but life with the sergeant was sheer hell!

Mr Wee shouted to them at 10 p.m. precisely every night. They were supposed to get into their beds, and then he switched off the lights for the night. He stopped at the second room to shout at the sailors to go to bed, while some sailors switched on the lights in the first room. Mr Wee ran to the first room, shouting at them, and so forth. However, they all wanted to listen to the radio until midnight, play cards or tell jokes, because they were young and Mr Wee was old.

The same thing would happen in the morning. If one sailor was late getting out of his bed, Mr Wee would be angry with him. So they thought of something which would madden the sergeant.

One night, about 10 p.m., all the sailors went to bed in the first room and the second room, while Mr Wee was looking at them. He switched off the lights and went out. About 10.10, five sailors got up and switched on the lights. They inserted four candles on the steel tubes of the sixth bed, which was the top. The sixth sailor remained in bed. They lit the candles, switched off the lights, and jumped into their beds. One sailor shouted for help. The sergeant ran into the room. He shouted when he saw one of the sailors who appeared dead. He shouted more when he realised that the sailor was not dead! He was alive and laughing, and all the other sailors were laughing. So Mr Wee laughed at the joke.

Two weeks later, they annoyed the sergeant again.

The sergeant did his rounds in the rooms and he went out. Soon after, six sailors got out of their beds. They switched on the lights, filled a bucket with water, and put the bucket on the door frame, leaving a gap between the frame and the door. They got in their beds and switched off the lights.

A sailor called for help. The sergeant ran quickly into the room and the bucket slid on to the poor sergeant, wetting him all over. He shouted at them and said that they would be jailed, because he couldn't accept jokes like that. No jokes for the sergeant any more.

It was October 1961. Simon practically ended his military service.

It was time to play jokes on his fellow sailors who remained with the Navy.

It was 5.40 a.m. He got up and wore his naval uniform for the last time. He did not wear his boots, because of the noise they made on the floor, and his fellow sailors were sleeping. Simon went to the second room with a box of black shoe polish and a thin brush to allow him to paint beards and moustaches on the sailors' faces. The operation went well and he went away to his room.

It was six o'clock. The sergeant came into the rooms, shouting as usual, and he switched on the lights. One sleepy sailor noticed that another sailor had a black face. The second sailor pointed out that the first sailor was black in the face too. More sailors discovered that their faces were all black, thank to the shoe polish, and some of them put the blame on Simon.

'It is Simon. He can't get away with this, no way! It's a war!'

Some of them were mad and started to fight with him, until Mr Wee calmed them down.

At ten the following morning, twelve sailors were due to be discharged by the Italian Navy, including Simon. Two years and one month or 750 days or 18,000 hours or 1,080.000 minutes or 64,800.000 seconds of his time, almost without pay, almost without work, apart from learning to make war for sergeants, officers, captains (with or without boats), admirals, and the government. First, Simon needed his discharge papers from Manfredonia.

At 11 a.m., twelve Italian sailors, in single line, stood outside in the brilliant sun and near the seawater. They had twelve clean uniforms, twelve clean navy caps, and twenty-four shining boots, all in order. Simon saw the inspection officer who would inspect the sailors, Simon being the last in the line. He was sure that the inspecting captain was the same wicked captain as the one in Rome, who punished him by sending him to Manfredonia. He had the posture, the same wicked face with a crooked nose, the same mouth, and the same devilish smile.

As he was getting nearer to him, the wicked captain said, 'Ciao, Sailor Simon! Did you like my punishment in the Italian south?'

'What punishment? Here, I had sunshine every day, the blue sea, and the gorgeous Tremiti Islands. I did some oil painting for the sergeant. I swam every day. The food was beautiful, with the special black buffalo white *mozzarella* cheese, and I saw my girlfriend in Rome every month. I assure you, Captain, the Navy looked beautiful from down here. The punishment was not a punishment at all, Captain.'

His speech made the wicked captain furious, like an angry devil. He saw the captain clench his teeth. His nails bit into his flesh, his nostrils flared, and his feet dug a hole to hell!

Chapter 8

After travelling for many hours in Italian train compartments, suffering from heat and cold, Simon saw through the window the Sasso Marconi village and the Church of the Madonna of Saint Luca dominating the town.

When he got home, he found his mother, father, brothers, and his Irish fiancée, who had arrived from Rome a few days ago. Everybody was happy because he had finished his naval service. It was almost like his father returning from the war in Greece with a long black beard and one bullet through his right foot. Simon didn't have a long black beard at the time. He had a short black beard while he was in the navy. However, a sergeant did not like the beard on him and he had to remove it.

Apart from the beard, he felt that he should find work for him and Alice, with some urgency, because his parents were not rich. Within one week, Alice found work as an English babysitter, while Simon worked in his father's garage, for the time being.

One day he saw his father talking to a customer about work and how it was very difficult to find work for the younger generation.

'My son learnt English for two years in London. He cannot find any work in this town,' his father explained.

'This is strange! My company is looking for a good English translator right now. We will talk to your son if he visits us on Monday.'

On Monday, Simon visited the company. He liked the people, the people liked him, and by Tuesday he had the job. The company made automatic machines for industry, with a drawing office, workshops, cleaners, a female cook, an office staff, and, of course, a management formed by two brothers. It was Mr Braga Policarpo, the big chief, and Mr Braga Secondo, who looked after the workshop. The company was Italian and the name was BPBS Co.

His place was in the office with a manager, an accountant, and two office girls. His duties were to translate Italian into English and English into Italian on his typewriter. He would do invoices, leaflets, and customers' letters. At times, Simon would talk, on the phone, with foreign customers or customers who visited them. The office had one window that occupied the front of the building on the via Emilia, which ran from Rimini to Milan and vice versa.

The company's midday meals were very good. Some workers walked to a bar to get an espresso coffee every day. The road formed a four-way crossing opposite the bar, and it was very dangerous because of the cars which ran at high speeds.

One day Simon saw a black car approaching at a high speed. At the same time, he saw a man riding his motorbike crossing the via Emilia. The black car crashed on to the rider, who fell on the road. The motorbike swivelled about uncontrollably. The rider went over and over on the tarmac and died. Simon was very shocked by the rider's glassy eyes when he passed on to another life.

On three occasions during Simon's life he saw those glassy eyes. The first time was the mule being killed by a bomb during the war. He was sorry but a mule is a mule.

The second time was when a university student jumped from his fourth floor room and his body smashed a few inches away from Simon on the pavement. He was immensely shocked to see the man's scared eyes when he fell to the ground. The morning paper said that he was afraid of failing the university exams, so he committed suicide!

The third time was when the rider died in front at the bar.

At the end of the day, he got a lift home with a friend. He related to him the story about the incident at the bar, the dead man, and the ambulance. He noticed that Vito, a fitter who worked at the company, was serious and sweating and he stopped his car.

'Listen, Simon. Two years ago I had an incident on this damned road and I ran over a seven-year-old boy with my car. Simon, I survived but the boy was dead. Two years ago I had wavy black hair. Now I am bald. I suffer every day of my life, because the boy is dead.'

It was sad. However, if Vito had been going slowly, the incident could have been avoided.

Apart from the road accidents, their lives were quite normal. His fiancée taught English to a three-year-old boy, the son of a rich Bolognese family. He worked too, and they wanted to marry, with the flat, furniture, a wedding, and a honeymoon. Maybe by the sea? But Alice had thousands of seasides in Ireland. Then the lakes? But Alice had thousand of lakes in her country. The mountain places, maybe? Yes, because Alice had seen the High Mountain resorts in Italy, and she liked them.

At last they decided in favour of Sappada. The mighty Piave River starts here. Then it was Austria, Auronzo, and Saint Stefano di Cadore, Cortina, and thousands of resorts. So, one day in June, they set off, Alice, Simon's brother, his girlfriend, and Simon, on the road which would take them to Sappada.

He was driving his father's Fiat 600, and he took the road to Belluno, then Padua, Treviso, and Vittorio Veneto. Later, the terrain became mountainous, following the River Piave at Ponte d'Alpi, Longarone Pieve di Cadore, and Sappada.

Before Sappada, they stopped at a country inn to eat, enjoying fabulous local food. Later, they stopped at a famous beauty spot, a sort of rock funnel, 150 metres in diameter at the top and 70 metres deep, without trees or bushes. At the bottom ran a green shallow river. It was beautiful and awe-inspiring, at the same time, to see how nature shapes the mighty rocks. But they were terribly hot and were sweating, and they decided to climb the funnel and get out from that terrible place, which seemed like hell. Within an hour, they arrived at their hotel.

The hotel was nice, being run by the nuns, who looked after them very well. They had a beautiful meal and some local wine, and they looked at the pine forest, the deer, the squirrels, and the wild boars.

After having booked the room, they returned to the city.

The news was that Simon would marry Alice in September, and on the big day Alice wore a white dress and a white veil, white shoes and carried a bunch of orange flowers. She was very beautiful, and touched by the sun, which give her a special aura because she was happy. They listened to the Wedding Mass. The ceremony was concluded with two gold rings and the kisses between her and him.

Outside of the church, the guests received the rice—for luck—thrown by the people, on a day which was wonderful for Alice and Simon. It was a day which they would remember all their life.

Having being married on one day, on the next they started a new adventure, which was honeymooning at the Sappada hotel. Alice and he took walks through pine forests, climbed rocks, or followed the Piave River, which was beautiful. The river starts among the Alpi Carniche on Peralba's Mount. It crosses the Cadore plain as far as Belluno and flows into the Gulf of Venice after 220 km, but the honeymooners walked 20 kilometres from their hotel to reach the point in the forest, where—on a marble post—was a written sign, in Italian, which said: QUI NASCE IL FIUME PIAVE (The Piave River starts here).

The beginning was among wet leaves, which changes into a puddle. It changes again into a small waterfall. Then it changes into a brook, which feeds a big waterfall, and then into a big mighty river. It was amazing. Simon was amazed, too, to see his Irish wife with her black hair blown by the wind, her happy face tanned by the Italian sun, and her happy laughter, carefree, because Simon was there.

However, they were very tired every day so, after their evening meal, they snored in their bed every night. The bees, which were supplying the honey, flew against their bedroom window and shouted, 'You are supposed to start babies, not snore!'

Alice and Simon could not hear the noise which the bees were making, because they were too tired.

Towards midnight, Simon's granny, who went to heaven to visit Saint Peter, came down into their hotel room. Alice slept, but Simon was awake. He saw his grandmother pull up a chair beside the bed . . . he had a heart attack! She was wearing a black dress, a grey apron with a small floral design, black stockings, and black shoes, the same as when she was living.

He sat up in bed and she spoke to him.

'Ciao, Simon.'

'Ciao, Granny, but why are you down here?'

'Because I want to give you three lotto numbers and . . . . .'

'Granny . . . Granny . . . the numbers?'

But his grandmother had disappeared. The chair was near the door. Alice slept soundly and he had been awake for hours.

The morning came and Simon woke his wife to tell her his adventure the previous night, but she only laughed.

'Simon, your grandmother called you in a dream!'

'Alice, I assure you that my granny was here, alive!'

'It was a dream, Simon.'

'I get goose pimples when I think about her—why?'

'I do not know about that, Simon. Last night you complained of a tummy ache, which caused the dream.'

Maybe Alice was right. Nevertheless, he saw his grandmother alive in his hotel room—it was true!

Their honeymoon at Sappada came to an end. No forests, no nuns' food, no walks, no rock climbing, and no Piave River when they left on the road to the city. The city offered plenty of work, and on the fifth day after they got back, Mr Policarpo Braga, the big chief, called him in his office to talk. The big chief was fifty years old, fat, big, and nearly bald. He wore a dark grey suit and smoked cigars all the time.

'Simon, would you like to travel to America with me?'

'To America? I don't know! When?'

'In one week, for a week. You can translate for me when we visit our American customers, who operate in the pharmaceutical industry. There's the "Lightcap Co.", which makes pharmaceutical capsules, and "Caplet Inc.", which fills the capsules with various products. Are you coming to the USA with me or not?'

'You are the boss around here, Mr Braga. I will ask my wife when I go home. I will let you know the answer in the morning.'

'OK. Caplet Inc. needs to order 200 machines for filling capsules, and I must have that order!'

When the evening came, Simon mentioned to his lovely wife the news about America, and she said to him, 'If you must, then you must do that, Simon.'

His wife was very good to allow him to travel to the USA with Mr Braga. He was sorry to leave Alice at home just fifteen days after they were married. On the other hand, a trip to the USA for business only happened rarely, in those times.

In the morning, he said to Mr Braga, 'My wife said, "If you must then you must do that."'

'OK. Then we shall leave on Saturday at 5 a.m. from Bologna. At 8 a.m. we shall arrive in Milan, and later, we'll go to Milan Airport at Malpensa in Mr Pere's Mercedes car. Mr Pere is our agent for Italy. You and I will then leave for New York. My brother and Mr Pere will remain at Milan. Is that OK, Simon?'

'That's all right, but you are the boss, Mr Braga.'

Saturday came. Alice would stay with his parents while he went to the USA, and she would pray to all the saints, together with his mother, father, two brothers, aunts and uncles, cousins, and his friends, who were living, for a safe journey.

It was September. It was cold and foggy, but after three hours, the sun came up, leaving three feet of fog on the ground and the Boeing 727 had no difficulty in taking off.

Simon hadn't seen a Boeing 727 plane before or any other planes or an airport. He had seen a toy plane many times, but this plane measured about 45 × 35 × 19 metres; it had three jet engines and six doors. The stewardesses were very good in helping the passengers with the food, drinks, magazines, and sweets. Simon was not afraid of flying over the sun or the moon, the clouds, the birds, and other planes. It was terrific for him and his first flight ever!

After eight hours of flying over Spain and the Atlantic, the brakes stopped the plane on the runway, which caused havoc among the passengers, especially the children. Mr Braga was sweating all over—his hands, cufflinks, shirt, trousers, and face. Simon did not know if the sweat was caused by heat or rage or fright.

It was late evening when they got out of the Boeing 727. Mr Braga was looking, among thousands of people, for two people, who were his American agents, and within three minutes he spotted them.

The first man, a Mr John John, had been to Italy to see the company. The second man, a Mr Jeff Jeff, had not been to Italy. The two were mulattos.

Mr J. John and Mr J. Jeff wore dark suits, black hats, and black and white ties. Cigarettes hung from their mouths. The two men were like two gangsters taken from a thriller. But later, the two 'gangsters' seemed nice with their big hands across his back, saying, 'Do you like New York, buddy?' or 'Do you want a cig, buddy?'

John John spoke the Italian language so-so, and Simon could not remain serious because JJ was so funny.

Jeff Jeff did not know Italian, but he laughed all the time. Mr Braga talked in the Bolognese dialect to them, and Jeff would answer, 'What?' all the time. There was a lot of confusion.

After the talking, Jeff walked to the car park and, within ten minutes, he came back in a black limousine. It looked like a jet, eight metres long by four metres wide, plus the fins!

They got into the limousine. It had soft alligator leather upholstery, a wooden dashboard, and pockets inside the doors. Within half an hour, the limo drove up to the Executive Grand Hotel in Manhattan. Central Park, the Top of the Sixes Restaurant, Mamma Mia's Restaurant, the Empire State Building, and many shops and many theatres were all within easy reach.

Manhattan is an island, forming New York between the Hudson River, East River, and Brooklyn.

Three hundred years ago, the Red Indians lived here in peace. Now, Europeans, Asians, Africans, Americans, Australians, and Indians live not in peace . . .

The hotel had many porters in multicoloured uniforms, black hats, fake gold, and black and shiny black shoes. Simon's boss gave tips of ten, twenty, or fifty dollars to the waiters, chambermaids, and managers, because he did not want people to think that he was a 'miser' from Italy.

After they had changed into fresh clothes, the two 'gangsters' took them to a fish restaurant near the sea in the moonlight. The moon was very beautiful and it was very sad to see what the human species was up to with theft, rape, civil wars, battles . . .

The restaurant was, in fact, an inn with old boards, bad doors, old posts, toilets, and old chairs on the second floor. The first floor had many old wooden posts that supported the second floor, and . . . the sea was full of large grey and black sharks!

The fish they ate—not sharks—was terrific, all right, but Simon was thinking all the time of his wife in Bologna. Was she all right?

On Sunday, they slept until 10 a.m.

After breakfast, Mr Braga and Simon walked down Fifth Avenue, until they eyed the Empire State Building.

'Mamma mia!' his boss shouted, looking at the building 'I'll bet that mass of bricks is one kilometre in height! (In Italian—Simon's boss couldn't understand English.)

'The building is 443 metres, actually, without the aerial,' said Simon.

'How amazing! Then it's four and a half times Bologna's Two Towers, which are ninety-seven metres!' he said and they decided to enter the massive building.

Since it was Sunday, the queues for the tickets halls and the lifts were enormous, but within one hour, they got into a lift—pressed like sardines in a box in the midday heat—which took them up to the eighty-sixth floor in forty seconds. In *forty* seconds? Yes, in forty seconds! The lift must have a very good stop bar to ensure that the lift actually stopped, or otherwise it would go up to the moon.

The view from the eighty-sixth floor of Empire State Building was terrific. You could see over houses, skyscrapers, the Hudson River, Manhattan, the Statue of Liberty, Central Park, and the Chrysler Building Tower; rich people, poor people, children, priests, cardinals, dogs, cats, ships, inns, restaurants, and churches; buses, taxis, vans, coaches, and cars all crammed into the streets of New York, creating the thin, yellow fog, which can send all people down to hell, instead of creating the healthy air the Red Indian population lived on.

However, Simon's big chief was near the parapet and he was thinking, while the wind ran though his few grey hairs. His hands were in his pockets, because he was cold. Simon was thinking, too, with thick black hair. He was thinking that if one fell from the eighty-sixth or fifty-sixth or twenty-third or twelfth floor of the ESB, one could save one's soul but one would have no brain, head, legs, feet, shoes, socks, pants, and trousers. He got a fright because the ESB swayed with the wind. There were white clouds and he was cold. When Mr Braga shifted his position from outside to inside the ESB, Simon was quick in following his example, and they hopped into a lift.

In forty-two seconds the lift took them from the eighty-sixth floor to the ground floor plus six floors below, and then came to a stop. The lift ascended to the right level, when the passengers could get out of the 'rocket'—but where? In heaven or in hell? Should they go left or right?

The big chief tried hanging on to Simon, and Simon tried hanging on to Mr Braga, like two drunken men.

Within five minutes, they managed to walk straight down the pavements, passing millions of people talking, shouting, and laughing. There were Africans, Asians, Russians, Europeans, Australians, and Indians, because it was New York, the great city.

The adventures made Mr Braga ravenous. They entered a snack bar on the right-hand side of the Hudson River, where the barman sold them two cups of coffee, snacks, and hot dogs. Hot dogs were not really 'hot dogs'—the animal. They were long fresh thin loaves with hot long sausages and mustard. They found that these were very good, almost as good as a plate of Italian spaghetti with tomato sauce on top.

Afterwards, his boss wanted to cross the river on a motorboat, like a two-year-old child.

'Mr Braga, the river is very deep and you cannot swim!'

'I will manage by clinging on to you.'

'You cannot do that. You are very fat and we would sink to the bottom of the river!'

'No, Simon. My fat will support me. So, would you hire one of those motorboats for me, please?'

'You are the boss, Mr Braga!'

The Hudson River flows into the Atlantic Ocean. The skipper drove his motorboat up to the harbour, which is on the other side. He explained that the red skyscraper they saw was built by an Italian company. Another Italian company had designed and built that white shopping centre. Another Italian company built that housing complex. All along the river's right and left shores, there were buildings made by Italian companies, which made them feel important.

They finished with the motorboat and strolled to the hotel. There, after a cup of tea with Mr Braga, Simon went up to his room. He slept, dreaming of an immense ship which carried the ESB to Africa, maybe Egypt, where thousands of mummies prayed to their god to change them back to humans. They were so tired of being mummies. Their god resembled his big chief, with his big fat stomach full of hot dogs and Coca-Cola, saying to him, 'Simon, you seem like a mummy. It is 7 p.m. and I want to eat, please.'

'*The Mummy! . . . The Mummy!*' he was saying, between sleep and being awake.'

'It is me, not a mummy. I am alive, Simon!'

'Sorry, Mr Policarpo. You want to eat? Where?'

'John was saying that there is a restaurant called 'Te topo o sei sei sei.'

'*Te topo o . . .* ? Ohhh! The Top of the Sixes Restaurant. OK, but we need a taxi, because I would not like to walk in a town like New York by night.

At 8.30 p.m., they arrived at the Top of the Sixes restaurant, which was a skyscraper, all lit up. The restaurant was on the last floor, which rotated slowly. It was terrific. Simon's boss did not like the rotations and one of the waiters stopped the floor turning, until his chief took his seat at the table. The waiter started up the rotations and the situation became normal.

The other guests and Simon became very interested in the lights of New York, in the white clouds, in the night air, and in the birds flying over the city. On the other hand, Mr Braga was very interested in the smell of the birds after they'd roasted in the oven, with potatoes, carrots, and peas, together with a beefsteak, boiled cauliflower, beans, bread, and lettuce. He had, also, two bottles of Chianti wine, two Cuban cigars, and two grappas.

'Mr Braga, why do you eat so much? I have had one small steak, some lettuce, some bread, and one glass of wine, that is all.'

'Because I am hungry and happy, Simon. In your case, you eat too little and you are unhappy.'

'Because I am missing my wife, away in Bologna, Mr Braga! Do you miss your wife?'

'Me? No, because my wife tells me off about the food every day, like you! I prefer New York . . . . .'

On Monday morning, John and Jeff turned up at the hotel with the limo and the cigarettes hanging from their mouths. They wore black suits and black hats, as usual. They were saying that the Lightcap Inc. was expecting them around 10 a.m.

When they arrived at the gate, the attendant, as black as a piece of coal, but as nice as a piece of white sugar, sat them on a red and blue settee, like the Bologna football team's colours.

He telephoned to a manager in the factory and, within two minutes, two managers showed up. The lines were numerous and very long, all making pharmaceutical gelatine capsules. The gelatine was supplied by old bones: chicken bones, pig bones, cow bones, donkey bones, and horse bones. The hot gelatine, in liquid form, ran on to the machine bed, where twenty or thirty steel nozzles deposited the gelatine on to twenty or thirty steel cups and the capsules were formed. The cycle was ended when the capsules were emptied into cardboard containers.

The lines were interesting. The factory was interesting. The workforce used by Lightcap Inc. was interesting. However, his boss was ravenous with hunger after watching the lines for two hours. The manager came to his rescue and, within fifteen minutes, they stopped at an inn, away from the factory, among tall trees, lakes, shrubs, birds, a few swans, and a fountain, all sited near the restaurant. The inn was famous for barbecue steaks and onions, and Simon became famous for translating from Italian to English and from English to Italian, all the time, at that inn, without any food or drink. The customers and Mr Braga were talking and shouting at the table, while they were eating or drinking, which was not fair on Simon.

Later in the hotel, Simon dreamed of the barbecue steaks, fried onions, and red wine from Italy.

Mr Braga had another attack of hunger at 8.30 p.m., so they went to an inn called *Mamma Mia*. When they got in, they could smell fresh garlic, fresh onions, sage, black pepper, sea salt, fresh rosemary, fresh Italian tomatoes, and boiled ragout. The wines would be Sangiovese and Albana from Bologna's hills, Frascati from the

Roman hills, and Chianti from the Florence hills. Simon thought that Italy and the Mediterranean countries were fabulous, with their foods, wines, fruit, flowers, blue and green seas, great mountains, hills, music, glaciers, and their people.

After the aroma of the Italian cuisine, they sat at a table ready to eat, and Mr Braga asked the waiter, 'Do you serve Italian spaghetti?'

'Yes! Spaghetti with the Bolognese sauce or spaghetti with clams the same as in Italy.'

The waiter was not Italian at all. Maybe he was French with an African mother, or Dutch with a Chinese mother. He did not know that spaghetti is not dressed with a 'Bolognese sauce' ever, because Bolognese sauce does not exist in Bologna or in Italy.

The inn was beautiful. Various artistic plates were hanging on the white walls. There were lots of small coloured lights, giving a warm atmosphere. Various people were talking in Neapolitan and Neapolitan American, Sicilian and Sicilian American, Irish and Irish American, and other less important languages.

On Tuesday morning it was time for the visit to Caplet Co. of Boston, Massachusetts. Boston is an industrial centre, on the Atlantic Ocean, between New York and Maine, in the northern part of the United States, near Canada. The Caplet Co. was a big global pharmaceutical company, tied in with Lightcap Inc. to fill and to sell a variety of medical stuff in capsule form, from aspirins to brain powders, from sex granules to pile oils, from light shock pills to machine-gun bullets.

The attendant found a manager, and all three of them went to his office. They were joined by two other managers to see the factory. There were many capsule-filling machines by BPBS of Bologna and other machines from Kaput, Hell, in Germany that were operating at high speeds. The world of capsule-filling equipment was, in those times, dominated by their factory and the German competitor, nobody else. The Caplet Co. was in the market for 200 capsule-filling machines for the United States and other countries of the world. Simon's boss had be in America, then, to seize the iron while it was hot.

The Bologna machine had intermittent motion with two hoppers, one dedicated to the capsule and one dedicated to the capsule caps. There was a third hopper dedicated to the product—powder or granules or liquids—which flowed to an intermittent motion plate, which distributed pharmaceuticals into the capsule bodies. Then the cap hopper distributed the caps to the filled capsule. The cycle was terminated. The capsules then spilled out from the machine into a cardboard container.

The factory was very interesting, but suddenly Simon felt an itch on his head, then on his hands, on his legs, and on his backside. He was itching all over his body, and his boss said to him, 'Simon, do you have lice?'

'No! But I am itching all over my body.'

One of the managers said, 'Maybe you are affected by the antibiotic powder floating in the factory. I am sorry. Your boss does not seem to be troubled by the itching, does he?'

'Mr Braga is not affected because he is too fat,' Simon said in English to the manager.

Later, his itching went away, but changed to another sort of 'itch'. His translating took hours upon hours, in three languages, English, Italian, and the Bolognese dialect, with no time to visit the loo! During their meeting, the three managers asked about the machine prices, spare parts prices, delivery, fitters, guarantees and discounts, and . . .

Mr Braga got the order for 200 capsule-filling machines. An order confirmed by mouth. Later the Caplet Co. would confirm the order in writing and, in due course, Mr Braga would visit Boston with Mr Pere, who would put all the details on the order.

John and Jeff drove them to the hotel, then Simon and Braga walked to the Fifth Avenue cinema and theatre. They saw a ballet plus a cowboy film. The ballet was *The Nutcracker*, which was beautiful. The film was fairly good and in English. Simon's boss was interested in the cowboy film, but he wanted it translated into Italian by Simon. He kept asking, 'Who is he? And who is she? Why has the man killed another man? Who is the Indian?' The boss spoke to Simon all in Italian because Mr Braga couldn't speak in English.

An American woman, who was sitting behind Simon, complained about the noise.

'Your friend is bothering me a lot. I can't hear a word with the noise that your friend makes!'

'*Signora*, will you be quiet! I want to see the film!' said Simon's boss, pulling a cigarette out from a packet.

'Mr Braga, it's 'No Smoking' or 'Vietato Fumare' in this cinema, or any cinema in America.'

'Why? In Italy, people can smoke in cinemas, theatres, bars, restaurants, trains, churches, and -'

'Shush!'

'Who is that?' asked the boss.

'It's the woman sitting behind us. Mr Braga, it is better that we return to the hotel. It is late, and tomorrow—Wednesday—John and Jeff are collecting us at 6 a.m. for the airport. Tomorrow we shall fly to Milan and then to Bologna. We shall see the Two Towers by night, which are beautiful. The ESB in New York is good, but the Two Towers in Bologna are fantastic; to think that they were built about 900 years ago! I am amazed, Mr Braga. I wonder if the ESB will be here in 2864. I doubt it!'

'Simon, the Towers are OK, but the order for 200 machines is better, a lot better!'

It was 10 a.m. Mr Braga and Simon were looking at the shadow of the Boeing 727 on the tarmac. The huge wheels jumped every ten metres on the tarmac grooves, until the aircraft stopped on the big runway. The aircraft jets increased their power to the maximum, and then the captain let off the brakes. The Boeing 727 surged forward. The pilot turned to the right on the way to Europe.

It was 11 a.m. New York time when the stewardesses served breakfast. In Europe it was 5 p.m., time for high tea. It was eight hours' flying time to Milan, plus three hours to go to Bologna. Then Simon would greet Alice, his Irish love, and he would eat breakfast at 7 a.m. on Thursday, after five days spent in another continent.

Poor Alice, who had fallen in love with an Italian guy from Padua, transferred to Bologna. When Alice was born, her father died. Her mother struggled to survive with four children. It was a struggle for food, clothes, schooling, and health. Alice grew up. She liked her local school very much. But the village did not have any work. An aunt found work for her away in a Dublin hospital, when she was a teenager. She trained to be a staff nurse. Later, she moved to London and she worked in another hospital, never forgetting her mother, her brother, and two sisters, visiting them in Ireland or meeting them in London.

Then one night Alice and Simon met in London for the first time. They talked. They laughed. They were very happy. They got married and so on.

The company was going places after the order of 200 capsule-filling machines from the United States. The autumn came, with wet days and nights. Winter also came, and one night Alice and Simon were wakened by a flake of snow falling against a black sky. Then there were hundreds, thousands, and millions of snowflakes against the black sky. It was magnificent.

In the morning, Simon got out of bed at 7 a.m. on the eighth floor of a block of flats, together with his wife, for breakfast. Watching the snow and the ice from a high place is beautiful but scaring. That day there were no humans, no cars, no buses, no vans, no coaches, and no horses at all, because they didn't have the courage to walk or to drive on the roads in that condition.

Simon also saw a few vans and coaches reversed on the side of the road, but he was determined to walk to the factory ten kilometres away for his work.

'Simon, it is impossible. The road is tremendously icy!'

'I will be careful, Alice.'

'You are mad! You will fall, for sure, and no ambulance will pick you up on the road.'

'No ambulances on the road, Alice.'

'You are impossible!'

'Do I get a hug before I open the door?'

'Nooo! You are a stubborn fellow. Ciao, Simon!'

He got a hug from Alice before he went out. The road was empty and extremely quiet. The snow and the ice spread a white mantle which covered the landscape of trees, fields, ditches, roads, and houses. It was fantastic, but the sun dazzled him. The white snow dazzled him. The Siberian cold froze him. His eyes, ears, nose, hands, arms, backside, legs, and feet were numb and shaking. Nevertheless, he walked without falling and got to work.

At the factory, he found that three stubborn fellows—like him—had walked to work, but the offices, factory, toilets, kitchen, and garage were empty of people because the place was freezing cold and without heating. His wife was right. He was a stubborn fellow. He returned home to Alice, who said, 'I did warn you, Simon. Snow, ice, no food, no work . . . and you must have been away some ten hours.'

'Six hours, not ten hours, Alice.'

February came round. March came round and a pain came round. If two pains happened in the same place and at the same time, Simon would not have survived because the pain was deadly. It was above his left urethra, which received the liquid or urine from the left kidney. The right urethra was OK, but the left urethra was faulty; hence, the great pain. The inventor of the human body should have been careful to leave these passages free. If the passages are not free, the body creates hell!

When he had an espresso coffee at the bar or wrote a letter to his Japanese customers or kissed Alice, suddenly his pain hit again and he felt that the stones were walking into his tummy with a terrible discomfort. He flushed the stones with bottles of mineral water, so his windpipe, stomach, kidneys, and bladder got the benefit, but one day a big stone got in his penis, causing a dreadful pain, and he flushed it out with bottle after bottle of special mineral water to ease the passage of the stone.

The stone resisted and travelled down into his penis, until it shot away into his hand. What satisfaction! What relief! The stone was black, very hard, the size of a 10-mm bean with over twenty hard calcium spikes. Those were the cause of his pain.

That was the way in May 1965 with his pain. That month also, he asked his boss for a pay increase from 72,000 lire a month, to satisfy his wife's hunger and his hunger, plus the debts for the furniture, holidays, and car. But his boss did not agree, watching the smoke of his Cuban cigar drifting out of his window, while his brother, the office director, and Simon listened to the big chief.

'I am sorry, Simon. There is no increase for you here. If you want, I could send you to the sales office in Milan with a wage of 300,000 lire a month. Do you like that idea?'

'And my wife?' Simon said.

'I must look after my wife and you must look after your wife—that would only be fair, Simon.'

'And our flat?' Simon insisted.

'There are many empty flats in Milan! Look, Simon, I am a hard man who has thick hairs on his chest.'

'Like an orang-utan!' Simon butted in, while his boss's brother and the director shifted on their chairs, embarrassed.

The big chief continued, 'My brother and I were broke a few years ago. We used our brains and now we have a great company with sales all over the world. Do you understand, Simon? If you want lots of money, you must sell our machines in France, in England, in China, and in America.'

'I sold 200 machines in the United States with you, but the money is the same—72,000 lire a month!'

'Then you must change your residence from Bologna to Milan.'

'I would do not that because my wife and I hate Milan. I do not accept your offer, and I will move to a better company in Bologna.'

Simon left Mr Braga's posh office. Secondo (Policarpo's brother) and Signor Avanti (the office director) had said nothing during the meeting. He thought that they were afraid of Policarpo, the orang-utan who had thick hairs on his chest.

He knew that Secondo was in a hurry to be home at midday. His wife and relatives were ready with cakes and presents for his birthday party. Secondo took his grey Fiat Dino car and shot out of the gate, speeding off down the *via Emilia Levante* to the city. But a man on his motorbike, coming from a side road, crashed into Secondo's car, which somersaulted into a wet field.

Some people called an ambulance quickly to take him to the General Hospital. The doctors tried to save him, but Secondo died. Life is strange. First, there is life. In a split second, there is death. He was forty-five years old and full of life.

The *via Emilia* (331 km from Milan to Rimini) is very dangerous because of the amount of traffic, with cars, motorbikes, lorries, coaches, and buses. In olden times, the people called it, 'The Roman Road'. It carried cows and horses and other animals. It also carried peasants, farmers, and Roman gentlemen and ladies in their carriages or on foot. It was not dangerous, apart from the highway robbers.

The road was designed and built by Marco Emilio Lepido, who was a Roman consul in 187 BC.

The company's office director, Mr Avanti, used the road every day from the city to the factory and vice versa. One day, it went all wrong for him.

As usual, he drove to work in his car. He stopped and his left indicator arrow was flashing to allow other cars coming from the eastern side. The office staff and Simon saw, through the office window, a French car approaching at great speed and crashing on to the director's car. The French car was in a mess. The director's car was in a mess. The French driver was shocked. His wife was sobbing and mumbling in French. Their two children were crying in French, until an ambulance arrived to take Signor Avanti away to the hospital.

A police car arrived to do a report on the accident. The French people were very nervous and the French driver was saying that the director had not switched his left indicator on and so caused the accident. Simon translated in French and the company's workers said that they were sure that the director had in fact switched on the left indicator. The accident was caused by the speed of the French car. The story of the indicator arrow ended there. The story about Signor Avanti went on for another six months in the hospital and at his home. Later, he could drive to the factory all right, but he was not the same man. The via Emilia was the place of tragic accidents like this and other such scenes.

Chapter 9

In August, Simon left the BPBS Company and started work at the MIF Co., which made pharmaceutical packaging machines. His wages were 126,000 lire per month, against his previous wage of 72,000 lire per month, so he rode a high and wild horse, thanks to the money.

The company was formed by the Ignazi family. The bosses were a father and his son—Signor Ignazio Ignazi and Signor Zeno Ignazi. The father was the inventor of the first cartoning machine and he was fifty-five years old, but he died the following year from cancer. The son was twenty-seven years old, a cultured young man and a businessman.

When Simon went to the new company for the first time, he met a man whom he had not seen for years. They were at the same school, used the same wooden bench, the same teachers, and the same books. His friend, Ivo, was very intelligent. He lived together with his sister when his parents died. Ivo was a director at Ignazi's company. Simon was an ass during his schooling days, but he became a selling agent for the same company. Therefore, one could be saying that 'will' counts, not the 'school'.

At Ignazi's company, he worked in the translating and selling offices, writing to overseas customers with letters about quotations, order acknowledgements, selling appointments, and the visits of customers.

One day, Mr Ignazi junior sent him to Manchester to sort out a payment problem and a selling problem with the English agents. They were not good, but their salesman, Mr Harry Gray, was good. Simon took him away from the UK company and the sales started doing well.

Pakex '65 was starting in London. It was the first time at a packaging exhibition for Simon. He found that the fifteen days of unloading and reloading the machines, involving the exhibition, fitters, people, customers, bad food and worse coffees, the noise of the machines, the heat and cold, just to show a couple of machines, was too much, and he was very tired when the exhibition was ended. But Mr Zeno was satisfied after Pakex '65 and asked Simon, when he returned to Italy, 'Would you like to help our French agent to sell more machines?'

He asked his wife first, and when she said it was fine, he said to his boss, 'Yes'. It involved putting the flat up for sale, plus the furniture, and finding a new house in France.

Later, his boss changed his mind. Not Paris, *no foie, no beurre, no La Seine* but Bologna again! This involved leasing a new flat, new furniture, and work at Ignazi's company. However, they were happy to be in Italy. The sun, Italian wine, the spaghetti, the fish, the seaside, and everything else was fine.

Christmas and New Year came round. They went to the mountainous part of Italy for their holidays to ski, but they were not able to ski, so they went to Ireland! Alice wanted to spend her holidays with her mother, aunts, and uncles, and Simon worked visiting Irish customers in December. He would join her in Cracklegs once he'd finished working in Dublin. Cracklegs is a farming village of about 3,000 human souls, and many animal souls, on the Atlantic Ocean, among blue lakes, green, yellow, or brown forests and sandy beaches, which are beautiful.

After his business in Dublin, Simon left for Cracklegs. The weather was bad, with enormous grey, brown, and black clouds, ready to soak anybody and anything, especially him, because he did not have an umbrella. He got a green train, like the Irish grass, and almost everything else was green, from girls' frocks to boys' trousers, from pub doors to pub windows, from garden gates to cowsheds, from men's caps to shopping bags.

The train stopped at Londonderry Station, in Northern Ireland, occupied by Scottish and English Protestants for 300 years or more.

The barometer indicated 'wet'. Simon got the green coach in the Free Republic of Ireland, or Eire. He passed over the large river that divides north and south. He breathed 'free' air, even though it was loaded with the smell of cow and sheep dung. He admired the Irish countryside, full of high and low wet places, from woods to houses, from barns to cars, from trees to bushes, from animals to rivers.

At the first southern town that he reached by taxi, it was raining. It rained on the taxi. It rained on his suitcase. It rained on his seat, while he sat down, and it rained on the light suit he'd bought in Italy.

The taxi followed the main road. The bends went in and out, high and low, through small villages and through the rain. Suddenly, the road went up through a series of hairpin bends, until the taxi encountered a rainstorm and tornado force winds, between high and low mountain ranges that were full of granite stones and boulders.

The taxi driver was Irish and he spoke to Simon in English for the first time during the trip. 'We're used to this kind of weather, especially over the pass!'

'I do not like tornado anywhere,' Simon mumbled from his seat.

The taxi driver nodded a 'yes' and drove on, until his car left the rainstorm and the tornado behind. In front, his car met thin rain. There was a lake on the left-hand side, a few houses, and a road sign which said, 'Cracklegs—1 mile'.

On the main road, they found Cracklegs village, with some shops and many shoppers. There was a petrol station, more houses, another beautiful lake on the right-hand side, three pubs, a Co-op, and an old thatched house before one leaves the village.

As the taxi man was able to talk, he talked some more and said,

'I would like the address in Cracklegs, please.'

'You must cross the village until you would see a house with a thatched roof on your right-hand side. At the top, take the right lane over a small bridge, and you will see the cottage on your right-hand side. That is the cottage where my wife's mother lives, OK?'

The taxi driver got mixed up with the roads and the streets and the lanes. Eventually, he found Mara's cottage.

Simon's wife called 'hello' from the cottage door, standing with her arms folded, and she said jokingly, 'What are you doing here?' Then they laughed and kissed, at last.

Eventually, a beautiful sun came out and shone on Mara's cottage. They went into the kitchen. Mara greeted the taxi driver and Simon from her armchair, and right away she got up and made ready tea, milk, and biscuits for the taxi driver. The man talked to the ladies about the storm, the rain, the sun, the Cracklegs people, the sheep, the cows, and the pigs, not minding about Simon, drenched as he was with rain and cold. He took half an hour to have his tea, biscuits, butter, jams—and more tea and more biscuits. His talking, laughing, or joking was terrible, like an automatic grinder.

Finally, he got up, walked to his taxi and disappeared, at last . . .

'I am sorry, Simon,' said Alice. 'We must look after strangers first. Here's our tea now—that's all right, Simon?'

While Simon dried his pants, socks, shoes, trousers, coat, and shirt by sitting on them, Alice asked him various things about the trip: Dublin, the train, the coach, the pass, the tornado, and Cracklegs.

He was curious, at the same time, about Mara, his wife's mother, who was well built, with strong bones, grey/white hair, thin, calm, smiling, and beautiful, for all of her sixty-one years. She was sitting on her armchair, next to the range, drinking her tea with milk and sugar, keeping a few biscuits in her apron. She pretended to look outside the window, but she was looking at Simon. Mara was delving into her mind for the reasons why Alice had chosen to wed a young Italian man. An Irishman would have been better, maybe! And Simon was wondering what the women thought about him.

Three people were thinking, eating, and drinking, looking at the range, where the boiling teapot sent the steam up to the cottage's wooden ceiling, which was high and dark from the smoke from the range. At times, they were looking at the mixture of coal, turf, and logs burning in the furnace or on the floor outside the furnace. Simon sensed that she kept her range on, continually, winter or summer, to cook, to make a drop of tea, to dry clothes, and against the cold and dampness, especially during the chilly nights. The teapot was like a steam train with a continual whistle, which would not stay quiet.

Over her range, Mara had a string to dry clothes on, and over that, she had a black wooden board on which stood several religious statues and pictures of the Madonna, Jesus Christ, and the saints. The Irish people are very pious, almost like priests and nuns, apart from those who follow another route to get to the devil quicker with their bottles of beer, gin, and whisky.

In Mara's cottage there were four internal doors, leading to the other rooms. One door led to the 'guests' tea room', mostly for priests and nuns. The second door led to Mara's room. The third door went to the 'pantry' and the fourth door to the spare room, which had a bed.

In the kitchen, there was one window, the entrance door, and Mara's sitting place, conveniently near her range, her radio, the turf bin, and her small table.

Mara had four children: three daughters—Betty, Ann, and Alice—and one son—Pat. Betty and Ann were working in the village, but Pat was out in the garden. Their mother had a good husband, but he had died of a serious disease.

Her cottage was built on 1848 by her grandparents. The bricklayers used stones and boulders, without mortar, excavated from the local mountain. The mountain was bare with short yellow, brown, or green grass. Most Irish mountains are conical, which resemble Italian Christmas 'panettone' cake, but they'd would be very hard to eat!

Outside, Mara had two fields for potatoes and onions. Irish potatoes are very good and Irish onions are very hot, like the Irish people. There was a beautiful lake near the cottage and it was very quiet, with several white swans. Simon did not see any fish there ever. However, he saw fishermen down at the lake, hoping to catch a fish.

Over the lake, far away, you could see the Turf Range Mountains, which resembled an old man lying down with his fat chin and his fat belly. Near the village, you can see the Atlantic Ocean. There are many very beautiful bays with brown and black rocks, and fine yellow sand by the blue and green seawater.

On a day with fine weather and with no wind, the view is terrific. If it is windy, the view is foggy due to the moisture floating in the air. If the weather is bad, the view is terrible. If it is a night with a moon, the view is beautiful. If it is a night with no moon, the view is sinister.

Betty and Ann, Simon's wife's sisters, had good weather with them and were coming home to high tea.

'Hello! How are you?' Betty greeted them. 'And this would be Simon, the Italian? Ummm! A small man.' Betty looked at him from his head to his feet, from the left to the right, which must have taken her one second. She was cooking some sausages in a frying pan, without talking to him, and looking at the painted kitchen wall. Simon thought then that for Betty he was less important than the pork sausages with sage and onions!

'OK, Miss Betty' he thought to himself. 'I am not a small man, at 1.71 tall, without shoes. I wonder how tall her boyfriend is!' Simon preferred Ann, with her black hair. She was slim, very nice and pretty, like Alice, but shy. Ann was the youngest of the sisters and Alice was the oldest. Betty was very jealous, especially of her oldest sister. Simon thought then that Betty could take a man and skin him to his bones, without removing his trousers, pants, socks, shoes, coat, and tie! She liked the 'big boss' image.

After his first day in Cracklegs, Alice and Simon went out walking in the sunshine—or in the rain—because it made no difference at all. They would stroll from Mara's cottage door to the fields in the sunshine, but suddenly it would rain cats and dogs, plus the wind, which could become a tornado. Sometimes they walked to Alice's relatives, near her mother's cottage. They met grandparents, uncles, aunties, cousins, nieces, and their families. Irish people are family-minded, with seven boys and five daughters, or even thirteen daughters and eleven boys. They are good workers, very nice, calm, very quiet, and sober—apart from the drunkards, like the rest of the world!

Another day, Paddy came to Mara's cottage. Paddy was engaged to 'Miss' Betty. Simon saw him outside the window, when Simon was enjoying a plate of sardines with fresh onions and boiled potatoes taken from Mara's fields.

Paddy? Betty's fiancé? He imagined that Betty's fiancé was handsome, young, and tall, with two big shoulders like a bull. When he looked at Betty and she looked at Simon, Betty was embarrassed about her fiancé, because Paddy was not handsome, not young, but was almost bald and with narrow shoulders.

'So this is Paddy, the Irishman? Ummm!' thought Simon.

However, Paddy and Betty took them around the country to cosy inns, country pubs with music, and many towns and villages in their car, a red Beetle. Simon and Alice can say now that Betty and Paddy were very nice to them. Ireland is beautiful, in the sun or the rain. Irish people are very nice, sober or not sober, and Simon loved the turf fires in the fireplaces or stoves, because turf gives off a nice clean 'vintage' perfume.

Alice and Simon's holiday was ended for now, and they said goodbye to the turf, the cows, the sheep, the pigs, the Irish mountains and lakes; the Atlantic Ocean, the green after green, and the Irish people. It was farewell to Betty, Paddy, Ann, Pat, and Mara, with her white and blue cottage, while the chimney sent the black Irish turf smoke out across the windy Irish sea towards Londonderry. They saw Protestant crowds, but why did the Protestants protest? They did not know.

They saw English people at London's Heathrow Airport, always calm, holding a black umbrella every day, even if the day was sunny in summertime. Anyway, they boarded an Alitalia Airways jet plane to Milan. They savoured two beautiful Italian espresso coffees at the thought that Simon's mother would be preparing green *lasagne* with home-made ragout when they returned home. The *lasagne* is a favourite Bolognese dish, and if *lasagne* is prepared and roasted properly by the cook, the dish is heavenly.

Apart from the *lasagne* and two cups of good espresso coffees, they needed to return home and to their work. If they wouldn't get any money: no money, and no presents for Simon's brother and his fiancée, who were getting married in September.

His brother got the crazy idea to marry while he was sitting on the toilet in his parents' house, reading a Mickey Mouse comic, in which Mickey got married to Minnie.

And his brother did get married with red roses, white lilies, two rings, confetti, a wedding dinner—and the honeymoon, of course.

After the wedding, Mr Harry Gray, the sales manager in England, wanted Simon to travel to England to visit some customers and get more orders.

In winter in England, the temperature is low, but not usually freezing, because the Central American Stream Gulf sends mild currents to

Ireland and to Great Britain. It is the damp atmosphere which causes the problems and the fog, apart from Cornwall, which is dry and windy. Simon could still remember looking at the sea at Newquay, admiring the multicoloured waves, walking on the pavement.

But he did not notice a concrete telephone pole, rising from the ground to a bunch of telephone wires. Simon bumped against the pole, the bump was terrible, and he was nursing with creams and ointments for a month.

Simon was young, just twenty, and now felt old at twenty-eight, because he did not have a son or a daughter, but Simon took a decision to have a family when he returned home.

During the trip to Britain, Simon got a few orders for the companies in Bologna, left England, and took a flight home.

After many months, Alice found that she was pregnant.

Simon was happy because to have a child is paradise, and the line is continued.

Alice was tremendously happy, and she went visiting all the city's shopping areas to buy 1,001 things, which she and her child would use, from some dummies to hundreds of toys, from a pram to blankets, together with the cushions, the sheets, and the dresses.

Six months later, Alice got labour pains.

They ran to the hospital and, after more hours of labour pains, their son was born. Alice was happy. He was happy, even though he was smoking non-stop in the hospital, like a chimney which had caught fire!

The baby had eight fingers and two thumbs, ten toes, two beautiful eyes like his mammy, one straight nose like his daddy, two nice legs, and two chubby feet, so they could not complain.

Every day Alice weighed him on the scales, fed him at various times, and weighed him again. If he was underfed that day, Alice got the 'pump' to pump him again. If he was overfed, he vomited over her new dress, and 'the mammy' shouted at him and Simon!

Apart from being fed, he did wee-wee and made shit all the time.
In between getting him off to sleep and getting him up, they had to
find a name for him.

Alice was talking and he was listening, because she wanted an
Irish name or maybe an English name for him, not an Italian name.

'Why?' said Simon.

'Because an Irish or English name is more natural to give to our
son. For example John or Stephen or Victor.'

'It is the same thing. Giovanni or Stefano or Vittorio. As we are
living in Italy, we ought to find an Italian name for him. Do you
agree?'

'Then, when we're living in Ireland, will our son change to an Irish
or English name?'

'Yes!'

'You must be joking, Simon! We'll call him John.'

'John?

'Yes! John.'

The Big Chief had spoken! And their son became known as John.
A man who had two names: John, when he was living in the northern
part of Europe, and Giovanni, when he was living in the southern part
of Europe.

When John was four months old, they took him to see Mara, his
Irish grandmother, by plane from Milan to Dublin, and then from
Dublin to Cracklegs by car, which gave them the chance to admire
Ireland's scenery, which is beautiful. They drove through Dublin's
outskirts to Sligo via Boyle, Longford, and Mullingar; then to the Bull
Gap before Cracklegs.

Granny Mara was very pleased to meet her first Irish-Bolognese
nephew, who was silent all the time, apart from smiling at her, Alice's
sisters, Mara's friends, and her relatives, because John was a baby
with a good disposition towards everybody.

While they stayed at Mara's cottage, they went out to visit Alice's
relatives. They had children of their own. They had some cattle, sheep,
dogs, cats, stables, a garden plus many fields. John seemed to enjoy
himself in the sun.

Upon their return, they would stop to see the Atlantic Ocean, a castle, a river, or a lake, ready for tea with some biscuits or to eat their lunch with granny. The life was very nice and quiet in that part of the country. In another part of the country, there was a war between the Irish people, which was shocking.

A few days later, he went away to attend an exhibition for his company, which was exhibiting cartoning machines. Alice would keep her two eyes on John in Cracklegs and he drove the 250 km to Baile Atha Cliath—Dublin in the Irish language.

He splashed through many puddles filled with muddy water, ran into round hole, square holes, big ridges, and ditches, and it was raining, windy, or sunny. At times the sun blinded him, but it would rain again every ten minutes.

Dublin is beautiful and full of interesting things, like the grand river and many bridges, the O'Connell Bridge, churches, hospitals, the Dublin Zoo, and millions of pubs. Irish people will enjoy a pub, and they do not work, do not eat, do not drive, and do not make love without a pub near to them, where they drink a pint of beer in peace first. Later, they are ready to work, apart from Masses at 7 a.m, 8 a.m., 10 a.m., and 12.30 p.m., and then they go to the pub, again, to eat chicken and fried chips and drink beer. In the evenings, they go to the church singing 'Ave Maria' with the priest, thinking about the pub, which draws men, women, priests, monks, and teenagers to drink beer, whisky, and gin. But babies drink milk or water, while a local band plays an Elvis Presley number and the people dance away. An evening at a local pub is very relaxing . . . if the people don't fight! But if the people do fight, well, they would carry on all night dictated by the beer or many beers.

The exhibition was a success for Simon, including two machines, which would remain in Ireland. He packed his exhibition bag, travelled to Cracklegs to kiss his Alice and John, who remained in Ireland, and went back to Italy because . . .

. . . because Simon had to pack his bag, again, for another exhibition in Johannesburg, the major South African industrial and commercial centre. The town had a population, in those days, of

2,100,000, mostly black Africans, English people, and immensely hungry lions, poisonous black tarantulas, big bats, and shiny omnivorous cockroaches.

Simon left from Fiumicino Airport near Rome on a beautiful day. Later, he could see Sicily on the right-hand side, and Libya was appearing in front. After an hour, the jet flew over Libya, and after another two hours, the plane flew over the Tropic of Cancer. The passengers were eating, drinking, and looking at the elephants, lions, black and white zebras, laughing hyenas, wild desert people, desert wells and oases, because wild Africa was living down there.

The jet plane went down to meet Johannesburg Airport's approach runway, after flying above the Central Africa Union, Congo, the Equator, which divides the earth, Zambia, Botswana, and the Tropic of Capricorn.

It was 4 a.m., ten hours from Rome to Johannesburg. It was better than flying from Milan to New York. However, he was in South Africa, a continent famous for wild heat, *and* he was freezing cold! Apart from the Rome-Johannesburg flight's sleeping passengers, sleeping crew, a few black sleeping porters, two black sleeping customs officers, two white men sitting at the airport bar, and the black barman, there was nobody else at the airport, which was cold, dark, and weird. The two white men were sipping two African coffees mixed with brown rum. Simon knew one man, because he had travelled to Italy on business some time ago. He was Mr Swan, the South African agent to the Bolognese Company. He was English. Simon did not know the other man, who brought their car round, a big black limo, and they departed for Mr Swan's house.

During the trip, Mr Swan kept talking about England and South Africa. He preferred SA because of the money and sunny days, plus a villa with a swimming pool, black servants, cars, and parties.

But Mr Swan was saying that a robber could easily enter a house and steal from the kitchen or the other rooms. First, he spreads butter or grease over his entire naked body. If you catch the robber, he slips out of your grasp and he runs away from the house.

'These robbers are very fly,' commented the agent as he drove into his villa.

The villa was in the country, near the town, and it was beautiful from the view Simon had of it. He saw many tall green pine trees, which were black in the darkness. There was a nicely shaped lighted swimming pool, a front gate made of iron, several wooden seats, several bushes, three black servants, and Mr Swan's beautiful South African wife, who was white.

It was 6 a.m. when Simon got out of the limo, and he went straight to bed, because he was very tired.

When he woke up, he saw a black woman. Simon asked her, 'Do you know the time, please?' It was an English phrase he'd learnt in London from an English teacher.

'8 p.m., bwana,' she replied, in poor English, probably taught by the lions that live on the veldt.

'Really? I've slept for fourteen hours!'

While he was talking with the woman, Mrs Swan entered his room, smiling, more beautiful and looking younger than before. He thought that his English friend was lucky to have such a gorgeous wife. However, Simon was lucky to have a gorgeous wife too! God couldn't have created a more gorgeous wife than Alice.

Later, Mrs Swan was talking to him and she said, 'Simon, you are invited to a party with our friends in your honour, tonight. I thought that you would welcome a good night with us.'

'It's marvellous, and thanks!'

When they arrived there, Simon found young girls, women, and men. There were sandwiches, cakes, biscuits, water, milk, oranges, whisky, and rum, and then . . . the dances, damn it!

A white girl was introduced to him. She was about twenty years old and her hair was jet black. She was medium height, slim and nice about the face. Below her face, she was a pine plank of $140 \times 40 \times 20$ cm, with two small triangular beans that were supposed to be her breasts.

After the 'how are you' greetings, she got him on the dance floor and started to dance close to him, and she told him that she did not like physical love, but she liked 'platonic' love, which was invented by Plato 450 years before Christ was born. Her love would be ancient.

Hymen, the girl who liked Plato, did not want platonic love on that night. She wanted physical love, with Simon, and she took her decision there in the dance room. Nevertheless, he took his decision there too and he said to Hymen, 'You are a nice girl and a good girl. However, I have a nice wife, and a good wife, who is waiting for me in Italy, 9,941 kilometres away from here, with our son. Do you understand, Hymen?'

But Hymen did not understand at all—or perhaps he did not understand at all—and she said to him, 'Simon, could we go together in the garden. It is very hot in the room. OK?'

He thought, 'If I go out into the garden with her, she will kill me with a thousand kisses and more. If we stay in the room, I will save myself sexually.' So I want to stay inside! And they remained inside. Hymen was terrible with her anger. She was fuming behind her ears. Her mouth had a wild itch. She seemed to be a dragon with ten horns, five feet, and three heads, until she left the room where people were dancing.

The dancing people and the other guests, waiters, servants, Mrs Swan and Mr Swan were all conscious that she and he had a problem with Hymen, so Mr Swan went up to him and said, 'Problems? Hymen is my secretary and it seems that she likes you, but she likes platonic love. Do not worry, Simon . . . . .'

Platonic love? Simon thought. 'I am worried because that girl wants *physical* love with me *now*, not platonic love!'

The Johannesburg exhibition started on Monday, and it ran until Friday with many machine exhibits. Hymen was present on the stand every day, and she ignored him because she wanted physical love sessions with him. Simon liked physical love, however, with his wife, not with Hymen or any other girls.

On the last day of the exhibition, a South African company gave Simon an order worth 999,000 rand, and the customer wanted to pay him in kind, which was: three elephants, two giraffes, and one lion, or five beautiful belly dancers. His boss refused the order because the animals and the belly dancers need to eat every day. Sorry!

When Simon was not at the exhibition, he walked along the streets of Johannesburg to see the shops and the people, the town and the parks. The people were mostly black, brown, or occasionally blacks, but white with white hair. They were albinos, who had poor pigmentation in their bodies. They were all good people. But the people who crowded the pavements of Johannesburg, smoking marijuana cigarettes non-stop, were not good people. He saw, with disgust, white men's toilets separated from black men's toilets. If a black man dared to urinate in a white man's toilet, the police could send the poor black man to prison, or worse!

Before Simon left Johannesburg, he wanted to buy an elephant, which he saw downtown in an animal shop. It was black. The shop assistant was sure that the elephant would not fit in the seat of the plane. So his choice went to a black ebony elephant measuring $35 \times 20 \times 15$ cm, and the man put it in a strong box. On the plane, he sat next door to his elephant, which looked down from the jet's window down on to the savannah. He saw some herds of elephants, lions, zebras, giraffes, and monkeys. He saw baobab trees, rivers, mountains, Tuaregh wearing blue robes, campfires, and camels drinking water from a well in the Sahara desert.

The glimpses of Africa were beautiful and gave him a deep sense of completion.

When he arrived at Rome Airport, he proceeded to the Italian Customs desk and an Italian Customs officer, or a *carabiniere* in the Italian language, dressed in a grey/blue uniform, stopped him and said, 'What are you holding in that box?'

'An elephant' Simon answered.

'An elephant?'

'Yes, but it is small.'

'It will grow! By law, anyone who imports animals, living or dead, into Italy, commits an offence punishable with prison. Do you understand, mister?'

'OK, but Mr *carabiniere*, my elephant is made of ebony!'

'I do not know this *boni, bum,* or *bani,* mister. I will try to telephone my chief. I have the number here: 00000000. Hello? Hello, sir. I have a passenger who wants to import an elephant from Johannesburg. Yes, sir. No, sir. The passenger insists that the elephant is small. Right . . . right. Ohhh! The elephant is made of ebony? You are right, sir, and I am stupid, very stupid, sorry, sir!'

The *carabiniere* blushed from his head to his feet, and he said to Simon, 'Your elephant can be imported into Italy. Good day, mister!'

There is a continuous joke involving the Italian *Carabinieri* Force making them very stupid. However, the *carabinieri* aren't stupid and are valid in fighting the crooks, murderers, and the various problems created by the scum.

After his adventure with the *carabiniere*, they went—him and the elephant—to Cracklegs, after travelling by plane, bus, coach, and taxi from the deep south to the far north of the earth.

After a week of doing nothing, apart from talking, drinking tea, eating soup or meat, talking again, walking out in the fields, sleeping, and visiting relatives or friends, Alice and Simon went to Italy to work in peace.

However, they could not have any peace!

One morning Alice and Simon were eating their breakfast at their kitchen table. They thought that their son would be playing on the lounge. They did not hear any sounds from the lounge, so Alice got up, calling him, 'John . . . Joohn! Are you there?'

John was not in the lounge. His wife checked their bedroom. No sign of John. He checked the cupboard, the toilet, and underneath their bed. Alice checked the landing and he checked the roof. No sign of their son there either. They were panicking.

'John, Jo—ohn! Holy Madonna, where is John?'

The only place that they did not check was their balcony. The balcony had a big green wooden toolbox fixed to the inside of the railings. If John had climbed on to the box, he could have fallen outside the balcony and would have died, after falling thirty metres. Simon was sure that he would see his son killed or badly wounded on the rough stone slabs of the garden.

But their son was not killed or badly wounded on the rough stone slabs of the garden.

Their son was in the kitchen—safe and sound—hidden underneath the table and keeping very quiet.

John was 1¼ years old at the time. It was a terrible fright for them.

It was June 1970.

Chapter 10

Simon's company now wanted him to travel to Greece to see the agents and to sell a couple of machines to their Greek customers.

'Well, OK,' said Simon to his boss,' but I've travelled quite a lot for you, and I am not happy. I cannot see my wife, son, mother, father, brothers, and friends ever—apart from Christmas and New Year. I would like, please, to take my wife and my son on this trip. I will pay for the expenses of my family.'

'You are dead right!' Mr Zeno answered. 'Go with the gods, Simon!'

So they travelled by air with Zeus, his daughter Athena, Dionysus, Aphrodite, Apollo, and Hermes, and he was happy.

Before they got the flight to Athens, a doctor gave them three yellow fever injections. Alice and her son were OK, because they ate and drank normally in Greece. Simon, however, did not have any food or drink for twenty-four hours. The yellow fever injections did not work for him.

The next day, he was feeling a bit better. His company's agents took them out to see Athens, the Aegean Sea north of Crete, very near Italy, and the Mediterranean. They saw the yellow sands, blue rocks, big brown crabs, multicoloured fish, fishing boats, and rich men's yachts. They thought that Greece was a terrific place with the sun shining every day. Simon's father did not like the country because he had seen Greece during the Second World War.

The agency director was Mr Popodolunosos, who had a wife, Tracia, and a beautiful daughter. The beautiful daughter, Tessa, had a husband called Pelo. Tessa and Pelo were the mother and father of Epapinondus, their son. Their names were not easy to pronounce for an Italian man or an Irish girl. They were nice people, who took them out to eat grilled and boiled fish or barbecued lamb chops, which were delicious, to the sound of 'Zorba the Greek' dances.

Next morning, they decided to hire a car, without the agents, to see Piraeus Harbour, the Parthenon, the Erectheum, and several museums. Later, they went outside the city and saw the Greek countryside as far as the Ionian Sea. They found a country inn, which was very clean with white tablecloths, shining cutlery, and an upright clock resting on brown floor tiles, and a log fire. The inn was empty of customers. The innkeeper served them Greek bread; Greek wine, water, tomatoes, and Greek goats' cheese salad and Greek lamb chops done on the fire. The lamb was delicious.

But Simon overheard the damn voice, 'What about your work? Your company sent you here to sell machines to the Greek customers, not enjoy your bloody self!'

'It's you, Mr Voice! I have spent three days seeing Athens with my family, and now I shall work before we all return home. OK, Mr Voice?'

The 'voices' did not scare him—no way!

In the morning, while Alice and John were asleep, he went to meet Mr Pelo and Mr Popodolunosos (help!) down in the hotel lobby. They had a car and went to see their agent's main offices, then some Greek customers, until evening. He thought that his wife and son would spend the day with a late breakfast, seeing the Imperial Guards, the beautiful gardens, and the ancient monuments. It was chilly early in the morning, but in the afternoon, it was milder in the Greek sun.

In the evenings, Simon joined his Alice and his son for a Greek meal in the hotel. For three days he was busy working with orders, invoices, price lists, and catalogues, but he had the pleasure of talking with his family at evening and night. He thought that if a company had to send a director, a fitter, or a bricklayer abroad, that company should give an option for the man to be accompanied by his wife, because everybody was then happier, even the company.

However, they caught an Olympic Airways flight to Milan, with the gods above safeguarding them against the perils of such a voyage.

John played with his toys or drew in his exercise book because he was an intelligent boy.

So they went to Greece, enjoying a phenomenal trip through Greek history, among beautiful statues and monuments. He lived their blue sea, hot sun, gorgeous food, and their infectious happiness—and his happiness when some Greek customers gave him some orders for the Italian packaging machines.

From the airport they took a taxi, from the taxi, a train, which rushed them through the cities of Lodi, Piacenza, Reggio Emilia and Modena, and then they arrived at Bologna, the town which is responsible for *tortellini*, the Italian pasta filled with pieces of savoury meat. One day Simon had witnessed a rustic grandmother preparing *tortellini*, which is a speciality of that region. She would make flour, eggs, salt, water, and yeast dough and a savoury sausage meatball. Then she would wrap one small rhomboid piece of dough combined with a small piece of meatball and leave it on a clean wooden table to dry. Later, the *tortellini* are ready to boil in chicken broth before people eat them. If the *tortellini* are well made, they become one of the dishes which the gods talked about in the heaven.

Apart the *tortellini* from Bologna, Simon called at his company the next day, and there was a surprise for him. He was to travel to Japan for the 1970 Osaka Fair.

'Osaka is on the same latitude as Sicily,' commented his boss 'over in the Orient. Marco Polo in 1275 travelled from Venice to Peking by ship and on foot, with his father and his uncle. However, you shall fly there. And when you have finished with the Osaka Fair, you shall fly to Manila to visit our agents for the Philippines and to sell a few machines there.'

'That's all right, Mr Ignazi, but I want my wife with me for this trip *and* you can pay for us both. OK, Mr Zeno Ignazi?'

'OK, OK. You can call me 'Zeno', not Mr Ignazi. After all, we are the same age, Simon.'

'But you swim in billions of lire, and I swim in dirty water!'

'If you continue like this, you could swim in billions of lire,' said Zeno.

At home, he spoke to his love about the forthcoming trip. Nevertheless, Alice refused to go to Japan. John was 2½ years old, at the time, and she would feel better at home.

Simon's mother intervened to change the scenario, while she ironed a pair of pants for his father. She said that she wanted to look after their son while they were in Japan. So Alice felt a lot happier, and they left for the Orient.

The flight from Milan to Copenhagen went smoothly, and they stayed at a central hotel. Copenhagen is on the east shore of the island of the Sjaelland. The city and the suburbs were populated by 1,254,289 people, at that time. With the bridges, narrow streets, barges, canals, many inns, and bars, Copenhagen resembled Venice in Italy.

They went along the harbour at night. There they found an old and beautiful inn, to eat wonderful fresh fish, looking out from the restaurant's window, amongst noisy dock porters, ship's captains, and sailors.

In the morning, Alice bought a beautiful multicoloured mat showing Copenhagen, and later they boarded a jet plane, which took them on the long journey to Anchorage. Here, they saw brick and wooden houses, huts, immense pine forests, deer, bears, black and white penguins, sea lions, snow-covered mountains, and massive ice fields. The aircraft flew from black clouds to bright sun, until they reached a zone almost without snow and ice.

They arrived at Anchorage after many hours' flying, and they had another long journey on the same plane to get to Japan.

The trip was terrific so far.

From the plane Alice and Simon could see giant polar bears twisting their heads and necks non-stop. The pilot made several turns over the airport and the aircraft landed on patches of dirty snow and water.

The noisy brakes came into action on the tarmac airstrip, near the small airport and a bar.

It was 8 p.m. and still clear. The aircraft flew into an accumulation of black clouds thirty minutes after they departed. At 9 p.m., the jet was deep in a tropical storm or hurricane. The passengers saw big white flashes of lightning, which lit up the black sky non-stop. They were afraid in the big aircraft, which behaved like a toy plane handled by a crazy child. It was very frightening for everybody. Simon gripped his seat non-stop and dramatically, when the aircraft went spiralling down, hopefully not to meet the sharks, waiting with their mouths open.

But the aircraft and the pilot saved the situation. In another fifteen minutes, they came out of the hurricane, while the crews were cleaning up the mess of bags, toys, pens, teacups, and dirty sandwiches. Through the windows, Alice and Simon saw the remaining lighting flashes far away over the dark sea, on the way to the Aleutian Islands, then Tokyo.

Tokyo Airport was beautiful, but it was dark, because they arrived at night, with red, green, yellow, and blue scintillating lights, due to the tropical rain. With its beautiful tiny gardens, interesting museums, and the Olympic Centre and other buildings, created by Kenzo Tange, Tokyo was able to live again, in spite of the earthquakes and the American bombs of 1945.

Outside the airport, they soon realised that the Japanese people are quite different from the people of other countries. The colour of their skin is yellow going to brown. They are tremendously busy, walking, bicycling, driving cars and vans, and working like crazy ants. Their eyes are oval, but beautiful, especially the girls, and resembled cats' eyes. Their babies resemble dolls. The Japanese men are 'real men', using 'karate' or 'kung-fu', when they fight.

Japan is a country which suffers noticeable earthquakes, almost every day and night, and it happened to them during their stay in Tokyo at the grand Oy Chy O Hotel.

Alice and Simon occupied a small room with two single beds. At 4 a.m. precisely, Simon woke up. One second later, he bumped his head on the ceiling, because the ceiling was so low. Two seconds later, his wife found herself in the position that he found himself one second earlier, and she shouted, 'It's an earthquake, Simon!' The Italian wardrobe, Chinese chairs, American beds, German table, Austrian lockers, Japanese TV, French bidet, African rubbish bin, and two Spanish slippers were all dancing about in their room to a

Chuck Berry rock 'n' roll beat. Three seconds later, his wife and he, fully clothed, took a lift down from the seventeenth floor to the hotel reception, with a tremendous scare lasting a whole week and more for them.

The hall was full of people wearing only pyjamas or kimonos or actually naked, because the hotel guests were terrified by the earlier earthquake. They thought that more earthquakes could happen that night. The hotel staff told them that they were in the safest place in case of earthquakes. The hotel could withstand earthquakes. If their hotel could not withstand earthquakes, then they would say goodbye to Mother Earth. On the other hand, Alice and he did not wish to say goodbye to Mother Earth, so they opted to leave the Oy Chy O Hotel.

Outside, they found that their hotel was in a beautiful and immense park. As they continued their walk, they reached a river, canal, or a lake, with several geese and white and black swans. On the other side of the water, they saw an immense castle. It was Hirohito's mansion, as a porter had told them. There were other Japanese people—waiters, chambermaids, dock workers, barmen, and lorry drivers—on the canal bank. These people were praying to the Japanese gods to maintain Hirohito in good health forever; at 5.30 a.m., each morning, they might have heavy rain, stormy winds, blazing sun, or terrible earthquakes. Having prayed for ten minutes, they were happy to go to work, until the next morning and prayer time.

At 9.23 and eighteen seconds, the earthquakes were ended for that day. Their hotel withstood the earthquakes for that day, but in the morning or in the afternoon or in the night, earthquakes will happen for sure, because it is Japan.

They left the hotel with their luggage and took the 200 kmh 'Bullet Train' to Osaka. They saw the Pacific Ocean, which was beautiful, apart from being stormy. They saw the snow-capped Mount Fuji mirrored in the sea in the morning. Mount Fuji enchanted them.

When they arrived at the station, the same story continued with work. Two Asian men, from their Japanese agents, the Tse Mac Co., came to greet them in the station hall. The first fellow, Mr Hakodate, was slim, short, with black hair, yellow/brown skin, and talked some English language.

The other fellow, Mr Suzuki, was tall, a muscleman, with black hair, yellow/brown skin, and talked good English. Nevertheless, he said 'l' instead of 'r'. For example, if Mr Suzuki wanted to say 'rate', his mouth would say 'late' or if he wanted to say 'right', his mouth would say 'light'. So a conversation between an Italian and a Japanese man would often be very confused.

Mr Hakodate was married, fifty years old, and had no kids.

Mr Suzuki was thirty-one years old, married, and had two kids. They were Asian men, very intelligent, very nice and courteous to Simon and Alice.

After they had rested for a while in their hotel—The Sakai—they went out with the agents to a Japanese restaurant to eat Kobe fried meat, which is a speciality of Japan. Kobe is a town near Osaka, where farmers sell cows after being fed hay and beer, so the animals get immensely fat! The farmers use strong ropes to keep the cattle in place before slaughter, then a restaurant owner gets the meat.

When the meat is fried on the Japanese steel plate cooker, the fat dissolves, leaving a piece of meat and, together with cooked onions, peas, carrots, and hot pepper, the customers can enjoy a juicier, tastier, and very tender steak (almost like Italian Tuscany meat), sitting on wooden seats in a Japanese inn. It was a very good meal and the atmosphere was very nice for the guests.

When they got out from the inn, they saw many men at work with planks, concrete, pumps, bricks, and machines in the middle of powerful lights, immense noise, and terrific dust. Those men were erecting bridges, railings, concrete walls, digging holes, placing ironwork and explosives for motorways and passages, which were built by night.

Humans can achieve anything in peacetime. In wartime, humans destroy everything that they have built before. To Simon, it was a sign of total stupidity.

The Osaka Exhibition was a success for the Italian stand and other stands. But a fair is a 'calamity' for the sellers, fitters, painters, electricians, and porters who must attend the exhibition. Many go for nights without sleep, endure long journeys, have little food and little drink, and are without their wives, all this for the bosses.

At least Simon was accompanied by his wife in Japan and he did not mess about with geisha girls at night. The original geisha was a lady trained in dancing, singing, refined talk, and ceremonies, not the geisha girls who take a lot of money from businessmen and tourists.

When the exhibition ended, Alice and Simon travelled to Kyoto, the ancient capital of the Japanese kingdom, where they filmed beautiful flowers, mini ponds, red and yellow bridges, Lake Biwa, Mount Hira, the River Yura, the Kurama Hills, and Japanese paintings. They thought that Japan was a beautiful place.

Their agents gave them a small Sankyo radio before they left Osaka.

Next, they flew to Manila, where they met their agents for the Philippines. They drove a long Buick white limo with black panes, a cool system, and red hide upholstery, which would be a dream in Italy.

The 'chauffeurs' were Mr Lee and Mr Yung, the directors of the company which sold their machines.

While Mr Lee was driving, Alice and Simon were looking at the people, the open coloured buses, and the white or yellow walls, which ran along the streets.

'Prisons?' Alice asked Mr Lee.

'They look like prisons. Nevertheless, they are villas!'answered Mr Lee' The owners are afraid of robbers and killers, who climb the walls or break open the gates. It is a tragedy.'

'Do the people call the police, Mr Lee?'

'The police? You must be joking, Alice!'

A Filipino porter took their suitcases from the limo, but Simon did not trust him at all. His face and his manners were odd, like a gangster. Anyway, Mr Lee shouted at them, from the car, that he would collect them at 8 p.m. to take them to a nightclub.

While Alice changed to a fresh dress in their room, Simon went out of the hotel to get some fresh air, which as hot as hell, and he strolled down the steps.

The square was almost empty, apart from four young Filipino men, who approached him—one from the left, two in front, and one from the right, gripping a knife. The men wore coloured scarves. Maybe they intended to assault him, thinking he had some money, but he did not want to find out and ran to the hotel. Simon was frightened when a hand touched his shoulder. The hand was not a Filipino hand. The hand was Mr Yung's hand, and he said, 'It is time for the nightclub, Simon. It is dangerous to be out of the hotel without friends. You must be careful!'

The nightclub was nice. Several beautiful Filipina soubrettes served them food and drinks, always smiling. The men were strong but small. The show was performed on the floor by four young Filipino men holding four long bamboos. One gorgeous female was in the centre, dancing in the middle of the bamboos, while the music became frantic. The girl skipped over the bamboos without falling, and the guests were applauding or whistling, to show that they were pleased with the performance.

Later, the girl invited a man, about fifty years old, to dance and to skip with her in the middle of the four bamboos. The dance was frantic. The man was falling on the bamboos and the guests laughed and whistled at the poor fellow, while the guests ate French pâté on toast, drank Scotch whisky or brown rum, and they all laughed.

The poor people—alas—crowded around the pavements by the nightclub, hoping that a few crumbs of bread and water would come their way, but the police were there too to keep them off and to protect the rich. 'Life is not fair,' Simon thought.

In the morning, Mr Lee and Mr Yung drove him to see their sales offices. He met a couple of customers to sell a few machines, but it was very hot. Simon was wearing a tie. However, Mr Lee and the others did not, owing to the heat. There was air, but the air was boiling! In the meantime, Mrs Lee, who was Chinese, took Alice around Manila's shops and, by midday, Alice, Simon, and she regrouped at a Filipino restaurant, near their offices, where Mrs Lee wanted to eat a raw hen chick.

'A *raw* hen chick?' asked Alice.

'Yes, a raw chick, hardly coming out of the egg. Do you fancy one, Alice?'

'You must be joking!'

'And you, Simon?'

'It is a raw chick? Uncooked or cooked—never!'

Mrs Lee swallowed and laughed at a raw chick with its red blood running over the plate, which a waiter was serving to the Filipino guests.

'Simon, do you see those eggs that another waiter is serving another group of people? Those eggs are one hundred-old eggs.'

'One hundred-old eggs, never! They would be mouldy and smelly, Mr Lee.'

'They are not, Simon. These eggs are heavenly for us. Try one!'

'Not me, Mr Lee. Sorry! Down in Italy, we are used to fresh eggs hardly coming out of the hen's backside.' And the Filipino guests were roaring with laughter.

The Philippines trip was very successful and Simon collected three orders for the machines. Alice and Simon left Manila, the volcanoes, the earthquakes, the massive heat, and the massive poverty, and they travelled by plane to Hong Kong.

At first they were not sure that the city was Hong Kong, because the buses were red double-deckers, like those in London. However, the people had slanted eyes and yellow skin, wore round straw hats, and only spoke Chinese. Therefore, they were Chinese people! Then the city was red, the hotels were red, and there were several massive posters of Mao Tse Tung holding his *Red Book*.

Was it Hong Kong or Communist China?

They registered and occupied a room in a hotel in the city. They went downstairs to drink two Chinese perfumed teas, which were very good. Then they went out to the port of Macao, which was massive, with a beautiful tropical sunset that they did not remember having seen in any part of the world. They jumped on a boat full of people, and Alice was captivated by the sunset's colours on the sea: the yellows, the browns, the reds, the greens, the blues, and the violets were fantastic.

They saw Chinese wooden boats, the skyscrapers of Hong Kong beyond, and thousands upon thousands of people along the harbour.

The people were mainly Chinese, with their straw hats, mixed with Europeans, Americans, South Americans, and other Asiatic people. They were talking, shouting, and laughing, non-stop.

Later, on their way back to the hotel, they looked around at many stalls. The shopkeepers sold many goods, from live piranha fish in their plastic bags to black tarantulas, from fresh fish to cats, from dogs to mummies, from live chicks to monkeys, from fruits to books, from jade or marble or wooden statues to cycles, from Japanese radios to German TVs. It was very interesting. The shops sold the same stuff, but dearer.

They were hungry, so they went to a nice Hong Kong restaurant with marble tables, coloured paintings, and statues. Two or three waitresses serviced them with several coloured small plates of roast and boiled chicken, pork, meats, fish, vegetables, and sauces, which were very good. That is why Marco Polo remained in the Orient for sixteen years! He liked Chinese food a lot. And Alice and Simon liked their food very much, sitting on the balcony of the restaurant, looking at the tropical sunset over the Asiatic city. It was enchanting.

They left China and boarded another flight to Bangkok. At the airport, thousands of people were feverish with the terrible heat and 100 per cent humidity, with sweat running down men's trousers or ladies' gowns. Many passengers with their families were piled up against the walls, sprawled on the floors, waiting for their flights, tired of the heat, plus the smell of human sweat. It was awful.

They ran to another jet plane, which flew over mountains, lakes, and seas—Thailand, India, Pakistan, Iran, Iraq, Syria, Turkey, Greece, Italy—and landed in Rome. Alice and Simon had travelled right round the earth—from Europe to the North Pole, from Asia to Europe again. The trip was wonderful, and Simon had orders for several machines, which he had sold in the Orient.

It was the summer of 1971, and Simon was worried again because Alice was getting fat, while she was usually thin. His wife had eaten well, being in Italy, but it was not the food.

She was pregnant again.

When she was sure that she was pregnant, she let herself loose in the shops buying dresses for herself, baby shoes, costumes, sheets, pillows, blankets, pram, and toys for their baby. Alice and Simon were very happy to add another son or daughter and in December, their son was born, three days earlier than Baby Jesus. Stephen was long and thin, with dark hair. He was beautiful and healthy.

His mother walked miles, taking his pram along the river every day, to get some pure air for her baby. She used ten woollen blankets and five woollen caps, because the temperature was icy in those months.

Simon helped Alice with their first child and he helped her with their second child, dressing him in the morning, putting him to bed, and other things.

A child belongs to two people—a mother and a father—not to the husband who goes to the pub every day and night, or to the wife who has to look after their child. That would be unfair on the wife.

January came with snow. February came with snow. March came, and still there was snow. Then came April—without snow! And Alice, Simon, and their sons migrated to the Empire of the Saxons. Why? It was because Simon's boss was not happy with the sales achieved by Mr Harry Gray, their English salesman. The Italian company was forced to employ Simon to sell the machines in Great Britain and Ireland from London. Simon was a very good salesman, he would earn more money, and he would make his wife happy, because she liked London. Their sons would learn English.

The only person who hated the move was his mother, just as she had when he travelled for the first time to England. She said, 'Simon, you live here with Alice, your sons, your house, and your relatives. The sun is splendid, the sky is blue, the sea is green, and the mountain is brown. Why must you leave your mother crying?'

'Mother, I love you dearly. I need the money too to keep my family alive. We will return for sure, Mother.'

His father kept quiet, and he was not pleased. He was a home bird. He liked Italian spaghetti, a small steak, goats' cheese, fresh fish, and fresh garden lettuce, home-grown tomatoes with olive oil, sea salt, and fruit. He enjoyed two glasses of Sangiovese wine at midday. At night he ate light meals with his wife, like Simon's family. Not some bacon, bread, and fat sausages and tea with milk that the English, Irish, and American people eat for breakfast, for lunch and for high tea, every day. It could lead to massive indigestion or heart failure. The Mediterranean diet is the secret, *but* no late nights, no drinks, no smoking, and no loving, like a saint.

However, Simon didn't like to be a saint. Simon wanted to keep their flat in Bologna, but the landlord wanted the flat for his son later. So they put their furniture in a London warehouse, waiting for a proper house. In the meantime, they would live in a hotel in Windsor, near Queen Elizabeth's castle.

An Irish customer, who worked in London, found the accommodation for them. Windsor was beautiful with old trees, ancient fountains, and many Italian people. However, the hotel was very old and on its last legs. It had ancient, dark, and dirty paintings, worn out carpets and a lift from ancient Rome, when Caesar was in power! The cuisine was not modern at all. The cooks cooked hard steaks without salt, pepper, oil, and spices. Their room and the furniture, toilet, windows, and doors all dated from long before Christ was born. It was a 'Windsor tragedy' for them, especially for their kids.

One day they invited Mr O'Connor, the Irish fellow, to lunch at the hotel. He was fat, maybe over 100 kg. He wore a grey suit with a black tie. The crotch of his trousers reached his knees and he was like a clown. Simon wore a pair of Italian black trousers and an Italian grey jacket with a dark red tie, effectively a two-piece suit. Alice wore a blue dress and looked very smart.

They ate. A waiter brought three black coffees with yellow milk that seemed a disaster—steaming hot and in a deep glass, which must burn your fingers and your hand.

Mr O'Connor said, suddenly, 'Your coat is suited for horse racing, Simon. English customers do not like a two-piece suit when they talk about business. You should wear a proper three-piece suit.'

'That is strange! I've sold many machines in England, Ireland, the USA, Africa, and Asia, wearing only business two-piece suits, never a three-piece suit, Mr O'Connor.'

In the following years, his customer bought fifteen machines from him and he was wearing two-piece suits, because Italian suits—two-piece or three-piece—and Italian machines, were very good and without fault.

To carry out his sales work within Great Britain, he hired a car. It was a Jaguar! Yellow and fast. However, it shook from the foundations to the roof when he drove it. Simon hired another car. It was an orange Audi, big, beautiful, and smooth, like a velvet glove.

He had a car, but he did not have any flat or house at the time. One became available in North London within a month. The demi-detached house had three bedrooms, a toilet and bath upstairs, a lounge, a bar, kitchen, and WC downstairs. There were two gardens and they paid ten pounds monthly, which was not too bad at the time.

Next door there lived a nice Neapolitan family with two young boys. The wife planted onions, potatoes, and flowers. Her husband home-made white and red wine for his family. When Alice and Simon had a sample, the wine tasted like vinegar, because the husband used sour grapes.

The street was full of elms, plane, and oak trees and led to a village called Freeze Waters with many shops, a barber, schools, churches, and a park. London was not far away by bus or underground. In short, they had a good time there, but they had three bad accidents in their house.

One morning Alice and Simon were woken up by thick black smoke in their bedroom. Alice jumped from the bed, coughing, and ran into the next room, which was also full of black smoke. She grabbed the boys from their beds and opened the window for some fresh air. In the meantime, Simon ran downstairs to find that he had left Stephen's plastic milk bottle on the gas fire during the night. This had caused the smoke, which could have killed them.

The second accident happened because they left Stephen in the wooden porch, on a sunny afternoon, in his pram. One day, a window pane came out of the frame and fell just inside the pram, sharp edge down. Another five centimetres nearer, the pane would have pierced their baby and Stephen could have died. They were all lucky.

John was involved with the third accident a few weeks later, when he tripped down their stairs and ended up sprawled against their glass front door, which he broke down, but his head was very tough!

They survived the bad spell and lived normally for the time being. They bought a white new Audi 100 for their holiday in Ireland. John was three years old and Stephen was eight months old. They left London and drove up to Liverpool. Then they went over the sea to Larne near Belfast, in Northern Ireland. In the boat they slept on good berths, dreaming, while other passengers were busy drinking beer or whisky all night long. They were happy because they were going home to Ireland, visiting relatives and friends and resting from work in Great Britain.

It was Sunday morning. The sun was splendid with the dew and the grass shone. The road was not busy at all. They sang and laughed at the cattle or at the rivers in the sun. Unexpectedly, their laughter turned to concern for him. The steering wheel did not steer at all! The car would go to the left or to the right. He drove it slowly and eventually he stopped. Simon lifted the bonnet to look at the engine, wires, clutch, brakes and everything seemed OK. He looked at the engine, again, and he spotted the 'disease' with the car. The Audi mechanic down in Germany had not fastened the steering wheel nut correctly, and with the movements of the car, the nut had fallen into a ditch full of water on an Irish road, full of cows and sheep. Apart from themselves, there was nobody else and no telephone box, but, away across the moor, Simon could see a white cottage with the chimney wreathed white smoke—a sure sign that the cottage was inhabited. As he walked there, a man approached him and said,

'Do you have problems with your car?'

'Yes! I cannot steer. The gearing nut is lost in the ditch full of water. Can you help me, please? I need two 16 mm nuts and a spanner.'

The Irishman went away to his cottage and came out on to the road, saying, 'A few nuts and a spanner. Let's go!'

Simon did not know if the man was a mechanic or not. He fixed the Audi and he did not want any money.

They were able to reach Cracklegs, where everybody was dying to see them and their new baby—Alice's mother, Mara, Alice's sisters, relatives, and friends. They would prepare ham, roast chicken, boiled pork, Irish tea, cakes, biscuits, and jam when they would visit them. The Irish people are very nice, straight and likeable. The green isle is beautiful, always, and their holiday was very relaxing with the lake, the swans, the Atlantic Ocean, and the yellow moon. Also, there were sheep, cattle, pigs, thin rain, stormy winds, and many pubs, where one could get a drink.

Upon their return, they moved to Holmbush with their Italian furniture, not far from Freeze Waters, but farther away from London. Their new house was old. It was not a semi, but it was a detached house with two gardens, three bedrooms, a lounge, two toilets, a kitchen, a garage, and a study, which they used for work. It was a nice place. However, there was another accident in their garden.

John, his brother, and another boy were using an iron swing to play. Later, John got down from the swing and covered himself with a thin red tent. He ran towards the swing and bumped his face and nose violently against the swinging swing because he could not see. Their son shouted with the pain and fell to the grass, while Alice ran to the garden, shouting, because her son was hurt, bleeding, and crying.

They took their son to the local hospital. A doctor cleaned and disinfected the wound and applied seven stitches to John's nose. All the time, John remained calm with no tears. What a fright for his parents!

Next, Alice and Simon received a visit by his young brother to London. Conrad liked the trip by plane and met a lovely Irish girl. His brother liked the Irish girl and the Irish girl liked his brother, but the lovely girl remained in England and his brother returned to Italy. Conrad's mother and friends were worried that the Irish girl had 'stolen' the Italian boy, because he was handsome and nice.

Later in the summer, Simon's mother decided to travel from Italy to London to visit them. She went by train and by ship, which took her twenty-five hours. His mother was a home-bird, always. To travel to Great Britain with no knowledge of English or the French language, on her own, given the dangers in those times, she had to be courageous. She brought with her some gorgeous *lasagne*, another Bolognese speciality, which they ate with the Italian wine.

His mother was with them for a week, in the house and in the garden. She enjoyed cooking her Italian specialities. Her stay was very enjoyable because Alice was very fond of her.

His mother visited them again, bringing Simon's father with her, but the father was not happy in England. He missed Italy too much.

Alice's mother, together with her son, Joseph,- travelled by air to Dublin and London from Ireland too, to see the grand cities, going shopping, resting in the house or the parks, accompanied by Alice and her family. They said that their stay was wonderful, but they would be at home in Ireland.

A few years later, Simon's younger brother decided to marry a girl from the Italian Riviera, with sea, rocks and mountains, many inns, and very important shipyards. The Riviera is a place for holidays. It is beautiful and has the tastiest food and wine.

After their marriage they went to an inn, with the guests, to eat and to drink amongst beautiful flowers. Then they set off for their honeymoon by car.

In the meantime, Simon had bad piles; he was bleeding and pale like a white wall, but he had booked places on a ship to go to America, in August, with the whole family. Therefore, they had a problem. However, he took a chance and they boarded the *Queen Elizabeth II* for the trip.

The transatlantic liner was immense, beautiful, and grandiose, like nothing they'd seen in their whole lives. There were thirteen passenger decks, one immense funnel, and four Rolls-Royce/Alstom electric propulsion turbines. The ship's speed was 29.62 knots. She could hold 3,056 passengers and 1,253 crew. She was 345 metres long, 72 metres high, and had fifteen restaurants and bars, five swimming pools, a casino, a ballroom, and a theatre. The ship was a floating town.

Alice, her husband, and their family had a beautiful cabin which was sea level. Then they waited for the journey to America to start.

The last passengers and their luggage were boarded on the ship. The ropes, the chains, and the anchors were let off, amid the shouting of the crowds of the quay. The ocean liner slowly departed for another continent with a huge blast from the whistle on the funnel, amid the shouting of the passengers and crew, until it reached the lighthouse, and then . . . the open sea.

The *Queen Elizabeth II* took on board other passengers from France, and then she set a course across the Atlantic Ocean for New York. On the third day, the first Concord flew over the ship, and the crew and the people saluted the jet. The ship would stay on course for two days more, but the Concord would stay just two hours in the air to get to New York, which was amazing. A few years back, a cruise ship would take ten to fifteen days to reach America.

On the ship the food was very good with pasta, steaks, eggs, rabbits, fish, cakes, fruits, wines, and beers. Not a slimming diet! Their boys were on the go, eating, drinking Coke, playing, and swimming, with games outside and inside.

After lunch and dinner, Alice and Simon took walks on the decks, read, played games or drank tea. They looked at the sea, which looked like a very hot, unending yellow mass of salty water, which scared them, especially at night, with no waves, no breeze, no fish, because the fish preferred the cool waters deep down in the ocean. There was a pale, sweating, obscured, mad sun. The heat was unbearable, and they sweated during the days and the nights.

The foods, the pools, the ship, the shows, and the walks were all very good and they enjoyed the entertainments very much, but their holidays shouldn't have been in summer. It was Simon's fault in compelling a wife and their two boys to suffer a four-five degrees Celsius temperature, and with a mad sun.

However, after five days they could see the rectangular grey or yellow skyscrapers of New York, while they wiped off their sweat in the heat at midday. Later, they saw the Statue of Liberty, the Hudson River, and tugs came to pull the QE2 to rest against her quay.

The ship's adventure was ended. The adventure of discovering America was starting for them. There was a great confusion on the pier, with children crying and laughing, men and women shouting, and many suitcases being offloaded from the ship.

Simon called a yellow cab to deliver them to their downtown hotel, which he had booked from England. He saw porters, officers, captains, and the yellow hot vapours from the seawater. The cab driver took them there, but he refused to carry their luggage to the hotel. He was saying that he would drive them there, and a porter from the hotel would help to carry their luggage to the reception hall. He went away with his cab, leaving their suitcases on the pavement.

Cab drivers all over the world help their clients into the hotel, but this New York cab driver did not. Anyway, Simon got a hotel porter, but he wanted a tip before he helped them! However, he tipped the porter to get their suitcases in front of the lift, but was the porter expecting another tip before he used the lift to their room? He paid the man four dollars in total to get into their room. Was this the New York Mafia?

Simon and family did not sleep well during the night, owing to the heat. In the morning, they took a yellow cab to Fifth Avenue to look around the shops. The cab driver, who was Mexican, was anti—New York. The traffic, shops, foods, and the people were terrible, he said. Simon thought, 'Why was he living in the USA? He should be living in Mexico!'

Towards midday and because of the heat, they went to Central Park hoping for some coolness due to the trees and bushes, fresh water from the fountains and wooden seats in the shade of the big oaks. The park was like hell! No fountains and no shade, only the cicadas and the crickets calling for more heat. Then they got a motorboat on the Hudson River and the Statue of Liberty, because the river might afford a fresh cool breeze for them. They were wrong. The river offered flies and mosquitoes by the thousands. As a last resort, they climbed the stairs of the statue up to the dome, where they could see New York, which was beautiful with all the skyscrapers, and they took many breaths of pure fresh air.

In the morning, Alice wanted to visit some Irish families in Philadelphia by coach. They found the road and the cottage of the first Irish family. Having knocked a few times without any answer, they thought that the family were absent. Eventually, a man, wearing only a vest and black trousers, opened the cottage door saying, 'Hello!'

'Hello. We are from Ireland—Cracklegs. Do you remember, Jim? I am Mara's daughter and the boys are our sons, John and Stephen.'

'Now I can remember! Come in, please. It is very hot and humid in Philadelphia. I have asthma. My wife is at work. Do you want cool orange juices for you and the boys? I'd like to show you photos of my family.'

Jim took out the orange juices from the fridge and the photos from a cupboard, while he sat on his armchair, pulling an electric fan near him, and then he went to sleep, or he was dead!

Anyway, they drank the drinks and looked at the photos. Suddenly, Jim opened his eyes. He started to talk about Ireland, Philadelphia, and his wife, and he stood up. He accompanied them to the door and they went out on the road, saying, 'So long, Jim. We hope to see you in Ireland.'

After Simon, Alice, and their boys took a train to a place called Devil Hell, where only Negroes lived, but they did not see any Negroes or any other people. They did see shops and houses boarded up, a few dusted cars, and rubbish. There were trees with yellow or brown leaves, and dust being scattered by the wind.

The place was deserted.

The second Irish family lived in another village called Whites. A few miles took them there, under a fierce sun, because it was two o'clock in summer. Alice had the address of the second cottage, and they knocked at the door several times, but got no answer. Eventually, a man who lived next door opened his cottage door to say that the Irish family had gone to Ireland.

'It is very hot,' said the man. 'Come inside, please. My wife and I will prepare some fresh orange juice for you, while you can rest in the lounge, which is cooler.'

Later, the old couple showed them a few family photos, until they departed for New York by coach. Some old people are very nice. The two villages were three miles apart. Three miles between hell and heaven!

From Newark Airport, they went to Niagara Falls, which were a terrific, grandiose, and heavenly display by nature. They saw forests, boulders, caves, rivers, and the falls, tumbling down one hundred metres or more. Linking the United States to Canada, there was a beautiful bridge suspended over the mighty river, the Ontario. They took many photos of the bridge, the surrounding places, and their family, until they reached the Canadian shore and a bar, which sold many Indian souvenirs.

They went back to Niagara Falls on the American side, and at the bottom of the bridge they found other Indian souvenirs that were sold by Indians and a life-size bronze statue of an Indian warrior, which was beautiful. As they walked along the river, they saw a green hut and an advert which said: *The Maid of the Mist*. For a dollar you can see the falls from underneath. A mackintosh and cap will be supplied by the company. 'Happy trip!'

Moved by curiosity, they bought the tickets and the raincoats. Then they stepped on to a lift, which took them halfway down a rock shaft, ending on an open platform very near the river, and the noise from the falls was overwhelming but fantastic. The visitors had to go down some wooden steps, which were wet, slippery, and very dangerous, until they boarded the boat or *The Maid*.

A few sailors and the captain, smoking his pipe, sailed the boat underneath, in front of and behind the falls, while the river's great waves scared the passengers for half an hour. It was great fun.

There were three main falls, two on the American side and one on the Canadian side. After the great adventures of the falls and *The Maid*, they rested for a while beside the river, eating their sandwiches and drinking cool juices. Flies and mosquitoes were attacking them and their food every second; however, the Niagara Falls were divine, but the heat and the discomfort were diabolical. Because of the heat and the flies, the Falls would be better in May or October, not in July or August.

Another jet plane took them to Washington, where a lot of people gathered at a square in front of the White House with orange juice, hot dogs, and music, like a circus where a number of clowns were performing an act or many acts. The open space in front of the White House was very nice, with trees, bushes, a column, and a fountain of which people would drink.

Then Simon and family decided to go to Capitol Hill by coach to see how Abraham Lincoln was cool enough among the shady trees. The coolness affected Simon and he dozed off on the grass and dreamed of eleven white soldiers and one white trumpeter, all dressed in black. The soldiers were stopped by a marble pillar with these words inscribed in gold, 'The Unknown Soldier'. But the dream was not a dream. The soldiers and the words were real!

The coolness was nice around Abraham Lincoln compared to the heat around the White House.

It was time to return to the hotel, because in the morning they were going to the Walt Disney World Resort in Orlando, Florida, the American holiday State It had blue and green seas, sunny skies, great motels and restaurants, beautiful beaches and long scary five or six metre sharks.

In the round square, they met Mickey Mouse, Donald Duck, his three nephews, and Uncle Duck. They saw castles, the suspended railway, lakes, funny bushes, pirates, Princess Snow White, and the ugly witch and listened to nice music. They had a beautiful time during their two days at Orlando.

A further day was spent down south and they went to a big room in Cape Canaveral, equipped with thousands of switches, levers, computers, shaking seats, and belts. The entire scenario was of the astronauts being catapulted to the moon by an American spaceship with explosions, noises, and terrific sounds. It was very interesting but frightening. But did the American astronauts actually land on the moon? Simon was unsure and a lot of people were unsure.

However, their American holiday was almost over, and another plane took them from Orlando Airport to Miami Airport.

Miami was a gorgeous seaside town with palm tree avenues, hundreds of swimming pools, restaurants, inns, nightclubs, and bars, but they spent only a day, unfortunately.

Alice, Simon, and their family finally left America and, after eight hours, a Boeing 747 touched down at Heathrow, London, at 7 a.m., while millions of English people and others were having their breakfast: *cornflakes with milk, orange juice, English tea with milk, or English black coffee, 10 slices of burnt toast and yellow salted butter, 4 fried eggs, 10 fried sausages with greasy skins, 7 rashers of fried greasy bacon, 5 fried greasy tomatoes, and more tea or coffee, more burnt toast, and more tea or coffee* every day, while people read the greasy morning papers, burped, and shifted sideways to pass unwanted wind from their bodies every minute. No wonder English people die, every day, from heart disease! The above diet should be given to the hyenas that live in the African jungle, not humans!

Chapter 11

It was September 1978, and Simon had just passed the forty-first year of his life. The schools for their kids and their work for them had started again. But the pain from his piles was driving him crazy again, and he was getting weaker and weaker. Nevertheless, he had to work, to correspond with clients, to write notes and leaflets, do visits and so on, helped by his staff and his wife.

His local doctor, Dr Savage, visited him and prescribed a cream for the piles. Either the cream was no good or the doctor was no good. Simon's family were very worried, and he decided to change to another doctor who, actually, was a professor. The day was nice and the sun shone on the brown lino tiles, when Simon went to Meaday Hospital near their house. The waiting room was almost empty, and he prayed quietly to the Madonna on the wall, painted by Giotto.

The professor called him into his study, and when he had the test results, he wrote a note for Dr Savage at the local clinic. Why did Professor Balls look so worried when he wrote the note? Simon had to find out soon!

On the steps of the hospital, he opened the envelope to read the professor's letter, which said:

'Dear Doctor Savage,

The patient has a malignant colon cancer. If we operate now, he might have a long life. If we do not operate now, I am giving him three months to live.'

Simon was terrified because his local doctor had diagnosed him for piles. Instead, he had a malignant cancer in his bowels. Dr Savage would be great if he was a chimney sweep!

He walked to his car, started his car, drove down on the slip road from the hospital and on the main road, turned on to e village street, stopped his car in front of his garage, and went in and dropped the keys on the table automatically. He was thinking about the cancer, his wife, his sons, and a thousand and one things.

The phone rang. It was Alice.

'Simon, how are you? I hope that the tests are OK.'

'I will tell you when you are at home. Ciao, Alice.'

'Tell me now, please.'

'I cannot now. Ciao.'

When Alice got in, she suspected the tests were not good because Simon was not happy.

'Alice, the tests were not so good.'

'Why?'

'Because, because . . . . .'

'Why? Why, Simon?'

'I am afraid that I've got . . . . .'

'What . . . ?'

'Cancer, Alice.'

'*Mamma mia!* Are you sure? The professor is sure that you have a cancer?'

'The professor did not say that, but the professor knows that I have a colon cancer. But he does not know that I know . . . understand, Alice?'

'No!'

'The professor has written a letter to Dr Savage about my colon cancer. I have the letter and I have read the letter. If the surgeon doesn't operate now, I will die within three months. If I go ahead with the operation, I will survive, I hope!'

They decided to call it a 'cyst' instead of 'cancer' when talking about it with other people, because 'cancer' was too bad.

For their Christmas holidays, they decided to visit Simon's mother and all his relatives. His mother wanted to talk to an Italian professor and surgeon about his colon cyst. The surgeon advised them of new tests to be carried out on Simon at the hospital. So the day for the tests arrived, in the presence of the professor, and two huge fat nurses made Simon undress completely and put on a white apron.

'Open the gas tap,' the professor told the nurses, while his hand felt Simon's tummy with some force several times.

'We want to X-ray your stomach, bladder, and colon to see the cyst. We must move several components of your body. Do you feel any pain?'

His body was floating in the air, due to the gas. He felt terrible pain for half an hour and finally he dirtied the apron, sheets, and the floor.

'Do not be worried, Simon,' the professor said. 'I cannot feel a cyst or anything else. When you get home, eat a plate of *macaroni;* drink a glass of Sangiovese wine, and good luck to you!'

Should he believe the Professor of London or the Professor of Bologna? It was a complete mystery!

They returned to London to try living with their problems. But their sons were invited to listen to Christmas carols sung by the schoolchildren with their parents. When the carols started, Simon got agonising pains across his tummy. He could not stay in the church, and they went home to phone Professor Balls, who gave him an appointment the following morning.

He did all the tests again and showed him, on the X-ray plate, an area which should not be there. It had irregular edges, was grey to black, and ugly.

It was the malignant colon cancer!

Professor Balls had arranged a private hospital near to their home for him. His family, Betty, his wife's sister, and Paddy, the husband, were there on the first day. The room had a large window and a door, which communicated to all wards, offices, toilets, lifts, and corridors. Because his room was on the third floor, it had a view of the northern part of London with shops, churches, parks, houses, and the fog! The chilly fog came up from the Thames River, which drowned London every day.

Professor Balls came into Simon's room, sat on his bed, and said, 'Simon, in the morning I shall operate on you and try to cut out the cyst. I am sure that the operation will be a success. Maybe I'll have to use a 'plastic bag' for your bowel, because the cyst is very near your anus, do you understand?'

'I do understand that, but will it smell?'

'No smells. You would change your bag every day. Many people use these bags. Millions! I know an English singer who uses the bag. Presidents, doctors, and housewives use them. You must hope that your operation will be done without a bag. I will see you in the morning.'

The man was a very good surgeon, and Simon was very determined to win, in spite of his terrible disease. He was not afraid of the operation. Alice and the others were all afraid of the operation. Simon phoned a lawyer to make a will and he immediately came to his room. It was his first will and he was happy for his family, because if ever they needed anything, they could use his clean shirts, his clean trousers, his clean pair of socks, and his clean torn pants.

It was the day of his operation. Simon was into his bed but he was not asleep. Alice was holding his hand to give him courage. One nurse was giving him sleeping injections and two other nurses moved him to another bed with bars, like a sleeping lion (his zodiac sign). His wife managed to hold his hand without crying. She was a real woman, tremendously sincere and sweet as honey, but if you trod on her tail, she could become very bitter and bad to eat!

Two nurses shifted the bed to go up to the operation theatre, while Alice waved to him. He saw the corridor . . . Alice . . . cold . . . Alice . . . very cold and utter darkness.

After a three-hour operation, his wife was to wake him up by saying, 'Simon. Oh no! It's me, Simon!'

Slowly, he opened his right eye. He saw a bed, white sheets, a green blanket, and white plastic tubes. Then he saw a face bent over him. It was a girl, maybe white, brown, or black. And she was smiling at him! Simon opened his left eye and he saw that the girl was beautiful. It was Alice, but was it paradise or was it real?

Two other girls filled the room. They, however, were ugly, like two African elephants living in the jungle. So he was alive!

'How are you after your operation, Simon? It's been three hours!'

'Three hours? I am happy, but . . . the cyst?'

While he talked with his wife, Professor Balls came in, saying, 'How are you Simon? You were very good.'

'Excuse me, Professor, why all these plastic tubes over my body?'

'Within two days these tubes will disappear. Now you must rest. I got rid of twenty centimetres of 'sausage' from your colon. It was terrible, but there's no bag. Happy? When you are at home, bathe the wound with hot water and salt, every day. I will visit you at the clinic in one month, OK? Then, monthly or longer.'

Simon was fond of salt with cooked fish, meat, or spaghetti, but too much salt is bad for the diet. However, he would use salt with hot water to mend his wound. As his professor said, the tubes, wires, bottles, and pots would disappear. Therefore, he could use the toilet, could eat, drink, and walk around the wards.

Alice and their boys came to visit him every day. Betty and her husband, relatives, and friends would visit every two or three days.

His brothers came over from Bologna by air. They encountered snow, wind, and ice. Simon thought that was very good of them.

After one week in the hospital, Simon went home. During the winter the temperature was freezing. The ground was covered with twenty centimetres of snow and ice. He was at home, at last, instead of being at the clinic with nurses, doctors, professors, tablets, injections, and potato soup every day. He was reborn, but he wanted to forget the cancer as quickly as possible.

He bathed with hot water and salt. Later, he recommenced working in his office. He would be helped by Alice, who in addition worked from 6 a.m. to 1 a.m. the next morning. She looked after their boys, schools, shopping, cooking, washing, entertaining people, and entertaining him. Professor Balls visited him monthly to see if any other 'sausages' were growing in the colon or other parts of his body. He remained happy, and so the Professor moved the visits to three months, six months, and one year.

Is it a year?

Simon had won the 'first round' between himself and cancer. He hoped that he would win the second round, the third round, the fourth round, the fifth round . . .

In spite of their problems, their company seemed to be sailing splendidly. Later, they went to Ireland for their holiday, and then to Gabbice, a seaside resort on the Adriatic. In winter, they went to Cortina, a mountain resort, where they all took some skiing lessons and had several skiing adventures.

One day their son Stephen was going uphill using a ski-tow. Another young skier was in front. He let his rope and the metal hook go, which hit Stephen's crash helmet quite hard. Alice and Simon carried their son by car to Cortina hospital for his head to be tested, but his head was quite hard!

Their holidays were enchanting, with the seas and the mountains, in Ireland or in Italy.

They returned to London from Italy, but Alice began complaining about her throat. She had a red swelling on her right-hand side. They went to a doctor, who diagnosed her with a thyroid gland, which was rather large. Within one week, the doctor took a biopsy from her neck. The tumour was benign, but the swelling grew enormously.

Because they did not trust the doctor, they changed to a professor, who discovered that the first doctor had used an infected needle while he was doing the biopsy. The professor advised them that Simon's wife should have an operation as soon as possible. But it was almost Christmas and they decided to spend their holiday in Ireland, together with Alice's mother and all her relatives. At the same time, they were waiting for some furniture for the house in Cracklegs from the port in Dublin. They waited until 22 December, and the shipment had still not arrived. So on the following morning, Alice and Simon went to Dublin by car from Donegal, where they were staying.

The road was empty of cars, tractors, and farm vehicles because it was very early. They encountered rain, fog, and freezing cold and, in addition, Simon spotted that they were almost out of petrol, and Dublin was many miles away. He had forgotten to fill up the tank the previous night. They saw fields, hills, cows, bulls, sheep, lakes, and the fog, but no petrol stations. They were seriously afraid of being stranded in the Irish wilderness. Later, on the road, there was a white cottage that was let to two petrol pumps. They thought that they were very lucky!

Simon switched off the engine and knocked at the cottage door several times in the freezing fog. Hundreds of rooks croaked from the tall oak trees, but there was no answer. He turned around to Alice, still in the car, and said to her, 'Maybe the people are still in bed.'

Suddenly, a man half-dressed and rather dopey opened the door.

'Good morning! Petrol, please.'

'We are closed for petrol.'

'We must go to Dublin and my car is almost without petrol!'

'OK. I'll switch on the pumps. Full?'

'Full, and thanks for your help, since we are at Christmas.'

Simon paid for the petrol and they were able to proceed until Dublin's customs offices, but the customs offices were virtually closed for the festivities. A few bottles of whisky and rum, and a few hundred cigarettes to the men each did the trick. Some porters loaded their furniture on to a lorry bound for Cracklegs on 24 December. That evening, they assembled the Italian furniture with the help of their relatives. They all ate Christmas dinner on Christmas Day at the table, which had arrived in Ireland.

Unfortunately, it was not so great after Christmas.

Alice's swollen thyroid gland got very bad and she had an operation to cut half the thyroid away at Bart's Hospital in London. Alice was very brave to undergo such an operation, with the help of the professor and the nurses, and within one week, she was able to say 'bye' to the hospital staff and have Ovaltine drinks and carrot soup. She was annoyed about her scar, which compelled her to use scarves to cover the wound. She took this mishap with a smile on her face, talking to her relatives and friends.

One day, when Simon was still in the hospital after visiting Alice, he saw some doctors, nurses, and people looking up at a girl standing on a third floor windowsill, who was about to commit suicide. It was obvious what she intended to do. A doctor went to talk to her at the window, but she refused any help. The drama went on and on until the doctor went outside the window, still talking to the girl and in spite of danger to his own life. As quick as lightning, the doctor pulled the girl to her own safety in the ward.

Why commit suicide? She was twenty years old, and if she wanted to commit suicide, she could commit suicide at one hundred and twenty and still enjoy life before then!

Slowly, the wound on Alice's neck was getting better, and a few years passed without any problems. Simon worked. Alice worked. Their sons were at school. Their life was pleasant, but his heart took a bad turn and they thought it would ruin their lives completely.

When he was twenty years old, a doctor who had tested him in his clinic, said, 'Simon, you could climb Mount Everest three times and you would come back, because you have a sporting heart at 160 max blood pressure.'

He should have known that a blood pressure value of 120 max is right for a young normal human being, not 160! At the time, that doctor should have prescribed some blood pressure tablets to lower the reading. With a blood pressure of 160 at twenty years old, Simon would have a blood pressure of 600 at seventy years old, and he would have exploded.

And now, at forty-seven, he had angina pectoris, which could rob him of the life that he loved so much. That doctor had made a big mistake. However, death did not lay her black blanket on him yet!

Simon had a bed in the local hospital, next door to a man of sixty-five, who was preparing his soul before flying to Saint Peter's home. Three doctors and ten nurses helped him with gas pumps, hand massages, and much shouting. Finally, he died, and a nurse closed the curtains.

Another doctor came into Simon's cubicle. Simon was scared stiff because of the dead man next door. The doctor brought him the X-ray plates of his heart and said to him, 'We would advise you to undergo an operation lasting three to four hours on your heart. A three-vane drill, which goes very fast, will cut through your chest bones to free your heart. Your heart will be placed on a steel cup with liquid—not whisky or rum—while doctors alter some arteries and veins. Your heart will be placed in the original position, your chest will be closed with some steel stitches and then some bandages, and the game will be over!'

'Is it dangerous?'

'Heart surgeons have great experience. There is a small problem. If fragments of bone get into the blood system, the patient might develop a heart failure or a stroke.'

'From the frying pan into the fire, Doctor!'

Simon decided to have the operation at the Princess Victoria Hospital in London. It was clean and new, and the nurses were nice. It was a hospital with medicines, injections, beds, pots, staff nurses, doctors, and professors. Simon hated hospitals like everybody else.

Alice, their sons, and Betty and Paddy were there at the hospital. Birds, bees, and wasps were flying outside. Daffodils, violets, and lilies were in bloom because the season was spring. A female nurse finished injecting Simon's bottom and two male nurses carried him along a corridor. The injections worked and he was very dopey, until he went to sleep, with no dreams.

After his operation, he was still dopey and shaking about in bed. He saw two or three ugly male nurses, hundreds of plastic tubes, stitches and bandages, and beautiful female nurses. He had terrible headaches, chest pains, a terrible cough, and leg pains. He felt like doing a wee, but he did not, because he was not wearing his pants. He felt like running away, but he didn't, because he was caged like a lion in pain. He was freezing cold, like he was inside a fridge, or steaming hot, like he was inside a boiler. He saw a woman. Maybe it was Alice. Yes! She was talking to him, but the words were not clear to him.

Slowly, his senses returned to him. He had a terrible pain in his left leg. He pulled the sheets away and discovered that while the doctors had cut open his chest, they had cut his leg too from his thigh to his left foot.

Simon said to Dr Greene, the surgeon who had messed up his leg,

'You ruined my left leg during the operation. Why, Dr Greene?'

'We cut open up your left leg because we needed a leg artery, which is larger than the other arteries. Now, that leg artery goes around your heart. Three arteries are new. There are two leg arteries for each leg. One artery will be quite sufficient to take your blood around.'

'You are telling me that my heart *walks*?'

'No. You walk using your legs, Simon, not your heart!'

'I was wondering . . . . .'

Dr Greene talked and talked while Simon felt a terrible pain across his chest. So a doctor took some X-ray tests and discovered that, out of five steel stitches, one was broken. These stitches were sharp and one went through his skin causing him terrible pain, non-stop.

The doctor performed another operation on him, without anaesthetic, for a couple of hours, and he thought that he would die, because the pain was diabolical. However, he was not destined to die that time.

Two operations for him and one operation for his wife—great! By the time they were be eighty years old, they would have had one hundred—a record!

On the third day, Simon was feeling a bit better, walking and talking, eating hospital soup and drinking hospital tea. On the seventh day, he went home to eat spaghetti and drink Italian wine, which were much better. They tried to put together the broken pieces of his family life after all his adventures. They went to Sardinia to enjoy the Sardinian sun, which was beautiful and very hot, the blue and green waves, wonderful cooked fish, the bread with goat cheese, nice night shows, and trips out on the sea.

Then they went to a scorching Bologna in August, later to a windy Ireland, and lastly they went back to rainy and foggy London to start again their work.

And work did start because two Italian managers from the company wanted to travel to America on business with Simon and his wife, hoping to sell automatic wrapping machines to the Yankees. They reached Milan, where they were joined by the two managers, and they all joined the queue of passengers scheduled for the New York flight at midday. When Alice arrived at the passport desk, the female clerk said, 'Your passport is not valid! You are Irish and you must have an American visa to enter the United States of America.'

His wife was surprised and very angry.

'Why can't I enter the USA being Irish, but you can, being Italian?'

'I do not know, Alice!'

His wife was furious. Nevertheless, Simon did not want to leave Alice in Milan alone with all those gangsters. It was better that the two managers, who did not speak a word of English, take the midday flight, and he and his wife join them in New York, taking the following flight.

The couple hired a taxi to the American embassy in Milan. Alice went up, but the Americans wanted two photos. So they went to a photographic shop, and Alice returned to the embassy with two photos, came down with her visa, and they left Milan in the taxi. The driver had waited for them.

They knew that they were late for their flight. The taxi man drove like a hurricane through the lights—green or red or amber—and past pedestrians, dogs and cats, past cars, vans, lorries, buses and cycles, past policemen and the armed forces, until they reached the airport running, sweating, and breathless, losing their coats, hats, and plastic bags.

They were lucky because their flight had been delayed. The two managers were still in the departure lounge. Alice produced her visa and they all took the jumbo jet flight above the Atlantic Ocean. The weather was fine over the white clouds. The sun blinked at them.

On arrival, they took another plane to Augusta, Maine, where they rented a grand Buick car to get to the hotel. They needed to eat and to sleep because they were very tired after the airport, the taxi, and two jets.

On the following morning, the two managers and Simon visited their American clients. The company produced women's sanitary towels. They were trying to sell four lines to package, wrap, and multipack their products. If the company liked their machines, the Americans would travel to Bologna, buying the next twenty or forty or sixty machines from the company. The Americans are big and powerful. They have big fields of corn, they have bison, they have Indians, they have blacks, they have enormous mountains, they have big rivers, they have forests, and they have the mighty dollar, but they also have poverty, gangsters, robbery, killers and rapists, and so on.

That is why jails are full to the brim with prisoners every day, like in Europe, in Asia, in Africa, and in Australia.

The factory was enormous with one hundred lines or more and many workers, porters, draftsmen, and managers. Mr Selby, the director of the company, was very interested in the photos and drawings showing their machines, and their reference lists and prices. He wanted quotations. But first he wanted to eat and to drink at a local country inn without any machines, drawings, or photos.

A Negro waiter turned on the radio, which was playing a classical piece by Verdi, and Mr Selby was in love with classical music. He talked and talked about Beethoven, Bizzet, Aida, and Carmen, while he ordered brandies or cognacs non-stop. In short, Mr Selby was almost drunk at the table. The two Italian managers and Simon were sober, and he saw a good opportunity to sell their machines.

'Do you want our quotations, Mr Selby?' But Mr Selby was not stupid, in spite of his cognac.

'I want to take you, your wife, and your friends on a Spanish galleon in Augusta Harbor this evening to eat giant lobsters. My wife, I, and my friends will join us there. I need your quotations tomorrow.'

When Simon returned to the hotel, Alice came back from the shops and he told her about their clients, the dinner on the galleon, and his quotations, which he had typed for Mr Selby, adding leaflets and the reference lists.

At 8 p.m., they all arrived at the Spanish galleon, which was all lit up on the sea and looked beautiful. They ate giant lobsters and drank French wines. The two directors and Alice and Simon would have preferred small lobsters because they were tastier, like those that were taken from Italian waters. Mr Selby and his wife were talking with Alice non-stop about England and Ireland, the beautiful furs from Italy and Italian *spaghetti*, and Simon felt that the order was theirs.

Next morning he faxed his quotations. At 4 p.m., Mr Selby phoned Simon to say that he would order four lines from the Italian company. The Augusta trip was successful. He had never sold four lines in such a short time. Simon was sure that the merit lay with Alice.

The two Bolognese managers took a flight back home. Alice and Simon stayed behind for an extra day to see the forest foliage turn brown, yellow, red, and green because it was autumn. In France, in Spain, and in Italy, the leaves turn yellow or brown. In Maine, the forest colouring is fabulous.

They liked the six-lane motorways too, and the wooden huts, where Indian vendors sold various souvenirs, from wooden statues to Indian bracelets, from Indian warriors to drums, from horses to squirrels, from totems to coloured eagle feathers. He liked a deer made by an Indian artist, who covered a chalk frame with seven layers of shining hide. It was a representation of a hunter, who had shot the deer in the wood, with blood coming from the neck and leg.

He bought the deer. It was beautiful but a little sad for them, because they had suffered sores and pains, as the deer had. Unfortunately, the deer was dead. But Simon was alive, just!

Chapter 12

At the beginning of this book, the author states that after returning from the United States, they went to the exhibition in the Midlands to exhibit their machines from Italy. After the exhibition, Simon was sick at home and an ambulance carried him to the first hospital. The hospital did not have the right equipment and the ambulance crew went to a second hospital near Hampstead Heath. He was hospitalised because his sickness was severe.

Continuing the tragic story—after Simon's life adventures—Simon did not understand the disease. He was either very hot or very cold. At times he saw multicoloured lights, which were beautiful. Then there were shining clouds and he heard sweet music, and Simon was entering a coma. The doctors found that Simon was suffering from a severe stroke, which was affecting his body. He was not able to move his right arm, leg, and foot. His brain stopped the words from getting to his mouth. Simon could not talk any more. It was a disastrous mess, and the second hospital's doctors sent him back to the first hospital for a series of treatments, which might awaken his senses. If his senses did not recover, Simon might die or remain stupid for the rest of his life.

His wife and their sons were desperate because the stroke might kill him. He was fifty-four at the time. Alice and the boys loved him truly, being their husband and father. She had met him thirty-four years ago. Surely fate could not be so cruel! Who could advise Simon's mother, father, brothers, relatives, and friends of his stroke when he was nearly on his deathbed in England? Alice performed that task over the phone. She was very courageous. Furthermore, their family had another 'critically' ill patient in Italy. It was Simon's mother, and the doctors did not know how long she would last. Two people very ill at the some time in England and Italy . . .

If Simon became healthy enough, he would immediately go to see his mother, and if his mother was healthy, she would immediately go to see Simon, but the gods did not want this to happen. Luckily—even though it was very unlucky—on the seventh day, Simon came out of his coma. He opened his eyes on his hospital bed and saw his son, who tried to clean some froth on his father's mouth. His wife was talking to him, saying, 'Simon . . . Simon. Are you well, Simon?'

But Simon could not answer.

The words would not come out. He was desperate and terrified.

He soon realised that he was not able to talk to other people. How could he converse with his Alice, his sons, relatives, or friends? How could he laugh, joke, and everything else?

He was able to read, write, and watch the TV and to understand everything, but he was not able to talk; he had learnt English like an Englishman, apart from his own language, and a little German and French, so it was a cruel, diabolical, and malevolent turn of fate for him and the people who cared about him.

Soon after his stroke, he moved his head vertically and horizontally to say 'yes' and 'no' simultaneously, with great confusion. He tried to talk, but the words were stuck in his brain without being able to force themselves out through his mouth.

The first word that came out of his mouth was 'Jack'. The people were wondering about this word. Maybe he had turned mad or stupid.

Simon was not mad or stupid.

That word went back to the 1939-1945 World War. A bomber, maybe German or English, used to fly at a low level over the Italian countryside, every night, making an awfully deadly noise, which frightened all the farmers, peasants, and their children.

The people kept saying, 'It's Jack! It's Jack!' Simon was scared too, because he was only six years old.

Now, he was an adult and he was very scared, not of the bomber, but of his devilish stroke.

His wife came to the hospital, which was near their home, with their sons twice a day. She brought fruit, newspapers, crackers, clean pants, and kisses for him. Alice was very good and tremendously supportive. She understood very well that Simon was lost without her, suffering from a severe stroke and being unable to talk.

His brothers came to the hospital, too, all the way from Italy. He could not see them because he was still in a coma. They returned to their home without any good news for their parents, relatives, and friends.

Also, many English and Irish friends came to the hospital to joke and laugh, like they used to do at their homes, pubs, or restaurants. But Simon could not laugh or joke any more.

For fifty-four years he'd been able to talk and write in Italian, and in English, but now he could speak none of those languages at all.

Why? He asked himself. Was it that the work of a wicked witch?

Six months previously, Alice and Simon had stopped for petrol on a motorway. After filling up, they decided to eat a meal in the grill, and when a gypsy asked them for some money, Simon refused and the gypsy got angry. She did three crosses on his forehead, as if cancelling him from the world. Who was the wicked witch or the devil?

Simon had been extremely good to all sorts of people from white to black, from red to yellow, and to his parents, relatives, friends, wife, and sons. The wicked witch, or the devil, must be wrong! But, right or wrong, the damage had been done.

Every day and night, he would force himself to talk silently to the wall, to his bed, or to his wheelchair. They did not answer him, which was very maddening. One day his mouth said, 'Alice', which was terrific. Then he said 'Alice' one thousand times to his wife, lest he forgot it.

On another day his mouth said 'nice' and 'good'. He was overjoyed. However, he was only able to enunciate short words. He was not able to say, for example, 'remember' or 'philosopher'. The words were too difficult. He tried to remember words, sentences, situations, and faces in order to trigger his old and new memories. With that he might start talking again.

Would Simon ever talk properly again?

During November, he started coming down from his hospital bed to do gym exercises. Later, he was able to go to the toilet using the wheelchair and shave by himself. As a normal human being, he had shaved with his right hand and everything was all right. At the hospital, he shaved with his left hand, and everything was all wrong. He saw big cuts across his nose, throat, ears, and eyes, like a boxer who had lost fifteen rounds! When he saw himself in the mirror, he realised that he looked terrible and had lost perhaps 25 kg in weight. His mother would not recognise him, ever!

He was thinking of his mother. They left her feeling unwell, and he would ask Alice how she was often and she would always answer, 'Your mother is all right, Simon.'

But he had a feeling that his mother was very sick or dead. One day he asked his wife, 'Dead?'

'Yes, your mother died on the Madonna's feast day. Your father and your brothers were there at home. I did not want to give you any further worry, Simon.'

One night, his mother visited him in his hospital bed and she said, in a voice from beyond the grave, which scared him, 'Simon, come. Come, Simon. It is better here. Come . . . come . . . it is much better here!'

He saw her happy smiles and he answered, 'Maybe later. Bye, Mother!'

Simon's ward at the Meadow Hospital was intended to accommodate thirty patients with cancer from cigarettes, old men and men suffering from strokes. On Simon's left, there was a man of fifty who was a fierce smoker. The doctors made him to go without cigarettes, which were poison for him. Simon did not smoke. This man wanted cigarettes off him, every minute, because he was stupid or mad, and he dirtied himself around walking without his pants in the ward, non-stop. One day Simon saw that the man's bed was empty, without blankets, sheets, or pillows. Simon reasoned that this man had changed wards, or the doctors had sent him away, or he had died.

There was another young stroke patient who cried all the time. His parents or relatives were there, but he continued crying like a broken water tap. Eventually, his parents took him home.

There was also a sixty-five-year-old patient who was suffering from a back stroke, and laughed and laughed, like a silly hyena all the time. The doctors inserted a steel frame in between his back and his bed for two hours. With this frame, he was able to rest.

One stroke patient laughed, one stroke patient cried, and one patient dirtied himself with human shit. What a bad life when one is very sick. It's much better to drink beer and dance away all the night until the morning!

Every day, Alice and one or other of the boys carried him with his wheelchair to have some therapy or exercises. The Meadow Hospital in North London was an old and oddly organised place, with many wooden, concrete, and aluminium huts scattered over the grounds. It was a bit like a farm with stables where patients slept, ate, urinated and opened their bowels, and might get cured . . . then urinate and opened their bowels again.

Simon slept in Number 3 'hut', and he moved one morning or afternoon to Number 5 or 7 'hut' for the therapy and to meet domestic animals every day.

The weather was very cold and icy. He was afraid that his wife or sons would get a cold or flu. In fact, Alice had a bad bout of bronchitis. 'If Simon had died at the time he had the stroke, it would probably have been better,' he thought. His wife and their boys would suffer, yes, but they would fight and live again without a father and husband. Maybe a new husband for Alice . . .

He did mention to Alice his thoughts about dying. She got very angry and said, 'You, dead? You are mad. A new husband? Why? You are stupid!'

However, Christmas 1992 arrived, Almighty God, and Simon did not say 'Jack', but managed other words and sentences. He was unable to spell long words. He had another problem with his right foot, which was crooked when he rested it on the floor. The hospital supplied him with special shoes.

Having spent three months at the hospital, the doctors sent him home on Christmas Day. His son drove him to their house, while Alice laid the Christmas table with his other son. It was very satisfying to be at home, without doctors, nurses, matrons, and priests with their sermons.

After his 'holiday', he returned to the hospital for one month. Then he was moved to another hospital in East London, about one or two hours away, subject to the traffic. That hospital was supposed to cure strokes, but if you can believe that, you can believe everything, like the moon is full of ice cream or the Earth is a cube.

The hospital had four floors and was very modern. It had a very big garden, 300 priests, and 1,710 nuns. There was one doctor, who had a very busy time with all the patients.

A nurse took them into a room. The walls were green. A picture of the Virgin Mary was hanging on one wall. There were four beds that were painted yellow. The curtains were dark blue, and Simon felt 'black' and desperate. Why had the doctors moved him to such an appalling set-up? He did not know.

The priests were severe. The nurses were harsh and ugly. The nuns were old and sharp, utterly different from the young nun who had taught him at the nursery school. He was three years old then. The nun was so beautiful that he wanted to marry her. He knew another nice nun when he was growing up. She was his cousin, and she had a nice boyfriend, but her boyfriend chose another girl; so his cousin chose God. His cousin was very clever.

A bell rang to call the patients to eat in the dining room, where one could see the garden full of gorgeous flowers. One could also see the 'food'—soups salted like the Red Sea, hard steaks and frozen beans without spices, watery cold potatoes and rice pudding, which the nuns put in the plates. It was appalling. He did not touch the stuff, and the cats didn't eat it either!

'Simon, you must eat,' Alice would say to him. 'If you do not like the hospital grub, we will bring other food for you, like fruit, crackers, biscuits, ham, cheese, and chicken sandwiches. Will it be all right?'

One day Alice told him that their son, Stephen, had cried in the hospital. He was twenty-one years old. He could not believe that his father and his mother were so unlucky: several operations, hospitals, a stroke, and now the hospital's food was terrible!

On another day, Simon noticed a thick long rope coming from a ceiling in the toilet while he was sitting on the seat. He thought, 'If I pull down the rope, I can do several turns around my neck with one or two knots tight enough and can then strangle myself, because I am very depressed, right?'

'That is not right,' a voice was saying to him. 'You are 1.71 metres tall, so your throat will be at 1.55 metres when you stand up. It is a physical impossibility to hang yourself. You could climb on the seat, all right. However, with only one hand, you would hurt yourself!'

'OK! Then I will take twenty or thirty tablets for blood pressure, this evening or tomorrow evening, with a glass of water, my blood pressure will go down, and I will sleep until the end . . . . .'

'Be careful! Doctors have a way of resuscitating people. Don't do it, Simon!'

OK, he wanted to kill himself by hara-kiri, as the Japanese do, because he was very depressed. His mind was depressed. The stroke was depressing. Alice and their sons were very depressed. The church was depressing. The priests were depressing, the patients were depressing and, especially, the food serviced by the nuns was depressing! So he needed something else to make sure that Simon left this world.

Simon was wearing blue pyjamas with red bobbles. He had a long knife from the kitchen hidden under his dressing gown. It was midnight, and three patients slept. Another patient was near the window, which illuminated the garden. He was scared, with his mouth open and his chin trembling. He was trying to commit hara-kiri. That patient was him!

He lifted the green blanket and the white sheet. He rested the knife on his tummy. He inserted the knife slowly between the epidermis and yellow fat until a red drop of blood came out. More drops followed until a bleeding cut was produced. Instantly, the action brought Alice and his sons to his mind, because he did not want them to suffer. So Simon decided no rope, no tablets, and no hara-kiri. On the other hand, he was very depressed and he thought of cheating his depression by thinking some other grand thoughts: God? Eve and Adam? Paradise? The devil? Nature? Wars? These he found very interesting. He would dedicate many hours to thinking about his grand thoughts since he would be hospitalised for many months.

According to Simon's thoughts and the Catholic religion, the universe was black at first, and God stumbled about among thousands of metallic and earth bodies, which filled the space.

'Let there be light!' He said, and light was created, with thousands of suns and comets to throw light on the places He might go for His work, because He was God. He also created the Milky Way. He created planets with rings and without rings. He created the pale moons and other suns, but Earth was preferred by God because He could play with the wild animals, flowers, plants, and waterfalls, where He took showers when it was really hot. All those inventions were His experiences over millions of centuries.

One morning, God awoke very tired in His bed of white clouds. He had a bad headache and He was mad at himself because He did not know what else He could do for the universe. He was pleased with His work, but the animals could not talk and God wanted company. Living in the heavens for centuries, He got very tired, like an old man who grows a white beard on his face, which descended over his body, under his chair, and on the floor, reaching the Arabian Sea. If God created a goddess for himself, He would end His problems and would sleep peacefully. During the day, He would walk with His goddess, picking wild flowers and red apples, every day.

Instead, He thought of another idea.

Not a goddess. He'd create a being such as Himself, using soft clay, and then breathe life into the being. The being was a naked man with a black beard and moustache. He also had a brain for thinking, two eyes for seeing, a mouth for eating, ears for hearing, and a stomach for digestion. He also had kidneys, a tummy, genitals, and strong legs and feet for running. He taught him words to speak in Hebrew, for instance, 'Grimel', which means 'camel' in the English language, and He called him Adam, which means 'man'. God couldn't know other language because there weren't any languages in the world at the time.

Adam was a dark-skinned man, not white. However, he did not find any arguments in talking to God, apart from God's inventions.

'I have created 999 million suns. I have created 540,400 million planets. I have created 3 million moons,' said the Lord every day to Adam, but Adam became bored every day, every evening, and every night in Eden of the earthly paradise where all the fruits and plants grew. So Adam was as lonely as a sick polecat. God was against another man. Then, a woman, but God did not create a woman ever.

God knew everything in the past, present, and future. However, He had no knowledge about women at all! God took a risk!

One night, while Adam slept naked, God broke off the right side of Adam from his body! Apart from the pain, blood, and some shouting, Adam was compelled to walk and to run the length and width of the earthly paradise without his right side!

'Excuse me, Lord. Why did you hurt me by removing my right side?' Simon said.

God did not answer him because He was the Lord, but He breathed life into the separated side of Adam and the side became . . . a woman! Amazing! The woman had black hair, dark skin, black eyes, and a sexy mouth. She was about seventeen or eighteen, slim, naked, very beautiful, almost divine, and Adam fell head over heels in love with her. Eve, Adam's side, was the first woman in Eden.

'Eve' means 'who gives a life'.

God created two beings to make His bed, His tea with lemon, and the water for His bath. But Eve and Adam were lazy doing God's work and preferred walking in the forest, hand in hand, kissing every second, and doing all the things two lovers do. Moreover, God was jealous of Adam because he was a good-looking man, tall, tanned, and bearded, but God was a ghost, and He did not trust them at all. After He had created them and fed them with fruit and sweet wines and talked to them, now they were lying to Him.

'How dare they!' God thought.

The two swore that they did not lie to the Lord, but He did not believe them.

The story went on. The Lord cheated them by saying that they could use all the fruits that were growing in God's garden, apart from the apple tree in the middle of the garden, because it was the property of the Lord.

'If you eat those apples,' said the Lord, 'you will die.'

The devil (the devil?), who had changed to a serpent, said, 'You won't die! You will just learn about good and bad things, like God.'

Nevertheless, Adam wasn't interested in the 'bad things' and he wasn't keen to taste the forbidden fruit. Adam was scared.

Eve ate the forbidden fruit because she was not scared. Typical of women!

Suddenly, the sky exploded with black clouds, dramatic lightning flashes, and terrible bangs every second. The seas and oceans made terrible black stormy waves. The comets were extinguished. The sunspots became wildfire, and God drove Eve and Adam out of the earthly paradise because they had disobeyed Him regarding the forbidden fruit.

What was the forbidden fruit?

Simon thought that the forbidden fruit was sex between Eve and Adam or a woman and a man, which is fantastic, sublime, and divine, as they had discovered.

And the Ghost? The Ghost did not have any forbidden fruit because He did not have any goddess. Why did the Lord call the fruit the 'forbidden fruit', since He did not ever use the forbidden fruit?

'Sex belongs to animals, including the human species, not ghosts or gods and goddesses,' Simon thought.

So Eve and Adam were forced out from earthly paradise in Asia Minor or Asia Superior or some other place. They lived lonely and naked, lost among the wild animals, experiencing hot and cold temperatures, storms, erupting volcanoes, flowing lavas, and burning rocks, earthquakes, and seaquakes. How could they survive all those difficulties?

Eve was pregnant and, after nine months, the first baby boy was born, who was called Cain. In the following years, Eve's second baby boy was born, who was called Abel. Adam went out hunting or fishing; then he returned to his love and they ate some forbidden fruits all the time. So their family grew to ten, twenty, thirty, or forty sons and daughters.

Cain and Abel grew up as a farmer and a shepherd and, being about twenty years old, they wanted girls. However, there weren't any girls, apart from Eve, Eve's daughters, and Cain and Abel's sisters.

They all ate the forbidden fruits that give life and they committed incest many times over.

Later, Cain killed Abel. Why?

Maybe Cain was jealous of Abel's lovemaking with their mother. Or perhaps Abel stole Cain's apples, pigs, and cows. But later Cain committed suicide out of shame over killing Abel. Two sons got killed, making it one very unlucky family. The story of Eve, Adam, Cain, Abel, and their descendants resembles a fairy tale like 'Three Piglets and Bad Wolf'. And God resembles a bad wolf.

Nevertheless, fairy tales have a happy ending.

The fairy tale about the divine creation of man (and woman), the earthly paradise, the forbidden apple, and so forth has an unhappy, distorted, disastrous, and tragic ending, which has no end at all! That is the story of the human species or man.

The Lord said, at first, to them, 'If you eat the forbidden fruit, you will die.' Later, the Lord said, 'Go and be fertile and numerous, like the animals.' The animals use sex to multiply. Adam and Eve used sex to multiply, following God's word. So God said, 'Go and be fertile', but God did *not* say, *'If you eat the forbidden fruit, you will die!* You would stand for 'die' or 'fertile', not both.

Simon thought that the earthly authors, not God, said and wrote 'that' sentence in religion books on purpose, instructed by the clergy and their followers. It was a lie and similar lies are told to the honest people by the dishonest people for thousands of years.

To continue the above story or wicked fairy tale, God thought that Adam and Eve were good at first. However, their descendants ruined God's project because the human species are worse than the devils, and now the Lord and the devils aren't capable of mending the situation, apart from ruining the life of men, women, and children with wars, oppression, wicked persons, wicked kings, queens, presidents, and dictators, persecutions, sickness, and plagues—every day, month, year, and century. God spoke in Hebrew. On the other hand, there are hundreds of other languages and races. There are white, yellow, red, brown, and black races and thousand of languages and dialects. Are there other gods, with other Adams, other Eves, other Cains, other Abels, and everybody else?

That would be absurd.

The Lord took a risk with Adam and Eve. Simon thought, 'As soon as God realised Cain was no good, He should have quashed His project for good, but He was too late and the project turned diabolic'.

Much later, in those times when the Roman army was in power in Asia Minor, almost of the people were wicked and there were fights, thefts, murders, killings, rapes, dishonest people, and wars (like today, nothing has changed at all in twenty thousand years and more!)

So God sent down from heaven his son, Jesus, to calm the people and be peaceful. Actually, God's son was God Himself, and the Holy Ghost was God. Are there three ghosts or one ghost? This forms one mystery according to the Catholic religion.

Jesus was born with the help of Mary and Joseph, who was an old carpenter. However, Joseph did not father Jesus. Almighty God fathered Jesus from heaven, transferred Him down to the earth, because Mary was a virgin, but . . . became pregnant! It was another mystery.

The Catholic religion is made up of hundreds of mysteries! For instance, stories about how five loaves became thousands of loaves to feed 5,000 people listening to the word of Jesus in the field, or how Jesus changed water into wine at the wedding at Cana and other parables; they are true mysteries, according to the church!

Jesus was a carpenter like Joseph. He was very clever, just, and very good. Why are people not like Him? No robbers. No killings. No rape. No dictators. No wars, but everlasting peace.

Jesus was born in a cave in the desert, because King Herod was looking for Him to kill Him and other kids. Jesus was saved. He grew up and taught the Good Word through His parables. He performed many miracles among the poor people and said, always, that He was sent down from heaven by God, His father. But many people did not believe Him because no man could actually say that he was God's son. They thought that he was mad.

At thirty-three years old, Jesus had the Last Supper with twelve apostles, who ate bread and drank wine. At the end of the supper, Judas betrayed Him for thirty pieces of silver, but later he committed suicide for betraying Jesus. The Roman soldiers caught Jesus and He was tried by the people, who found Him guilty of pretending to be God's son.

Pontius Pilate, the Roman governor, said to the people, 'This man is just and he did not say anything wrong.' But the people insisted that Jesus was mad to say that He was God's son, which was a heresy. The people could rise against Pontius Pilate any minute, and they shouted at Jesus, 'Crucify Him! Crucify Him! Crucify . . . Crucify . . . . .'

Then Pontius Pilate called a slave to prepare a silver basin in front of him and pour some clean water into it. Pilate put his hands into the water and said to the crazy people, 'I have washed my hands, and I shall leave this man to the people.' This made Pontius Pilate a coward because Pilate could have saved Jesus from crucifixion, just as some people are coward to a friend and on many occasions of life.

Anyway, the Roman soldiers dressed Jesus in an itching velvet robe, and they put on His head a crown of thorns. Jesus' forehead was hurting and bleeding. Then they put a heavy wooden cross on His shoulders, and He walked and stumbled on the stones to Golgotha, near Jerusalem. He was followed by two robbers with their crosses, His mother, Mary, other women and men, crazy shouting people, and the Roman soldiers.

When they reached the place of the crucifixion, the soldiers crucified three men, with Jesus in the centre. They used big rusty nails on His hands and feet, but for the two robbers they used thick ropes, not nails. Jesus asked for some water to quench His thirst. However, the terrible soldiers gave Him poisoned vinegar, and they laughed at Him. He knew that He was about to die and prayed to His father in heaven, 'Can you save me, Almighty Lord?'

Simon thought that Jesus, His father, and the Holy Ghost were the same ghost. So why did Jesus call God? God is Jesus and Jesus is God or the Holy Ghost. It is another mystery for the people, who are guessing who this God really is, because the story is a confusing web on which a drunken, drug-addicted black tarantula spider walks to this day.

When Jesus died on the cross, big black clouds gathered in the sky above Golgotha. Lighting flashed, a stormy wind blew, earthquakes and seaquakes happened, and the volcanoes erupted. The animals ran away. The scared people thought that the end of the world had begun. The voice of the Lord said angrily, 'Why have you people killed my beloved son?' 'But it's You, God,' Simon thought.

The Catholic religion says too many wrong things, such as human beings are supposed to suffer in order to reach heaven. Whereabouts is heaven, purgatory, or hell? Is it on the right or on the left? Is it at the top or at the bottom? Simon thought that all those things form in our brain and are not real at all. They are fantasies. So are mysteries, miracles, sins, and souls.

After Jesus' death, the soldiers brought Him down from the cross and set Him in a cave putting a ten-ton boulder across the entrance in case Jesus left. The two thieves were left to the vultures. The crazy people and the soldiers went home. The holy women, some men, and the Apostles stood guard over Jesus outside the tomb. After three days and nights, Jesus resurrected Himself because He got fed up with lying in a cave, which was very hot, very humid, and very dark. He moved the ten-ton boulder, got an express train to the heavens, and said to the people, 'I stayed here for thirty-three years to calm and to purge you, but the purge did not work for you. I worked day and night on many miracles for you. I gave you cooked fish and gave you bread, wine, water every day. Now, you have crucified me with rusty nails! It is very unfair to me. I will depart from your earth and I won't listen to your prayers any more.'

Simon thought that Jesus Christ or His father or the Holy Ghost was right. Absolutely right.

That was the story of Jesus and the creation by God.

Then let Simon try to tell the story of a universe created without God in case the story is better.

At first, it was dark.

After millions of centuries, an immense bang was heard in the universe, much like millions of permanent fireworks which gave light. Millions of suns loaded with hydrogen and other gases, comets, dusts, stones, planets, and moons were born. The suns are made of fire. The universe was very cold, so the moons and the planets started to develop crusts from fire. There were high peaks, ditches, holes, immense valleys, and volcanoes because, without volcanoes, the planets and the moons would explode in the universe, creating millions of fragments. One fragment is the earth. Our earth was lucky, with many volcanoes, an atmosphere, winds, weather, and rain, which filled up the seas, oceans, rivers, and lakes, caves, underground rivers, waterfalls, and underground seas over millions of centuries.

Maybe there was one virus that was responsible for life—from viruses to bacteria, from amoebas to jellyfish, from worms to grasses, from ants to flies, from spiders to flowers, from bees to rats, from bushes to trees, from fish to cats. Dogs, horses, elephants, lions, whales, dinosaurs, and monkeys were created and . . . full stop!

The scientific brains are not sure of life. Was it the monkeys? Was it the Homo sapient or the Homo sapient sapient? 'Fantasies,' Simon thought.

'I saw a Homo sapient today reading the Wall Street Journal!' 'Really! These Homo sapients are becoming very intelligent.'

The monkeys and all animals are a different species from human beings, who can read, write, and talk. They can drive cars, lorries, trains, planes, rockets, and ships. They wear suits, frocks, shoes, and socks. They sleep on beds. They eat with forks, spoons, and knives. They use toilets. They work, paint, and sculpt hundreds of other things.

For centuries, monkeys have remained the same as they are today: hairy with long arms, long tails, and little brains. They go around stark naked, eat with their fingers, sleep in the trees, do not use the toilet, do not drive cars, do not cycle, do not read books, do not write, do not drive a rocket to the moon, and they do not talk.

It is no use looking for a missing link, because the missing link does not exist. Monkeys belong to the animal kingdom and men (and women) belong to the human kingdom. However, they do not know their past. Was there one virus which changed millions of times? The egg or the hen story? Maybe they came here from Mars or Venus, because over there it is very hot, or Jupiter, because it is very cold. A lot of mysteries! The human brain and body are other mysteries. Simon thought that humans could try indefinitely to throw some light on life, but they could not explain these and other mysteries. Maybe humans are not bright enough or the mysteries need not be queried by humans. Perhaps animals would have a better chance to explain those mysteries because animals live according to nature. Instead, human beings like very much any warfare, which involves famine, death, and destroyed buildings, schools, churches, and hospitals.

Simon thought that he was in Italy during the Second World War.

He could still remember the hardships, sufferings, bombs, and the hunger brought on by other human beings who were very stupid and thoughtless. Life should be lived peacefully.

Simon thought that—lying on his hospital bed, while a nurse gave him a brutal injection—if one chooses God and the religions, one suffers because of wars. If one chooses the natural universe—without God—one suffers because of wars as well. This world could have peace if all the people change to robots, without minds and without memories, but the people of this world would be stupid robots!

At the Oddfellows—the second nursing home—there was a nice lady doctor, who helped him a lot with his spelling. Every day Simon went to her study for half an hour, and she gave him extra time to encourage him. His stroke had cancelled—almost—his vocabulary. He was determined to learn the words again. His brain power was intact. The bridge between his brain and his mouth was faulty. His long-term memory was very good, but his recent memory was very bad. If he learned a new sentence now, he could forget it by tomorrow. It was maddening for him.

Writing a letter or a book on the computer was fine, so he had to do talking exercises by himself until his death.

Simon found a solution!

He stayed on his side because he was scared to be on the 'other' side. But he was scared to be on this side as well because the hospital food was pathetic. The toilets were very dirty and he felt like vomiting. The nurses washed him in the bath, and they laughed and joked, talking about his nudity.

Before, he was a fifty-four-year-old 'strongman' who worked, got married, raised a family, and had many friends. Recently, Simon had changed to a 'nothing'. On the other hand, he was not prepared to throw in the towel. He wanted to learn everything again. At the time when he had his stroke, he felt he was buried ten metres underground without a coffin. One week later, he climbed up to the surface; he could see the floor and his bed. Three weeks on, he said the first word

'Jack' in his second life. Five weeks later, he used his wheelchair in the hospital and he learned more words.

He changed hospital to the Oddfellows and went out into the garden with his wheelchair. Several times he took the lift up to the top floor, where he was having some therapy done. He spent some days at home and tried to walk without using his wheelchair. He used the walls, doors, chairs, tables, and the cats. He learned to use his computer again. It was real progress by some kind fellow who did not want to burn in hell!

On the other hand, Simon was very tired of staying in the Oddfellows Nursing Home. However, his wife and one son flew to Ireland to visit some relatioves, and his other son and Simon stayed at home. When they returned to London, Alice rang the Oddfellows to say that Simon did not want to stay there any more, and he returned home for good.

They lived in a house which compelled him to sleep in the lounge, due to his stroke, creating great confusion. They thought that it would be better to move to Cracklegs in Ireland, and later they moved there. The following four weeks were occupied with emptying the house of furniture, paintings, books, files, and flowerpots. In the general confusion, Betty, Alice's sister, arrived from Ireland. She confused them even more with an offer to 'help' them. She was very cunning indeed.

Later, Paddy arrived, called by Betty. He was nervous, smoking one hundred cigarettes a day or more, because he did not want to drive them to Ireland. Better for him to drink several pints of Guinness a day in a Donegal pub, without his wife! Their sons could drive them to Ireland very easily, but there was Betty, the big boss!

Eventually, they left London in two cars. John and Stephen were in one car and the other people in another car. They found the road to Scotland, which was nice and full of interesting things, until they stopped at Stranraer. The weather was very windy. Paddy was mad at them. Betty was mad at them, but Alice and Simon were nice to Betty and Paddy.

They took the ship to Belfast at 10 p.m. and at 7 a.m., the next morning, two cars left the boat and they proceeded along the road to

Cracklegs. Paddy seemed a bit happier because he had drunk two or three gallons of beer and smoked about 300 cigs on the boat during the passage over! Betty was still mad as usual. Alice and Simon were thinking about their life in Italy and in England . . . and now in Ireland with their sons. Three countries. Three ways of living: friends, foods, schools, and languages. It was a really diabolical situation for their family, and Simon with a stroke.

At Cracklegs, their life seemed quite normal with the help of Mara, her son, their many relatives, and many Irish friends. Betty and Paddy seemed friendly enough to them for the time being. They went to many Irish pubs, dances, music, and beers. The Irish people are cheerful and very strong hard workers, and honest and good helpers, like the Italians. Alice and Simon were very happy over there, apart from his various illnesses, such as colon polyps.

Another disease affected his heart, which could leave one dead suddenly without saying goodbye to one's relatives and friends.

He thought that humans should have two hearts, one for every day and one for emergencies.

Concerning hearts, his brother called on the phone with very bad news. Their father had died of a heart failure. Simon could visualise at the time of the Second World War, when he returned home, the kisses, the cries, the happiness, the dirty 'university', the food that his father provided for them, his bicycle workshop, the station, and the train to England.

Simon thought that his life train was arriving—almost—at the last station. On the other hand, he was not dead yet! He was still learning with the help of the London therapy, Italian therapy, and 'his' therapy. The doctors were not sure about his brain. Did it work or did it not work? That was the question because he could not spell words right.

At the hospital in Bologna, they gave him a 180-page test book, partly in colour and partly in black and white. The drawings were single or repeated. He had to find doubles for the colours or for the drawings in half an hour. He found 178 correct doubles, so he was happy, and the doctors were very happy about his brain.

Was it Archimedes' brain?

The doctors didn't know if Simon held a power similar to Archimedes; however, the doctors were not at all happy with the tests concerning his colon.

They found a polyp as big as an orange.

Simon liked oranges, however not those inserted into his bottom!

A few weeks later, the polyp was still growing fast again and the 'orange' changed into a bad cancer. The surgeon advised Simon to remove it quickly, otherwise he could die. So the surgeon operated on Simon and the colon cancer was removed.

It was July 1997, and he was fifty-nine years old.

They returned to Ireland.

At the time when he had his stroke, his wife asked the doctor if he could drive again and he said, 'No, you must be joking!' That doctor was wrong, because Simon is able to drive now.

In autumn 1998, Alice's mother died. It was a very upsetting moment for her relatives, her friends, and the people from the village. Mara was very good, Catholic, straight, proud to be Irish, cheery, and so friendly. She had almost reached ninety years old and seemed very healthy. The village people could not make out why she died. After all, she could have lived for over 100 years. She must have got a fright or wicked people that were nasty to her. Mara's funeral drew all the people of Cracklegs to the chapel and, later, to the graveyard. Another soul going up to Saint Peter, who must be very busy up there.

Down on earth, it was very cold in Italy, with two feet of snow. They shovelled the snow in front of their house, until Alice hurt herself in her back. She called a local lady doctor, who gave her a prescription of tablets and rest. But her backache got worse, because it was a back hernia and his wife went to a hospital. Simon was not worried about the operation. He was worried about the anaesthetic. He did not know why at the time.

Another professor was talking about an operation that would last two hours. In fact, the operation took four hours because the anaesthetic, given by the doctors or by the professor, went all wrong.

After the scare, they travelled to Ireland. However, the 'things' started happening over there!

It was night-time. His wife went outside to their garden to feed Sasha, his younger son's Alsatian dog. Alice got down three steps and suddenly screamed because of severe pains in her right foot and ankle. She felt a 'crack', she said, as if her ankle bones were broken. She sat on the first step and refused to walk, because her ankle would not support her weight. Her son came from outside and carried his mother inside their house, while Sasha wagged her tail furiously, because she understood that something was wrong.

Stephen called an ambulance from the hospital, twenty-five kilometres away. Alice's ankle was very swollen, and it was broken for sure.

After half an hour, the ambulance arrived and Alice went away. Simon, Stephen, and Sasha stayed at home, wondering about his mother and his wife in pain. Later, his other son rang from the hospital to say his mother was all right after X-rays and some severe bone realignments with appalling pain. In the morning, the doctor, Mr Foot, operated on her, using four steel plates in her right ankle. The doctor put her foot in plaster for six weeks. He did a good job, but why six weeks? The muscles and the tendons would stiffen up. Two weeks would be plenty. However, Simon was not a doctor, so he kept quiet.

Life must go on, and within seven days Alice left the hospital, Mr Foot, and the nurses. Nevertheless, she now had six legs! Two made of bone and muscle, and four made of steel to support her.

Ireland saw them for 1 ½ years and Italy saw them for six months.

But Alice got worse with her ankle, and they decided to hospitalise her for three days and to take off the four steel plates. This operation was done by an Italian doctor, who was young and very good. Alice walks fairly well now, but Simon had another colon cancer operation, the fourth, and he can say now that he is recovering well.

A pack of misadventures followed them over the years: kidney stones, urethra malfunction, piles, heart bypass, thyroid, colon cancers, angina pectoris, back hernia, and steel ankle plates. Plus the pains, worries, and discomfort for them and for their sons forever. On the other hand, many people live without problems. Was it luck? Was it destiny? Simon did not know.

However, their sufferings were nothing if compared to the world's suffering, with terrible diseases, famines, plagues, disorders, riots, and continual wars, which do not leave any place for safety. Too much money is set against poverty, stupidity, and ignorance. Those are the problems, which create crooks, thieves, rapists, thugs, murderers, and wars.

Thousands of centuries away from the monkeys (or some other species or aliens who landed here), the human species are at the beginning of their history, like babies, who dirty their pants every day, use thousands of atomic bombs, industrial pollutions, diseases, and wars to destroy themselves and the world.

Men (and women) must start growing up and become peaceful, without any wars and evil people, but when? It is now, or in another twenty thousand years, or in twenty million years, or never? Simon didn't know. The people do not know. Religion does not know. The scientists do not know.

Perhaps a solution cannot be found, and the gods will destroy the present human species (because they are no good) and create a 'good and intelligent' human species that will be similar to the gods.

Suppose the new generation of human beings turns out to be cleverer than the gods?

Then those human beings and the gods would be at war with each other for centuries or indefinitely.

The End

Lightning Source UK Ltd.
Milton Keynes UK
UKOW040017250912

199557UK00003B/36/P